AF424467

MESTIZO

The life of Martín,
the son of La Malinche and Hernán Cortés

Author: Manolo Palomares

This book could only be dedicated to my parents,
Dorita and Manolo, with gratitude and love.

Mestizo.

From late Latin *mixticius*. "mixed, blended."

Any person of mixed blood. In Central and South America it denotes a person of combined Indian and European extraction.
Encyclopaedia Britannica.

Index

The Manuscript. March 2023.

Just as in a word search a word appears clearly amidst a jumble of letters, so, before my eyes, an email stood out among all those waiting to be read in my inbox.

The week was starting, and the operations engineer was sitting in front of me, giving me the daily report. I did not want to seem rude and tried, genuinely, to pay attention. But it was inevitable; my gaze kept slipping from his report back to the laptop screen. There was the email that had caught my attention standing out among a list of blurred emails. The engineer finished his report, and I thanked him, promising to look for him later in the morning to review some topics.

I wanted him to leave my office. I just wanted to open that strange message.

As soon as he left my office, I got up, half-closed the door, and sat back down. I then reread the email's brief subject line: *From: Fernando Orozco. Subject: Martín Cortés Manuscript.*

I realized that this was the email I used for the company. The address I used for everything related to my novels was different. This one had been sent to my work email.

I did not remember any Fernando Orozco, the sender, but I did know who Martín Cortés was. Or, rather, who the various Martín Cortés had been throughout history. At least, I knew of three. No, wait, I was wrong. Actually, there were four, I thought, recalling one more. All of them lived five centuries ago.

I double-clicked on the email.

Dear Mr. Palomares, I tried to reach you by phone last Friday, but your office told me you had already left. They kindly gave me your email address since they could not share your phone number. Maybe it is better this way. I prefer writing to you, so you do not think I'm a madman or a stalker surprising you with an unexpected call.

1

I have read your novel about Hernán Cortés and want to take this opportunity to congratulate you on it. I even rated it five stars in the online store. Being written as a historical novel, I found it easy and enjoyable to read. I admit I am not an avid reader, and I can't offer a professional critique of a book, but I know I enjoyed it and could experience the conquest of Mexico through your words.

I do not want to beat around the bush, so I'll get straight to the point: I am a descendant of Martín Cortés, the Mestizo. At least, that is what my family has always said—that we are the descendants of the son Hernán Cortés had with La Malinche, who is so poorly regarded by my fellow Mexicans.

Along with the family legend of being descended from such prominent figures in the history of Mexico and Spain, a box containing a bundle of handwritten sheets has been passed down from generation to generation. No one has ever told us exactly what those fragile papers say, but it's rumored that they are the memoirs of Martín Cortés, the Mestizo. Honestly, I don't know if it's true. I am unable to understand the handwriting, though I confess I haven't tried very hard to decipher it.

A few months ago, when my father died from COVID-19, I was left as the only descendant of that family tree, which supposedly connects me to Hernán Cortés and La Malinche, who was baptized as Marina. Several historians contacted my father and grandfather over the years, trying to verify our relation to those ancestors. Some confirmed we were their descendants. Many other historians dismissed us, calling us frauds. The last person I remember coming to see my father for this reason was an Australian historian, to whom my father almost confessed the existence of that bundle of papers.

As I said, I am the only living member of my family. I am 24 years old and currently have no partner or children. I will soon be moving to Houston, where I am to start a job with a multinational company. I don't want anything to happen to me, nor do I want my family's history to be lost. I would appreciate it

I opened the attached file. It was a JPG image showing several lines written in pen. The handwriting was small and cramped. At the end of the illegible text was a signature that began with three figures resembling stylized eights. In the flourish that followed, I thought I could read the name Martín Cortés. I printed the email and the image.

Once at home, the first thing I did was review the books about Hernán Cortés and the Conquest of Mexico in my library. I could not find his signature in any of them, but I did find it on the internet. At the Miguel de Cervantes Virtual Library, I downloaded several files featuring the signature of Hernán Cortés and La Malinche's firstborn. I am not a handwriting expert, but after examining them closely, it seemed to me that the signatures were identical.

I discussed what happened with Claudia, my wife. She suggested I call Fernando Orozco, the sender of the email.

"He can give you more information and maybe explain why he trusts you to study Martín Cortés. After all, you're not a historian and have never worked with ancient texts."

I dialed the phone number. After about ten rings, the call was disconnected. My impatience made me think it was all a joke, or maybe Fernando had second thoughts about giving me such important documents. A few minutes later, my phone rang. It was the same number I had dialed before.

"Mr. Palomares?" I heard someone ask amid the noise of voices over a PA system. "Sorry I couldn't answer earlier, I was going through customs. I'll be boarding a plane soon."

"Yes, that's me. Don't worry. I assume you are Fernando Orozco," I said, hesitant to the person who had returned my call.

After the initial greetings and apologies for the loud airport speakers, Fernando went into a restaurant so we could talk better. The conversation flowed more smoothly than expected, despite not knowing each other in person.

Fernando wanted to entrust me with his confidence and wished to lend me a priceless sixteenth-century archive of Mexican and Spanish history. I was grateful for this, so my conversation was kind and empathetic.

He reiterated that he had no family left, although he did not seem affected by it. Undoubtedly, he was someone with a good head on his shoulders. According to him, his mother had died when he was still a child, and his father, from whom the lineage of Hernán Cortés and La Malinche was supposed to come, had passed away during the early months of the pandemic.

"They kicked us out of the private hospital because they had already robbed us of all our money, those bastards!" he recalled angrily. "The Mexican social security did not want to take us because they were overwhelmed. They only gave my father some boxes of medicine that turned out to be useless. The only solace in returning home with my dying father was that he could die in his bed, as he always wanted. Do you know something, Mr. Palomares? The last conversation he could have with me, since he was gasping for breath, was about the inheritance of this manuscript. He made me promise to guard this legacy well so that I could pass it on to my children in the future."

Fernando continued talking about his life. He would be moving permanently to Houston in a few weeks. He was a petroleum engineer and had been hired by an American company as soon as he completed a trial period at Pemex. During the phone conversation, I could hear the boarding alerts for his flight to the Texan capital, where he was heading to finalize the lease for a house and organize his upcoming move.

"It was clear from your email that you liked my novel about Hernán Cortés, and I appreciate your kind words, Fernando. But I feel that's not sufficient reason to entrust me with such an important archive as the one you say you have," I told him honestly. "I'm not even a historian. I don't know if I'll be able to decipher the handwriting in which it's written."

"That will be a challenge," he replied, laughing. "I've been unable to translate more than half a page. My expertise is in numbers and chemistry."

"Why me?" I insisted.

"Well... when I read the novel about Hernán Cortés, I decided to stalk you a bit," he confessed, somewhat embarrassed.

"Stalk me?"

"Yes, to find out things about you. Spy on you through your social media. Sorry for the intrusion," he apologized. "I looked at pictures of your kids and your wife. Don't think of it as some kind of harassment; it's nothing like that. I just wanted to get a sense of who you are. I found professional information about you online, which helped me contact your company, where they gave me your email address."

"Thanks. I think," I responded, unsure if it was the right thing to say after he confessed to investigating me and my family online.

"One of the things that caught my attention is that you also have mestizo children, just like my ancestor, Hernán Cortés."

"Mestizo?" I had never thought of my children in that classification. "Well, yes. Maybe they can be considered mestizo; at least the type of mestizaje that happens in the 21st century. They are the children of a Spaniard and a Mexican."

"Exactly, like La Malinche and Hernán Cortés. Though your wife isn't indigenous," Fernando said, laughing, "she's a güera[1], like you and your kids."

"That's true," I commented, left speechless.

Of course, it wasn't the racial mestizaje that began in the 16th century but rather a cultural or national mestizaje that happens worldwide in the 21st century.

"Understand, the mestizaje of your family isn't the main reason I chose you, of course, but it was the cherry on top. You, Mr. Palomares, are a writer, even if you don't make a living from it; that's what I believe. I didn't want a historian to write a thesis or essay, leaving the manuscript stored somewhere. I was looking for a storyteller capable of publishing this manuscript as a historical novel, as if it were born from your imagination and its true origin remained unknown or disguised as a historical account that had come into your possession."

"Honestly, Fernando, I'm overwhelmed by the idea of translating and writing a novel based on that manuscript."

"You know Spain and Mexico, like Martín Cortés, the Mestizo. To write your novel about the Conquest of Mexico, you surely had to gather and read a lot of literature, setting aside your personal opinions. It's evident in your novel that you aimed to be objective in the narrative. That's why I contacted you instead of the Australian historian who visited my father years ago, to entrust you with my family's manuscript."

"I'll be honest, Fernando. I'll try to help you with this, but I don't know if I'll be able to. Frankly, diving into 16th-century texts and trying to decipher the old Spanish grammar and flourishes will take a lot of time," I explained, considering that my job already took up a significant portion of my day, leaving little time to transcribe ancient texts.

"If you can't do it or it becomes a problem, we'll drop it. Promise," he said, remaining silent for a few uncomfortable

---

[1] In Mexico, a person with light skin or hair.

seconds. "So, what do we do? Should I send it to you or what?" he asked finally, with a casual tone.

"Okay. Send it to me," I said, after seeing my wife nodding beside me, listening to the conversation on speakerphone.

"Thank you. Send me your home address by message. I'll send you a custody agreement drafted by my lawyer, naming you as the recipient and legitimate guardian of these documents. Once I receive it signed, I will proceed to send you the box as soon as I return to Mexico. I also want to thank you, Mrs. Claudia, for supporting your husband in this. I ask for your patience," said Fernando, who had already assumed that Claudia was listening to our conversation on speakerphone.

"I thought I wouldn't have to share my husband with books again at night, but I see that won't be the case. I'll have to wait until Martín Cortés finishes telling him his life," my wife commented, not too pleased.

Two weeks after I sent the signed custody agreement to a law firm in Mexico City, a package arrived at my house via UPS. A bundle about the size of a boot box. I opened it in the presence of my wife and children. After removing the cardboard and plastic wrapping, a wooden parota box appeared. Once lifting the lid as if it were an archaeological discovery, I found a cotton cloth inside, woven in the traditional Mexican style, which wrapped what must have been the manuscript.

I untied the knot. Removing the cloth, I saw a pile of yellowed sheets that looked quite fragile. Very carefully and with my hands in cotton gloves, I took them out one by one, placing them in transparent plastic sleeves. I did not know if this was the usual procedure for a historian or archivist to handle such old documents—I doubted it. I did not want them to get stained or torn while moving them, as they were brittle.

Once I had taken out the parchment sheets, I stored the wooden box in the storage room, along with the cloth that had tied the manuscript inside.

During the following months and for half a year, every night after dinner, I would go up to the library, take out the old papers—as my children called them—and transcribe the text in 16th-century Spanish for two hours until midnight. On weekends, I would wake up early and translate for a couple of hours more until my wife and children woke up. This way, I avoided taking too much time away from my family.

In the first fifteen days, I managed to translate only two pages, which caused me anxiety and distress. At that pace, it would take years to translate the entire manuscript. With the help of a LED magnifying lamp and my wife's assistance when I struggled with a word, I gradually improved my translation speed, eventually managing to transcribe one page per night.

Months went by, and I continued the same nightly routine: dinner, clearing the table, library, taking out the sheets, translating the manuscript, copying the text, putting the sheets away, and going to sleep. While I immersed myself in reading and transcribing, Claudia would listen to a podcast with her headphones, read something on the sofa, or take a nap on it. When necessary, I would ask for her help to decipher a phrase or word I could not read. Despite using a magnifying glass, I started seeing blurry after a while. A visit to the ophthalmologist resulted in my first prescription glasses, shattering the childish pride I had always had in my excellent vision.

"Astigmatism. Quite normal for a man your age," he said, as if I were an old man.

It did not take long for me to realize that the narrative wasn't in order. I discovered that the pages were unnumbered on the first night. But the most significant discovery was the authorship of "The Life of the Mestizo," as I began to call the manuscript Fernando had sent me.

What I initially thought was an autobiography narrated in the third person turned out to be a mistake on my part. The signature of Martín Cortés that I had seen was authentic, but that document was merely an authorization granting permission for someone else to write it, hence the third-person narration used in the manuscript.

The author of "The Life of the Mestizo" was a younger man than Martín Cortés. The writer turned out to be Gómez Suárez de Figueroa, a captain in the Spanish army, who was twenty-eight years old at the time of writing. Of mestizo origin, like Martín Cortés himself, but born in Peru instead of Mexico.

The world would know him a few years later as Inca Garcilaso de la Vega.

I was paralyzed; what I had in my possession was the biography of the so-called First Mestizo, Martín Cortés, the son of La Malinche and Hernán Cortés. The writing had been done by Inca Garcilaso de la Vega, a Peruvian mestizo, the same man who later wrote great works about the American continent during the 16th and 17th centuries. In fact, he was known as "The Prince of Writers of the New World."

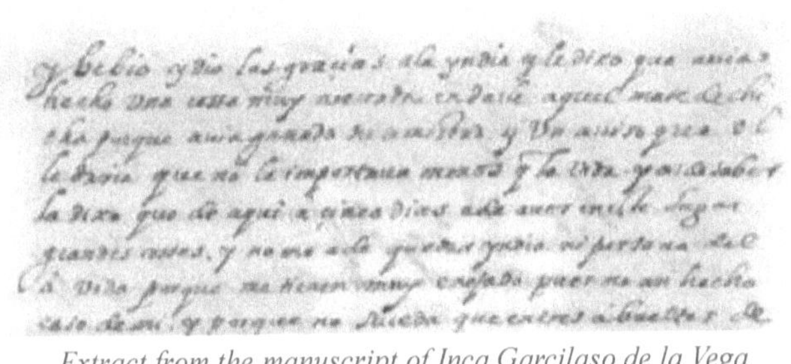

Extract from the manuscript of Inca Garcilaso de la Vega

Occasionally, I would write an email or call Fernando to inform him about the progress and discoveries I was making in the manuscript. Fernando congratulated me and encouraged me to continue the work. He insisted on the need to document the significance of Martín Cortés the Mestizo in the history of both countries, while maintaining the truthfulness of the narrative.

In September 2023, nine months after beginning the translation, I considered it finished. From the original text written by Inca Garcilaso in small script, I had almost a thousand A4 pages handwritten. It took me another month to organize the transcriptions, as I had been translating the pages as they appeared in their transparent sleeves. By then, I had a more or less chronological account.

Despite all this, it was evident that some pages were missing, leaving gaps in the narrative. Perhaps they were lost, or maybe they were never written, and the jumps in the story were because Martín Cortés did not want to mention those periods due to a lack of interest. I prefer to think it was the latter—that Martín chose not to mention those periods.

"Fernando, I can't write the story of Martín Cortés as it is. I don't intend to correct Inca Garcilaso de la Vega, but I believe he simply wrote down what Martín told him, without adding or taking away, and without providing a coherent narrative," I told him over the phone.

"What do you suggest?"

"It needs some rhythm. We should present it as it was dictated—in the form of memoirs—but intersperse dialogues with some of the narratives. This will help to better understand the narrative text, which is sometimes confusing."

"Go ahead, the hard part is already done!" Fernando said, recalling one of Hernán Cortés' phrases to his men in challenging times.

"In all conscience, I tell you that we will manage to produce a good historical novel from these memoirs," I replied, using the formula "in all conscience" that Hernán Cortés used to swear, returning his historical reference.

The story was in front of me. It had been dictated by Martín Cortés the Mestizo and written by none other than Inca Garcilaso de la Vega. I had to shape it. Give it some agility and coherence. Support some moments with dialogues, revealing the characters'

10

opinions better. Or imagining them, while staying true to the facts. I would try to write the memoirs of Martín Cortés the Mestizo, intruding as little as possible.

"How many more days are we going to stay up until midnight writing?" Claudia asked with saintly patience when she heard me finish the conversation with Fernando.

"I estimate at least two months, maximum three."

Claudia sighed, lay down on the sofa, and put on her headphones.

A year after receiving Fernando's email, in January 2024, I clicked the mouse on the printer icon. Seconds later, the machine began to spit out the pages with Martín's life story. The title on the first page could only be one: Mestizo.

Journey to Spain. March 1528.

The scent of avocado pit and vanilla flower in her hair. The smell of milk, saltpeter, and smoke on her skin.

Her mother used avocado to wash her hair and adorned it with vanilla flowers to perfume it. Both aromas lingered in the handkerchief she used to tie back her long, jet-black hair into a thick braid.

The smell of milk, smoke, and saltpeter on her skin was etched in young Martín's memory. This was how Marina, his mother, smelled. Or at least, this was how her son remembered her.

Martín had lived with her until the age of three at the palace in Coyoacán, where she had given birth to him. The day Marina had to leave to accompany his father, Hernán Cortés, to the Hibueras, the boy was placed under the care of Juan Altamirano, a cousin of his father who had a newly built house in Mexico City, the former Tenochtitlan.

Catalina Pizarro, an older half-sister of Martín and a bastard like him, showed the boy during his visits to the palace in Coyoacán the bedroom his mother had occupied. One day, Catalina showed him the chest where La Malinche, as many called Marina, kept her clothes. From there, Martín took one of her handkerchiefs, which he always kept hidden and sometimes took out to smell in secret, to remember her.

Martín lived at the palace in Coyoacán with his parents, Marina and Hernán. There, Luis Cortés was also born, a son of his father with Elvira de Hermosilla, who left Coyoacán a few months later, leaving her son in the care of a maid.

In the same building also lived three daughters of Moctezuma, whom Martín called "aunts" when he visited the residence. One of the daughters of the Aztec emperor had become pregnant after Hernán Cortés returned from the Hibueras, and a few months later, a baby girl named Leonor was born. She was the daughter of the conqueror and, at the same time, the granddaughter of the last Aztec huey tlatoani[2], Moctezuma II.

"Another bastard," Martín heard a servant say while washing the newborn Leonor, although the boy did not understand the meaning of the word: bastard.

The days he spent in Coyoacán were the best for Martín, as he could play with other children. When no one was looking, he would sneak into his mother's room to see her belongings. He had fun at the palace of Coyoacán, unlike at the house of his guardian, Juan Altamirano, where there were no children and he had to take daily lessons in Latin, basic literacy, and reading.

Martín was now six years old. He found himself alone and scared, sitting on a barrel of fresh water, at the port of Veracruz. He was waiting for his father, Hernán Cortés, to approve the two ships that would take them to Spain. All around him were the faces of unfamiliar men, but there was not one among them who did not know who the boy left sitting on the barrel was. A mestizo child with olive skin, honey-colored eyes, and brown hair.

Juan de Lepe, one of his father's servants, had left the boy there to find something to eat. He was certain that nothing would happen to the boy while he went for food. No man, whether Indian, Spanish, or from another nation, would take their eyes off him. Everyone's lives were at stake if anything happened to that child.

Everyone knew he was Martín Cortés, the firstborn of Captain Hernán Cortés. Baptized as Martín in memory of the conqueror's father and nicknamed The Mestizo because he was the son of Cortés and the Indian woman Doña Marina, La

---

[2] Emperor / King.

Malinche. To others, he was simply Martín Cortés, the bastard, though no one dared to say it aloud.

His father had arrived in Veracruz a few days earlier. He had not yet seen him, but Juan de Lepe had told Martín that the captain was around.

"Checking the provisions, the loading of chests with jewels and gifts he's carrying, inspecting the sails and ropes, and keeping an eye on the men boarding," the servant had remarked before leaving to find food for the boy and himself.

Martín watched Juan de Lepe disappear among some low buildings by the port, getting lost among the people and goods that hid the doors of the establishments. The insecurity and anguish of not seeing familiar faces grew in the boy's chest.

"So, you're Martín, right?" a young, strong man with a well-trimmed beard asked, ruffling his hair with his hand while smiling at him.

"Yes, sir. I am Martín Cortés," he replied shyly, recalling he had seen this man in his father's company at the palace of Coyoacán, but not knowing who he was.

"Who abandoned you here, boy? If I find out who it was, I'll have him whipped," he said, looking around, trying to find the one responsible for leaving the child alone.

"No, please," Martín begged, "don't whip him. I told Juan I was hungry and asked for food. He went to get me something. He won't be long."

"Juan de Lepe is the one looking after you? You've found a good tree to lean on, boy!" the man said, smiling. "I believe we've never been formally introduced. I'm Gonzalo de Sandoval. I've been with your father since he left Cuba to come to these lands. I was born in Medellín, like him, like your grandparents."

At that moment, Juan de Lepe appeared running toward them. He was carrying two folded corn tortillas with some steaming meat stew inside.

"So it was you, Juan, who left the captain's son here abandoned. You deserve to be whipped for that. If his father saw it before I did, you can be sure it would have happened," Gonzalo de Sandoval scolded Juan de Lepe, whom he had known as Hernán Cortés's servant for four years.

"I beg your pardon, Captain Sandoval. I kept him in sight while they prepared the stew in the tortillas to bring to young Martín. Would your grace like one?" he said, offering one of the two tortillas to the young captain.

"God forbid I take food from a child's mouth, Juan. Give them to him and don't leave him alone again. You wouldn't want his father to know," Sandoval said, winking secretly at Martín, which made the boy smile at the shared understanding.

"What should I not know, Gonzalo? What is being kept from me?" asked Hernán Cortés, who had arrived unnoticed, surprising the three of them.

Martín froze with a bite half-chewed in his mouth, holding one of the tortillas. His father was not the strongest man, nor the tallest, nor the roughest or loudest. However, when he was present, Martín could see how all the men transformed. They seemed to shrink. What left the boy speechless and fearful was observing his father's left hand, where two fingers were missing. He felt his stomach churn when he focused on those small stubs.

"Captain, nothing we can't resolve ourselves," Sandoval quickly responded. "We were talking about the journey to Spain we're about to undertake."

"Very well, Gonzalo," replied Cortés to the man who had been his youngest and bravest captain. "When did you arrive, my son? I had not been informed that your caravan had reached Veracruz," he said, glancing at Juan de Lepe.

"Captain, we have just arrived," replied the young Martín to his father.

"Two hours ago, my lord. We had not yet found your grace," Juan de Lepe excused himself.

16

Hernán Cortés approached his son and, putting an arm over his shoulders, brought his head close to Martín's and, after kissing him, whispered in his ear.

"Father, Martín. I beg you to call me father. We'll leave the title of captain for the other men, if you agree," Hernán whispered to his son, hugging him warmly, which helped Martín relax.

"Juan, when Martín finishes eating, find Captain Andrés de Tapia. He will tell you which ship I will be traveling on and where my cabin is. Set up Martín's bedding next to my hammock," Cortés ordered.

"It will be done, my lord," responded the servant, who had paled at the thought of being punished for having left the boy when he went to get food.

"Accompany me, Gonzalo. We need to see where to place the Indians who will travel with us. Moctezuma's children and the nobles coming with them cannot sleep with the sailors."

"I will check with Tapia to distribute them between the two ships, sir."

"Captains Andrés de Tapia and Diego de Ordaz will travel together. You will travel with us," commented Cortés as they walked away.

Martín watched his father and Gonzalo de Sandoval head toward the dock. The men working near the boats stepped aside before they reached them, making way. From atop the barrel, while eating his corn tortilla, Martín saw his father and Sandoval stop next to a man he had seen before. He must have been Captain Andrés de Tapia, as the three of them talked for a while, pointing at the ships and the goods waiting to be loaded.

"Juan, do you know if my mother will come with us to Spain? It's been a long time since I've seen her," Martín asked between bites.

Juan de Lepe was momentarily speechless, unsure how to respond to the conqueror's son. For a moment, he hesitated to tell the truth, but if no one had told the boy yet, he would not be the first to do so.

"I don't know, Martín. It would be best if you ask your father when you get the chance. He knows better than anyone who will be going to Spain on this journey," replied the servant, deflecting the issue.

The rest of the afternoon, young Martín spent watching the cages with fantastic animals waiting to be loaded into the holds. He saw ocelots and jaguars, armadillos, parrots and macaws, gannets and pelicans, quetzals and hummingbirds, as well as other birds unknown to the boy with fabulously colored plumage.

He saw many Indians boarding the ship. Some were as short as Martín himself, while others had skin as white as milk, which frightened him, reminding him of a dead person he had once seen before burial.

"Those are albinos, Martín. They were born that way, and they can't be in the sun for too long because they get sick. The others who are your height are dwarfs," commented Juan de Lepe upon seeing the boy's astonishment at watching them pass by.

Following these strange men, some Aztec ballplayers, dancers, and pole vaulters boarded. After them came the servants, merchants, and soldiers.

A group of four Aztec nobles presented themselves to Andrés de Tapia, adorned with headpieces, huaraches[3], and colorful maxtlatls.[4]

"Martín Cortés Moctezuma," said Andrés de Tapia upon seeing the Aztec noble, noting it on the passenger list, "you will board this ship," he indicated to Moctezuma's son the vessel behind him.

---

[3] Sandals.
[4] Loincloth.

18

"Gabriel Tecpal and Julián Quauhpiltzintli will travel on that ship," Tapia pointed to the other ship for the two Aztec nobles. "Lastly, Pedro Gutiérrez Aculan will travel on the ship behind me, alongside Martín Cortés Moctezuma."

The nobles, each accompanied by two servants, headed to the ship assigned by Captain Andrés de Tapia.

"Juan, don't delay boarding; we will depart soon, and few people are left on land," said Andrés de Tapia.

"That man's name was the same as mine. Are we family?" Martín asked innocently, having heard the Aztec noble called Martín Cortés Moctezuma.

"When he was baptized and became a Christian, your father was his godfather, and he asked to be named after your grandfather, Martín Cortés. That's why he carries your name and surname," Captain Tapia responded.

Martín watched the man with whom he shared name board the ship. He appeared older but still strong, wearing a beautiful headdress of green and white feathers that caught the sunlight as he moved with grace and dignity.

The ship's deck was filled with lashed wooden crates, barrels, and bundles of various sizes. Some men were sitting or reclining on the deck; others had gone below to rest. Beneath the aft deck was Hernán Cortés's cabin. It was modestly furnished, with a table nailed to the floor and four chairs. Juan de Lepe was finishing hanging two hammocks between the bulkheads, like those used by the Indians, for the captain and his son to rest.

That very night, once father and son sat at the table to start dinner, Martín could no longer resist the temptation to ask about his mother.

"Capta… Father, will my mother come with us to Spain?" he asked after they had barely taken a few spoonfuls of the corn and pork stew.

Hernán Cortés froze. After a few seconds of observing his son, he put the spoon down in his bowl. He had delayed the moment to tell him, but he could not postpone it any longer. That would only cause the boy more suffering.

Since he was three years old, he had been deprived of his mother's company. Marina had to accompany him on the journey to the Hibueras as an interpreter, and since then, Martín had only seen her on the few occasions when she visited Juan Altamirano's house after returning from the expedition. Hernán Cortés knew from his cousin Altamirano and his own daughter Catalina that the boy was always asking about his mother. Somehow, he had had a very strong bond with Marina.

"Martín, my son, Doña Marina—your mother—fell gravely ill a couple of months ago after she said goodbye to you when she learned you were going to Spain. She went to the encomienda of Xilotepec, but unfortunately, she became feverish during the journey. She suffered from intense fevers caused by smallpox for a few days. She did not suffer long. Marina passed away a few weeks ago. May God have her in His glory," he said, genuinely feeling the loss of the woman he had loved so much.

Martín felt a cold hand twist his stomach in a tight, painful grip. The tightness made him pale, and his bronzed skin turned ashen. He noticed his vision blur, and he began to cry silently, sitting in front of his father.

Hernán Cortés stood up from his chair and, rounding the table that separated them, went to his son, who was silently crying with his head bowed, still holding a piece of bread in one hand and a spoon in the other. Martín's numerous tears fell onto his small legs. Hernán Cortés turned his son's chair and taking him by the armpits, lifted him and held him tightly against his chest in a strong but tender embrace. Martín then broke into sobs against his father's shoulder and neck, while Cortés held him with his right arm and pressed him against him with his left hand.

"Father, I loved her so much," said Martín between sobs, with his head buried under his father's thick beard. "Tell me about her, please."

Hernán Cortés carried him to one of the hammocks and, placing him on it, sat down next to his son. He took a handkerchief from his doublet and dried the tears streaming down the boy's cheeks.

"First of all, Martín, you must know that Marina, your mother, loved you dearly. Nothing in the world made her happier than watching you grow. If she couldn't be with you longer, it was because I asked her to accompany me to the Hibueras. If she had requested to stay, I would have granted it," Cortés deceived himself in saying this, knowing he would never have undertaken that expedition without her. "There was no Indian, man, or woman, who did more for the Spaniards in the conquest of New Spain, and at the same time for her own people, who were oppressed by the Aztecs, than Marina. But her sense of duty and the love she had for me made her accompany me. She understood how crucial her presence was for me on that journey."

"Mother was good, wasn't she, Father?"

"She was magnificent, Martín. Your mother was kind, loving, and tender, yet she was also the bravest woman I've ever known," Cortés said sincerely, remembering her. "You, Martín, are very much like her. I loved her as I have never loved any other woman. Nor will I ever love another." Cortés omitted saying that he was a scoundrel not only for not marrying her but also for encouraging her to become the wife of Juan Jaramillo, one of his captains. "Did you meet your sister?"

"When she came to say goodbye to me, she was with a baby who could not yet walk. Was that my sister?" Martín asked excitedly.

"Yes, son, that was your sister. Marina had a daughter on the ship on her return from the Hibueras," he again avoided saying that she was the daughter of Marina and Juan Jaramillo and that, in reality, she was his half-sister. For now, it was enough.

Martín went to his hammock, and after undressing, he put on a nightshirt and lay down carefully to avoid falling. Juan de Lepe entered the cabin and cleared the table, with the Corteses' dinner untouched. He arranged the captain's and his son's clothes.

Lying in his hammock, Hernán Cortés watched as his son carefully took a handkerchief from a small fabric pouch.

"What do you have there, Martín?" Cortés asked.

Martín was startled, realizing his father had seen his little secret.

"It's a handkerchief from my mother."

"Really? Could you show it to me, please?"

Martín carefully got up and approached the hammock where his father was resting, who had a small lantern by his side. Hernán Cortés took the handkerchief and unfolded it. He saw the colorful embroidery on the cotton cloth and remembered that Marina sometimes wore it on her head.

"What a lovely memento of your mother, Martín. Keep it safe," he said to his son, handing the handkerchief back to him. "Wait, don't go just yet. It's not right that you have nothing of mine," Hernán Cortés commented as he removed a chain with a gold cross from his neck. "This cross of Our Lord Jesus Christ was crafted from the first gold the Indians gave us when we arrived in these lands. It's not grand, but it has been with me through every trial. I want you to have it now," he said, placing the gold cross around Martín's neck.

"Thank you, Father," replied Martín, hugging him.

Hernán Cortés watched his son head back to the hammock and lie down in it.

He remembered when young Martín was born, word spread in New Spain that the first mestizo of the Indies had been born. Hernán Cortés smiled at the memory. Since his arrival on the island of Cozumel, even before he had set foot on the mainland, he knew of the existence of a Spaniard who had been lost a few years earlier in a shipwreck and had started a family within a Mayan tribe. By the time he reached Cozumel, Gonzalo Guerrero, as the man was called, already had several children with an Indian woman. Other Spaniards had also had relationships with native women from the beginning, having children with them before the fall of Tenochtitlan.

Hernán Cortés had never bothered to deny the rumor that Martín was the first mestizo. Looking around, it was evident that mestizaje had happened quickly since the Spaniards arrived in these lands.

The next day, on the seventh of March, the two ships set sail for Spain from the port of Veracruz at dawn. It was the first journey to Spain for Martín and also for his father, who had not returned to his homeland in twenty-four years since departing in 1504.

The first two weeks went by without a hitch. Thanks to a fresh and constant wind, they made good progress as they passed through the Lucayan Islands[5]. Martín liked to sit on a pile of ropes on the poop deck because it was where he could best catch the breeze and where he felt least seasick. That day, the pilot silently handled the tiller, oblivious to the sailors' voices and the song of a man accompanied by a guitar. Hernán Cortés climbed onto the deck with some documents in hand and consulted something with the pilot. Martín observed his father's left hand as he held the papers. The sight of the incomplete hand made his stomach churn. He was missing the pinky and the ring finger.

"Have you never asked your father why he's missing two fingers?" Martín was startled by Gonzalo de Sandoval's voice next to him. He had not realized that the young captain was also on the deck.

---

[5] Bahamas.

"No. I don't dare, sir. It must hurt him to remember, and he'll get angry with me if I ask," Martín responded shyly, although inside he longed to know how his father had lost them.

"I'm sure he'd be pleased to tell you. Captain Cortés likes everyone to know the effort it took to conquer Mexico. Nothing about it was easy. Many men died. Too many friends and comrades. Many enemies died too, and they did so honorably, unlike some of ours who died sacrificed… and who knows what other horrors after that," Sandoval said, lowering his head as Hernán Cortés retreated to his quarters after speaking with the pilot.

"Would you tell me how my father lost those two fingers?" Martín asked eagerly, as he always loved to hear stories of battles and wars.

"It happened near Otumba, in July 1520, almost eight years ago," Sandoval thought for a moment, "it feels like a lifetime has passed since then. Otumba is a small village on the way to Tlaxcala. We had fled from Tenochtitlan on that ill-fated and sorrowful night. Do you know which night I mean, Martín?"

"My sister Catalina told me about it. It was the night the Spaniards left Tenochtitlan."

"Well, I'll tell you about it in more detail another day if you prefer, as I was in that hell too. As I was saying," Sandoval continued his tale, "we had left Tenochtitlan, escaping along the Tacuba causeway. More than half of our men died in that massacre. We spent several days fleeing, while the Aztecs harassed and pursued us, killing us slowly. No rush."

Sandoval leaned on the railing and looked out to the horizon. He needed the fresh air. Martín stood up and approached him. His head barely reached the handrail, and he had to peer through the gaps in the balustrade.

"We suffered hunger and thirst like I have never experienced since. Some men couldn't continue due to exhaustion and preferred to stay behind, waiting for death to find them before

24

the Aztecs did. Some died of thirst. Others from their wounds, as there was no man who wasn't injured. Your father was hit on the head with a stone that left him as if dead for a whole day. If he hadn't been wearing his helmet, he would have died right there, as his horse did."

"Was my mother there too?" Martín interrupted.

"Yes, Martín. She was there, alongside all of us, Doña Marina. She carried a small shield in her left hand to defend herself during the attacks. She tended to your father when he was nearly killed. The Spanish women attended to the wounded. There were María de Estrada, La Parda, La Bermuda, and La Milagrosa; also Doña Luisa, the Tlaxcalteca who married Captain Pedro de Alvarado. Have you heard of them?" Sandoval asked, looking at Martín, who was standing beside him, watching the sea, listening intently to the story.

"Yes, I've heard of Doña Luisa and María de Estrada."

"All right. There we were, fleeing from the Aztecs, as they kept killing us during the pursuit. It was like we were on a hunt, and we were the deer or boars. On the fourth day of fleeing, thirty thousand Aztec warriors formed up in front of us. We Spaniards were barely three hundred and forty soldiers, thirteen horsemen, including your father, and twelve crossbowmen, along with five hundred Tlaxcaltecan allies. We were the only ones left alive since we left Tenochtitlan," Sandoval recalled, sighing. "Your father had the soldiers form a circle, to avoid presenting a long front line, so the enemies would have to crowd to attack us, meaning only those in the front rows could do so. The battle lasted all morning, until noon. We had been fighting for hours under the sun, without water. Our tongues stuck to our palates, and sometimes we couldn't even speak to each other for lack of saliva. The horses were also exhausted, and some had already died by then. Worn out."

Gonzalo de Sandoval fell silent, his gaze lost in the sea. At that moment, he was not floating on a ship. He was years back, in the midst of the horror of that battle. Surrounded by suffering and hardship. By screams and death.

"Did my father lose his fingers there, Captain?"

"That's right, Martín," Sandoval replied, returning to the present. "The wounded and dead increased in the circle of Spanish and Tlaxcaltecan soldiers as they defended against the Aztecs, who seemed to have an endless number of men. In one of the charges we made with the horses, always at a half rein and in some cases almost at a walk, as the animals could barely go on, your father was struck with a macana. It must have been those sharp obsidian blades that severed his fingers," he said, recalling the terrible stones that cut like Tolosa razors. "According to what he told us later, he didn't realize he was missing two fingers until he tried to grab the rein of his mare with his left hand and couldn't hold it properly. Using his knees to press the sides of the mare and spurring her, he made her turn and charged at the Aztec warrior who had cut off his fingers. He pierced the warrior's head, driving the lance through one eye and out the back of his neck."

"What happened to the fingers?" Martín asked, his eyes and mouth wide open as he listened to Sandoval's story.

"No one ever saw the fingers again. There was no seamstress who could sew them back," Gonzalo de Sandoval replied, laughing at Martín's innocent question. "Later, your father saw among the Aztec warriors a group of three or four men wearing large headdresses and carrying standards. He understood that these were the captains who were directing the attacks against us. He made the rest of us aware that we had to take them down. We knew that when the Indians lost their captains, they soon faltered in the fight, and we hoped the same would happen then. It was our last chance; we couldn't survive if the Aztecs didn't retreat from the battlefield," Sandoval continued, feeling his mouth dry again at the memory of that day. "With the war cry of 'Santiago y cierra, España!' we charged at

26

the Aztecs, Pedro de Alvarado, Cristóbal de Olid, Juan de Salamanca, Alonso de Ávila, me, and your father, who reached the Aztec captain first, striking him to the ground along with his standard. As he tried to get up, Juan de Salamanca, who was behind your father's mare, cut off his head with a single stroke. Seeing their captain and the standard fallen into Spanish hands, the Aztecs began their retreat from the battlefield."

Martín was captivated by Gonzalo de Sandoval's story. He had not heard about the Battle of Otumba before and hearing it from someone who had participated in it filled him with excitement. He also wanted to fight for His Majesty in distant lands, win battles, achieve victories, and conquer territories.

"Now that I remember," Sandoval said, turning to Martín, "when we returned to where the few remaining soldiers were, your mother ran toward your father, still with her shield hanging from her arm. Seeing his hand bleeding and missing two fingers, she tore a piece of cloth from her huipil and bandaged his injured hand."

This image profoundly affected young Martín Cortés. He imagined it from then on in a thousand different ways: his mother tending to his father, wounded in battle after achieving victory. It was better than any chivalric tale his sister Catalina read to him.

The next day, one of the carpenters on board, at Gonzalo de Sandoval's request, made a small wooden sword for Martín Cortés. When it was given to him, the boy almost cried from the excitement of having his own sword and ran to show it to his father. For two days, the boy went around the ship fighting everyone, bringing laughter and joy to all the men, who pretended to duel him with their swords. Hernán Cortés watched proudly as his son leaped from port to starboard, and from stern to bow, shouting "Santiago y cierra, España!" and swinging his little wooden sword wildly.

But the joy on board did not last long.

A storm with strong winds and rough seas hit them for weeks, almost without respite. The storm's force caused the death of some of the animals they had in cages. The storms brought large amounts of water into the holds, soaking and spoiling much of the food they had brought for the journey. Only a few salted fish and bacon could be saved for the rest of the trip. Most of the bread, tortillas, biscuits, cookies, meat, fruits, vegetables, and legumes rotted. This made the journey more difficult, as they had to ration the scant food and water, since several barrels had also broken, mixing their fresh water with seawater.

As if that were not enough, several men fell ill during the voyage, including Captain Gonzalo de Sandoval, who, from halfway through the journey, had to remain bedridden and under the care of Hernán Cortés's servants. Little Martín, when the storm allowed and it was not too dangerous, would approach with his sword at his side to where Gonzalo de Sandoval lay. When he had enough strength, Sandoval would tell him about other battles he had participated in. While listening to Captain Sandoval's stories, Martín was distracted and did not think about the terrible creaking of the ship's wood being pressed by the waves and shaken by the storm.

When the storms that had battered them for three weeks finally cleared, four men had disappeared from the ship Hernán Cortés was on, and five from the ship Andrés de Tapia was on. Two others had died after falling from the crow's nest when the ships listed heavily due to a large wave, and the lookouts could not hold on properly.

Gonzalo de Sandoval. May 1528.

The journey proceeded normally after the storms, though Gonzalo de Sandoval did not recover from his illness. He showed some improvement only when the Spanish coast was sighted, and the ships turned at Punta Umbría, entering the Tinto River, before reaching the Port of Palos.

On May 20, the two ships that had crossed the vast sea docked. The voyage had lasted thirty-six days, the shortest on record until then, according to the pilot's report to Hernán Cortés. As soon as they moored, Martín disembarked with his father. He had expected to find a large, bustling city; however, the Port of Palos was as small as Veracruz, though dirtier and noisier than that of New Spain.

The shipyard and dock workers stared in amazement at the beautiful birds and strange beasts they brought aboard. Even though they were accustomed to seeing people from other parts of the world with their typical attire, they were surprised to see the Indians disembark, covered only in loincloths and head ornaments.

"You didn't expect this small port, did you, Martín?" asked Hernán Cortés, seeing his son's disappointed face. "True, it is not a bustling and large port like Seville's."

"Is Seville far, father?"

"Just a few days' ride on horseback; we will go there soon, and Seville will surely amaze you. It is the largest and most populated city in Spain."

The boy had to wait a few hours until his father was free. Martín waited impatiently next to Juan de Lepe, who was already happy and counting the hours, confident that Captain Cortés would give him permission to visit his village, which was not far away. Martín watched as the goods were unloaded along with the few animals that had survived. He was struck by the looks of surprise on the Indians' faces as they disembarked in such a busy port.

Before departing for Seville, and while the unloading was taking place and the carts and animals were being prepared to carry the cargo, Hernán Cortés wanted to give thanks for having arrived safely in Spain.

"Andrés, I leave you in charge of preparing the journey. Let the men who will accompany us settle as best they can on solid ground while the ships are being unloaded," Cortés instructed Tapia. "I am going with Martín to the Monastery of Santa María de La Rábida. As soon as the unloading is finished and everything is ready to start the journey, please send someone to notify me so I can return."

"I will order some men to accompany you to La Rábida, Captain."

"That won't be necessary. We are home now, and I fear nothing, at least here in the Port of Palos," Cortés responded with a slight smile. "It is important that Gonzalo rests as much as possible so he can continue the journey with us."

"He has already gone to the house of Diego Rodríguez, a local rope maker who makes rigging, cables, and ropes. He informed me that he would rest there until we started the land journey. The two Indians who accompany him have carried his chests to the rope maker's house."

"Very well, Andrés," said Hernán Cortés, then turning to Diego de Ordaz, who was waiting nearby. "Diego, I ask you to go ahead of us and arrange our arrival in Seville and our lodging. Notify the officials of the Casa de Contratación[6] of our upcoming visit, but do not tell them what we are carrying. It is best to avoid temptations," Cortés remarked. "As soon as you enter Seville,

---

[6] House of Trade.

30

find and send a doctor to the rope maker's house to attend to Sandoval's health."

"Yes, sir," replied Ordaz.

After bidding farewell to the two captains, father and son began walking along the dusty road lined with palm trees leading to the monastery. A fresh breeze blew from the river, making the walk very pleasant for young Martín in the company of his father.

"Son, we are going to the Monastery of Santa María de La Rábida. You may not know that Admiral Christopher Columbus left his son in the care of the friars here before setting off to discover the Indies," Hernán Cortés remarked as they walked. "He departed from the Port of Palos, the same place where our ships have docked."

Through the entrance of the white building, under a semicircular arch, they entered the monastery. Before the simple altar, father and son knelt and prayed before the image of Our Lady of Miracles, giving thanks for their fortune and the blessing of having survived the ocean voyage. Even Captain Cortés had harbored doubts due to the powerful storms that had battered them during the journey, but they had made it.

They spent a couple of days at the monastery, sharing a cell the friars had provided. They enjoyed good food in the company of the monks, and one of them took the time to explain some passages of the Bible to Martín. During these days, Hernán Cortés sent messengers to various places to announce their arrival in Spain.

On the third day after their arrival at the Port of Palos, Captain Andrés de Tapia arrived at the monastery and informed Hernán Cortés that everything was ready, and the men were prepared to begin the overland journey.

"How is Captain Sandoval?" Martín asked Andrés de Tapia, beating his father to the question.

"He seems somewhat better, Martín. He got up and walked along the dock, but he will have to make the journey resting on a cart I have prepared for him. Sir," he said, turning to Hernán Cortés, "when I arrived at the monastery, I encountered the two Indians who were taking care of Sandoval. They had been sent by the rope maker to inform you that we are ready."

The three of them walked back to the Port of Palos, accompanied by Sandoval's servants. Andrés de Tapia took advantage of Martín walking ahead to inform Hernán Cortés that the Sevillian doctor who had examined Sandoval had given him bad news. The doctor had told Tapia that it was likely their friend would die soon.

The next day, they set off for Seville. Martín rode a gentle donkey alongside his father's horse. Behind them rode Captain Tapia, and further back was a cart where Sandoval rested.

"Captain, I fear he is worsening. His fever has returned, and he is delirious. He keeps repeating feverishly that the rope maker has stolen some gold ingots from one of his chests. I suggest we stop in a town so he can stay there. This way he can rest and perhaps recover," a concerned Tapia informed Cortés after returning from the cart where Sandoval was traveling and checking on his condition an hour into the journey.

"Near where we are is the town of Niebla. Give the order to head there so we can spend the night."

Arriving in Niebla was a striking experience for Martín. Enormous walls surrounded the small town, and behind them loomed what appeared to be a castle. Powerful towers interrupted the fortification at regular intervals, and numerous arrow slits were visible along the wall. Huge gates adorned with arabesques provided access to the town. As they passed through them, Martín felt like a conqueror atop his mount with his wooden sword hanging at his side. His father had told him as they approached Niebla that the town had been occupied by the Muslims for centuries until the land was reconquered, expelling the Moors who did not convert to Christianity.

When they crossed the walls, they were greeted by the few locals who were present, who applauded and cheered as they passed. There was no doubt that, due to the proximity to the Port of Palos, the people of Niebla had known in advance about the arrival of the ships from New Spain and the illustrious man who had achieved the conquest of those distant lands.

After settling as best they could in the Castle of the Guzmanes, Gonzalo de Sandoval was accommodated in the inn of Pedro de Toro, in the outskirts of Niebla. Two muleteers sent by the Count of Medellín, from Gonzalo de Sandoval's hometown, had been waiting in Seville for his arrival. Both wanted to carry him on a stretcher, but Hernán Cortés asked them to stay in Niebla to care for Sandoval until he recovered, if he did.

The next day, Martín played with other children on the town's walls, imagining battles between Moors and Christians. Some boys had fresh memories of the war, as their fathers and grandfathers had often recounted the story of town's capture by the armies of the Catholic Monarchs.

"Martín, my son, I ask you to accompany me to pray for the soul of Gonzalo de Sandoval. My heart is heavy, because I know this good friend will soon leave this world," said Hernán Cortés after two days in Niebla.

After the mass held in the old mosque converted into a church, Martín walked with his father to the room occupied by Gonzalo de Sandoval, whom the boy had not seen since they arrived in Niebla. Beside his bed stood the town's priest, Miguel Jiménez, who had officiated the mass shortly before. Martín found Sandoval weak and emaciated. Upon seeing the boy, Sandoval smiled from the cot where he lay and extended his arm. They held hands and clasped them tightly.

"Don Gonzalo dictated his will today before Cristóbal de Barrionuevo, the King's scribe, with Juan Delgado and me as witnesses," Father Miguel Jiménez informed Hernán Cortés.

"Very well, Father. We must continue our journey. I entrust Gonzalo to you, whom I love as a brother," Cortés said to the priest.

"We will take care of him, sir," the priest replied.

Hernán Cortés knelt beside the bed where Sandoval lay and brushed the hair from his feverish, sweaty face. He leaned in and kissed him on the forehead.

"Goodbye, Gonzalo, my brother."

"Forgive me, Captain, for any fault I may have had. It was never my intention to fail you," Sandoval whispered.

"You have only brought me joy. I am proud and honored to have lived these years alongside you and to have had you by my side through so many experiences we shared." After saying his farewell, Hernán Cortés stood and left the room.

Martín, crying, approached the bed and embraced Sandoval. Though brief, they had shared good moments together. He felt saddened to lose his company because, in the times when he was not with his father, Sandoval had treated him with kindness, education, and respect.

"You have a whole life ahead of you, my young friend. Always keep your conscience clear, and you will be a good man, Martín," Sandoval ruffled the boy's hair in the same way he had since he first met him.

After bidding farewell to the priest, father and son, along with Andrés de Tapia, left the room and headed to the plaza of Niebla, where the entourage bound for Seville was waiting.

At the city's entrance, officials from the Casa de Contratación, whom Diego de Ordaz had informed, awaited them. They accompanied them to the institution's headquarters to deliver all the cargo they carried for inventory. Hernán Cortés was well aware of these royal servants and their far-reaching influence, often taking what was not theirs or accepting bribes to falsify inventory records. Therefore, he had a duplicate inventory recorded by a scribe while they were in Niebla.

Martín was now truly impressed by the grandeur of Seville. He had not known ancient Tenochtitlán, as it was demolished during the three-month siege by the Spaniards. After its capture, much of what remained standing was torn down to use its materials for constructing numerous residential and religious buildings.

In his young mind, he couldn't recall ever seeing a river as large as the Guadalquivir, nor one so full of ships. The wide and long sandy shore next to the city was broader than the beaches he had known in Veracruz. Thousands of people walked the cobbled streets of the city, of various races and speaking different languages. The streets were narrow and winding, filled with many merchant stalls, pack animals, and trash. He was surprised to see people throwing waste into the streets, where it mixed with the droppings of horses and other animals, creating a very unpleasant smell.

The gigantic and towering structure called the Giralda left the boy speechless. He had seen it as they approached the city and could not stop marveling at it. As they explained to him, it was the old minaret of a mosque. Now, beneath this tower that seemed to reach the sky itself, a cathedral was being built.

A few days after arriving in Seville, after his father had attended to numerous messengers, Martín learned that Hernán Cortés's presence had been requested by His Majesty, which filled the boy with pride. Before leaving Seville, they received the news of Gonzalo de Sandoval's passing.

As Captain Sandoval had written, his body was to be buried in the Church of San Martín in Niebla, and later his remains would be transported to Santa Cecilia Church in the town of Medellín. Hernán Cortés and Martín donned black clothes as a sign of mourning for the loss of such a good friend. With sadness in their hearts, and after offering several masses for Sandoval's soul, they continued their journey.

They departed Seville for the town of Madrid, even though the king was in a place called Monzón, to the north. The journey was uncomfortable for the boy on his donkey, but in each town they passed through or stayed overnight, they were received with great celebrations by the local representatives, who had already been informed of Hernán Cortés's presence by the advance party of the caravan.

After several days of travel, the entourage continued toward Madrid, under the charge of Andrés de Tapia, while Hernán Cortés diverged with his son and some servants. Days later, they arrived at Puebla de Guadalupe, a small village in Extremadura. There, Hernán Cortés met his cousin, Licentiate Francisco Núñez, to whom he introduced young Martín.

"Son, I must leave to meet with His Majesty. I need to refute certain accusations that have been made against me," Hernán Cortés said to Martín, who did not understand what his father meant. "My cousin, Licentiate Núñez, represents me in Spain, but now it is necessary for me to handle my own affairs."

"Will I stay here with him, Father?"

"No, Martín. Tomorrow you will leave for Medellín, which is eighteen leagues[7] from here. There you will meet my mother, your grandmother Catalina," Hernán Cortés said, smiling as it was the first time he referred to his own mother as a grandmother. "She will take care of you until I send for you."

Young Martín felt sad. He had never spent so much time with his father as he had on this journey, and he did not like the idea of visiting a woman he did not know, but he had no choice but to obey.

---

[7] One league is equivalent to 3.4 miles.

"Don't be distressed, son. When I was not with you in New Spain, I kept an eye on your life and attended to your needs. Now I will be away for a few weeks, but you will be in the company of your grandmother, who is a kind and loving woman. You won't suffer. I'm sure that in two or three days, you won't even miss me. And as always, even if your eyes do not see me, I will continue to watch over you," he said to his son, after which the boy threw himself into his father's arms, who hugged him tightly to his chest and kissed him on the head.

Illustration #1

Monastery of Santa María de la Rábida. Engraving from 1849

Grandmother Catalina. August 1528.

Life continued for Martín in the company of his grandmother, Catalina Pizarro. She was a stern and serious woman with outsiders, but affectionate and familiar with her grandson. In her, he found something like the love his mother had given him during the brief time they lived together.

After their frugal breakfast, grandmother and grandson would climb the hill each morning to the Church of Santiago, where Martín Cortés, the father of the Spanish captain and Martín's grandfather, for whom he was named, was buried. During the ascent, Catalina would ask her grandson to help her, claiming that her age made it difficult. Martín would take his grandmother's hand to assist her up the path. Catalina smiled gratefully at her grandson's gesture, though she did not yet need his help, as she had been making the climb alone for years. After mass, they would descend back to Medellín and return to Catalina Pizarro's house.

Soon after, an old scribe would arrive to continue the lessons Martín had begun receiving in Mexico City. Martín did not appreciate writing but enjoyed reading, as it allowed him to immerse himself in the chivalric books he loved so much. When he had read more than two pages, he would grow tired and ask his grandmother to read to him, and Catalina Pizarro, sitting him on her lap, would take the chivalric novel and read to her grandson.

In the afternoons, Martín went out to play with other boys in Medellín, and, like everyone else, they played at war. Sometimes they pretended to conquer Mexico, assigning among themselves the roles of those who had participated. Most of the captains who had accompanied Hernán Cortés were from Extremadura, like Pedro de Alvarado, Alonso Hernández Puertocarrero, Andrés de Tapia, and the late Gonzalo de

Sandoval, so their exploits and adventures during the conquest were well known to many.

In these war games with the other boys, Martín always wanted to play his father, but Hernán Cortés was the most coveted character, and he did not always get to be the Spanish conqueror. Being the captain from Badajoz, Pedro de Alvarado, was also a popular choice among the kids in Medellín. At the end of each day, someone was always injured by a wooden sword, with a scraped knee, or a bump from a 'malicious Aztec warrior' defending Tenochtitlan.

As was always the case in Spanish towns, each child had a nickname. It was common among them not to know each other's given names. Martín did not receive the Cortés family nickname and, if there was one, he never knew it. He had his own from the moment he arrived in Medellín: the Mestizo.

"Mestizo, it's your turn to be Moctezuma," said Tiñoso.

"Today you'll be Cuauhtémoc, Mestizo," Piches told him.

One day, a group of older boys from the town approached the square where the younger ones played with their wooden swords, bows made from the olive branches, and arrows taken from the reeds by the Guadiana River.

"So, you're the bastard," said a boy of about fifteen when he saw Martín playing with the other children.

Martín did not know what it meant to be a bastard. He remembered hearing the word from a servant in Coyoacán, referring to a newborn half-sister of his. In both cases, it seemed to Martín that bastard was an insult, something they would not dare say in front of his father.

"Bastard, come here and tell us about your mother, that harlot of Hernán Cortés," Julián the Trapper taunted, causing laughter among the three boys with him.

"Leave him alone, Mestizo, he's bad news. He's the Trapper," Morcillo advised.

With his head down and eyes on the ground, Martín approached the group of boys who mocked and insulted him. He dragged his feet through the dirt of Medellín's square, as if they were heavy, delaying his steps, perhaps hoping they would leave before he reached them. But they did not. The rest of the boys laughed at the insults the Trapper hurled at Martín. He finally stood before the group and stopped.

The Trapper approached Martín and gave him such a strong slap on the back of the head that the small boy staggered.

"Can't you speak, or do you only know the language of the infidels your mother spoke?" Julián the Trapper asked.

Without warning, Martín drew the wooden sword from his belt and struck at the Trapper's face. By ill luck, just as the boy was moving toward Martín to give him another slap, the tip of the sword plunged into the Trapper's eye.

Catalina Pizarro had to compensate the boy's father with six ducats, money with which those of ill repute could live for a year. The boy's family was known in Medellín for frequently poaching on the nobles' lands, which had caused his father to be imprisoned several times. Despite the family of Trappers keeping their nickname and profession, the boy injured by Martín was henceforth known by a new moniker: Julián the One-Eyed.

"Still, you haven't told me why you poked out the Trapper's son's eye out, Martín," commented Catalina Pizarro a few days later.

"Grandmother, he insulted me… or I think he did," Martín replied, embarrassed.

"I don't like blasphemies or rudeness. It's best not to repeat them if they are."

"He called me a bastard, grandmother," Martín confessed, not knowing if it was a rudeness or blasphemy. "It offended me when he said it, though I don't know what it means."

"Martín, that word can be an insult if used in a derogatory way. It means your mother and father were not married when you were born. Don't worry about it; I know your father is taking steps to rectify it," said Catalina, approaching her grandson to embrace him. "Do you know something? Before learning of your birth and that I was a grandmother, your father mentioned you in a letter, though he wasn't explicit. He referred to you by a nickname."

"Father gave me a nickname?" Martín asked, fearful of something humiliating.

"Yes, he called you Tiger," she replied, smiling. "I'm sure you'll be pleased to hear the story."

Catalina Pizarro rose from her chair and walked to a cabinet with many drawers. She opened several of them, searching among the documents inside for a while.

"Here it is!" she exclaimed, raising some papers in front of her grandson. "Your father wrote this letter to your grandfather Martín; may God rest his soul. Unfortunately, the Lord had called him when the missive was received, so he never got to read it or know that you had been born."

Catalina sat by a window to get more light and read the letter. She gestured for her grandson to come sit beside her.

"Your father hadn't told us that you had been born, and in this letter, he hinted at your existence."

"Read it to me, grandmother."

Catalina spent a few minutes reviewing her son's text until she found the part she wanted to read to her grandson.

"*'Sir, here in my house we have raised a tiger since it was born. It has grown and become the most beautiful animal one can imagine. Besides its beauty, it is calm and roams around the house, eating everything it finds on the table. I believe it could make the journey by ship, and with your permission, I will offer it to His Majesty.'*"[8]

---

[8] In italics, an excerpt from Hernán Cortés' letter to his father, Martín Cortés. In reality, Hernán Cortés sent an ocelot to Spain to be delivered

44

"Me, a tiger?" Martín asked, excited, jumping from the chair and spending the rest of the afternoon playing with his grandmother, growling, and making imaginary claws with his hands.

In December, a messenger sent by Hernán Cortés arrived. When Martín returned from his daily battle with his friends in the square—this time they had fought as Spaniards against Tlaxcaltecs—he was called by his grandmother, which surprised him since he had not yet shaken off the dust and dirt he always came home with after playing with the town's children.

"Grandmother, did you call for me?" Martín asked, peeking into the room where Catalina was.

"Yes, Martín. Please, sit here next to me," she said, indicating a stool beside her armchair.

"Have I done something wrong, grandmother?"

"Not at all, dear. A message has arrived from your father."

"Is father coming to Medellín?"

"The letter doesn't say that, Martín. He writes that he has been received on several occasions by His Majesty, King Carlos. He has been awarded the title of Marquis of the Valley of Oaxaca, although it has not yet been bestowed upon him."

"Father is a Marquis? That's good news."

"Indeed, Martín. In the letter, he informs me that he has requested the habit of the Order of Santiago for you from King Carlos and believes there are good reasons for your admission into the order," his grandmother said, though she did not seem pleased about it. "He also tells me that he requires your presence in Toledo as soon as possible since you will enter the Royal House of Pages."

---

to the king, but the animal died during the journey, and only the letter reached his father, causing confusion. Perhaps the grandmother thought her son was referring to a grandchild.

"What is a page, grandmother?"

"A page is a young man who enters the Court to serve the king or someone in his family. In this case, you will belong to the household of his wife, Empress Isabel of Portugal. She is the mother of Prince Felipe, who was born last year, and of Infanta María, born this year," Catalina explained sadly, knowing that her happy days with her grandson were coming to an end.

"But I don't want to leave, grandmother. Here I learn to read and write, and I'm happy living with you." Martín hugged his grandmother, who had already begun to cry along with him.

Two weeks later, the envoys of Hernán Cortés arrived in Medellín. Martín departed with them for Toledo, where his father was residing during his stay in Spain. Catalina Pizarro and her grandson, amidst tears, promised to write to each other as soon as they could.

Young Martín, who was seven years old at the time, stayed only at his father's residence in Toledo for a few days. At the beginning of the year, Hernán Cortés accompanied his son to the town of Madrid, heading to the newly opened Royal House of Pages. Here, the sons of noblemen and knights were trained in various disciplines and received formal education from the ages of six to fourteen.

"Son, here you will study and live with other boys. It is important not only that you learn but also that you live at the Court, where you will attend ceremonies, events, and meetings with members of the nobility," said Hernán Cortés as he left him in the large hall where the beds for the youngest pages were.

"Father, I have already learned a lot in Mexico and Medellín with the tutors. It would be better if I went back to grandmother and continued my studies with her," Martín suggested, making his father smile.

"That is not possible, my son. I have other plans for you. It is important that you learn and interact with the nobility. That is the best way for you to help me," said Hernán Cortés, placing his hands on his shoulders.

Martín understood that what his father was asking of him was important, even though he did not fully grasp it. He did not want to disappoint him, so he nodded. He would do whatever his father wished.

"Do not worry. I will learn as much as I can, and rest assured that I will be a good servant to you."

"I have never doubted it, my son. At the beginning of spring, I will return for you, and you will accompany me to a certain place."

"Whenever you wish, Father."

That same week, six more boys arrived and joined Martín. The seven of them would belong to the household of Empress Isabel. Four of the pages who joined along with Martín were, like him, illegitimate sons. The Royal House of Pages had been the best way to place the noblemen's illegitimate children near the Court, as only the legitimate firstborn sons would inherit the family title.

On January 15, their lessons began. The first class of the day was Castilian Grammar and Elementary Literacy, in which Martín performed well since the scribe had been teaching him letters for two hours every morning during the time he lived with his grandmother. After that first subject, they continued with Orthology and Calligraphy, followed by Basic Mathematics. At noon, the children were taken to a large hall where a long table awaited them, set with dishes of various sizes, glasses, cups, ceramic platters, and cutlery in front of each chair.

The children stood silently behind their chairs, waiting for the order to sit and begin eating. This behavior was expected of them and demonstrated proper table manners. They were all hungry. They had awakened with the first light of dawn and had only had a glass of milk and a piece of French toast. The dining room door opened, and a young man dressed in black clothes with a white ruffled collar entered. He positioned himself at the head of the long table and addressed them.

"Welcome to the Royal House of Pages. My name is Antonio de Toledo, and I am His Majesty's Chief Equerry, thus in charge of the Royal Stables and this Royal House," explained the man, observing the seven young pages, none of whom were older than ten. "After this meal, you will need to complete the tasks your tutors have assigned you during the study hour in the library. Then, you will have some time to rest before attending mass and returning to this hall for dinner. All of you come from good families, descendants of old Christians, so I trust in your good behavior in this Royal House, as well as your worthiness when you interact with Their Majesties. Inside these walls, none of you is more than another,"—*all are bastards*, he thought to himself—"Do not rely on your lineage or your ancestors to assert dominance over others. The only things that will make you stand out are your intelligence, culture, and education. Now, gentlemen, you may sit and begin eating."

At that moment, the chairs shifted, and everyone sat at the table. A servant standing beside Antonio de Toledo was summoned, and after a brief whispered conversation, the servant went to fetch Martín, who had already begun eating.

"Knight Martín Cortés, Master Antonio de Toledo has requested your presence," whispered the servant.

Martín rose properly and walked toward Antonio de Toledo, while the other boys paused their meal and watched.

"I ask you to continue your lunch, gentlemen," ordered Antonio de Toledo, gesturing with his hand, prompting everyone to return to their plates and resume eating.

Martín reached Antonio de Toledo and, after bowing his head, spoke.

"How can I assist you, sir?" he asked in a trembling voice.

"Are you the son of Hernán Cortés, the newly appointed Marquis of the Valley?"

"Yes, sir. Hernán Cortés is my father."

"So you are the Mestizo, the son of Captain Hernán Cortés and the Indian woman called La Malinche?"

Martín stiffened at the question, fearing disrespect toward his mother.

"My mother's name was Marina, sir. She was baptized with that name and was a Christian," he responded, annoyed.

"I did not mean to offend you with my question. If I did, I apologize, Martín. I was merely curious to know you. You may return to your seat and continue your meal."

"Thank you, sir," Martín said before retreating and returning to his place at the table.

Antonio de Toledo watched the young mestizo return to his seat. Although he did not mention it, Antonio de Toledo felt proud of Hernán Cortés's feats and accomplishments in the Indies. He had conquered a New World.

The Order of Santiago. July 1529.

Six months after his arrival at the Royal House, as everyone called it, Martín had already adapted to the institution's routines, as well as to his companions, all descendants of the most distinguished Spanish nobility, though most of them were illegitimate children. Occasionally, he received letters from his grandmother, and he replied that same week, telling her about his activities at the Royal House and his experiences. He hadn't heard from his father in all that time, until one day a messenger arrived to inform Martín that he should prepare a bundle of clothes, as his father would soon come to take him away for a few days.

"Mestizo, your father has arrived," said Botijo, also known as Alonso Pimentel, the bastard son of the Duke of Benavente, whose slow wit had earned him a nickname that suited him perfectly.

"Thanks, Botijo. Make sure no one touches my things," Martín replied distrustfully, then ran out of the large dormitory.

No page would have thought of stealing from another, as the punishment was expulsion from the Royal House and the stigma of being labeled a thief. Martín mentioned it to Botijo because sometimes they would take some of his chivalric books, and it annoyed him not to have them when he wanted to read. These books were among the few possessions Martín was reluctant to lend, especially those by Joanot Martorell and Garci Rodríguez de Montalvo, which his father had given him.

When they met at the entrance of the Royal House, both embraced. A servant took Martín's bundle and loaded it into the open horse-drawn carriage in which he had arrived. After bidding farewell to Licentiate Antonio de Toledo, who had been speaking with his father moments before Martín arrived, father and son climbed into the carriage and left.

"Where are we going, Father?"

"To Toledo. I want you to obtain the habit of the Order of Santiago, just like I have. I trust that the audience that will be held over the next few days will have a satisfactory outcome," Hernán Cortés informed his son, recalling that he himself had not been accepted when he first applied.

Martín watched the wheat and barley fields pass by during their journey to Toledo, absorbed in his thoughts. He knew that a couple of boys from the Royal House belonged to the Order of Santiago. Whenever they could, and when the occasion was suitable, they wore the beautiful red cross of the Order embroidered on their doublets. Another of his companions belonged to the Order of Calatrava.

Although they considered themselves equal within the Royal House, each knew the noble title of his family, even if he would not inherit it, or the Order to which they belonged. After contemplating this for a while, Martín decided he liked the idea of having the cross of the Order of Santiago embroidered on his clothes.

"I heard that in Medellín you wounded the Trapper's son. I knew his father when I was young, and I lived there. His father had bad blood even then, and I believe I'm not wrong in thinking his son inherited it," Hernán Cortés commented during the trip. "Your grandmother told me you attacked him because he called you a bastard. Is that true, son?"

"Yes, Father," Martín replied, ashamed and fearing a reprimand.

"You did well to defend yourself and confront him, even though he was older than you. Never let anyone disrespect you, Martín. You are my son and Doña Marina's. Together, your mother and I conquered Mexico. None of the families of the

52

pages living with you at the Royal House have achieved as much. You should be proud of who you are."

"I am proud of you both," Martín confirmed, raising his eyes to meet his father's.

Hernán Cortés pulled some papers from inside his doublet, unfolded them, and showed them to his son.

"It's hard to read with the jostling of the carriage, Martín. This is a papal bull," he said, showing him the documents. "His Holiness, Pope Clement VII, signed it a few weeks ago. This bull officially declares you the legitimate son of your mother and me. No one will ever call you a bastard again. Not you, not your sister Catalina, nor little Luis, who was born before we came to Spain."

Martín was pleased, though he did not fully grasp the significance of the papal bull. Hernán Cortés omitted mentioning that it had cost him a small fortune to obtain it, legitimizing Martín Cortés, as well as Catalina Pizarro and Luis Cortés, his other half-siblings living in New Spain.

Martín took the document and, despite the movement of the carriage, read its contents: "To the beloved Martín Cortés and Luis de Altamirano, students, and to the beloved in Christ daughter Catalina Pizarro, maiden..."

When he finished reading the bull, Martín felt better knowing he had been recognized by the Church as a legitimate son. His father put the documents back into the inner pocket. Hernán Cortés found it ironic that Pope Clement VII, himself the illegitimate son of Giuliano de Medici, had decreed his children's legitimacy.

The hearing before the tribunal of the Order of Santiago took place three days later. Eight men in white robes with the red cross of the Order embroidered over the left side of their chests questioned the witnesses proposed by Hernán Cortés about young Martín.

The first to testify was the captain and conqueror, Diego de Ordaz, who had participated in and distinguished himself during the conquest of Mexico. Gonzalo de Sandoval had told Martín that Ordaz had climbed to the summit of Popocatepetl volcano. The boy remembered seeing its snowy peak and columns of smoke in the distance when he lived in New Spain.

"Captain Diego de Ordaz, you are here before this tribunal of the Order of Santiago to determine the suitability of page knight Martín Cortés, present here, for membership in the Order of Santiago. Documents have been provided indicating the candidate's legitimacy," said the president of the tribunal, showing the papal bull, "as well as other proofs requested from the petitioner, his father, Captain Hernán Cortés, who is also present. Do you swear on your grace and the Holy Bible before you that the testimony you will offer is truthful?"

"I swear," Diego de Ordaz replied, placing his hand on the Bible.

"We ask you to inform us of the details of young Martín Cortés's life, his birth, mother, father, and the origins of both."

Captain Diego de Ordaz began his account, confirming the parentage of Hernán Cortés and his mother, Doña Marina, whom he said was the daughter of noble indigenous people from the province of Coatzacoalcos in New Spain. After his testimony and answering several questions posed by the tribunal members, the first session of four was concluded, one for each required witness. The next day, Captain Andrés de Tapia continued, and on another day, Alonso de Herrera testified.

After the witnesses gave their testimony on the Bible, confirming Martín's pure blood by asserting he had no Jewish, Moorish, or servant ancestry, Hernán Cortés and his son remained in Toledo, awaiting the verdict. They were summoned before the tribunal three days after the final hearing.

"After reviewing the information provided by the petitioner, listening to the witnesses' accounts, and having sworn on the

Holy Bible to the truthfulness of their testimony, this tribunal has determined that the candidate Martín Cortés Malintzin meets the requirements for membership in the Order of Santiago."

Hernán Cortés, emotional, silently wept upon hearing the verdict.

"Next, we will proceed with the ceremony where young Martín will be bestowed with the habit of the Order of Santiago and take the oath. Only candidates and members of the Order are permitted to witness this ritual," the president announced loudly, as part of the habit-imposition procedure.

Familiar with this ritual, Hernán Cortés could remain in the hall with his son as a member of the Order of Santiago, but the four witnesses who testified on Martín's behalf had to leave.

Once Martín had stripped off his clothes as instructed by the tribunal members, a white robe with the red cross of the Order of Santiago was placed on his naked body, over his heart. Lying on the cold stone floor, arms outstretched in a cross, the rules binding the members were read to him in Latin. These included obedience to the Order and subjection to the master, living without personal property "*in omni humilitate atque concordia sine proprio vivere debeatis,*[9]" marital chastity, prayer, fasting, clothing regulations, the duty to fight against infidels, and simultaneously, showing compassion to prisoners. Once the eighty rules of the Order were recited, Martín was allowed to rise and embraced his father.

Hernán Cortés hosted a small banquet at his residence in Toledo. The witnesses and other companions of the Spanish captain, now the Marquis of the Valley, attended to honor the youngest knight of the Order of Santiago, Martín Cortés Malintzin.

---

[9] With all humility and harmony you must live without your own.

On their return to Madrid to leave Martín at the Royal House, Hernán took the opportunity to share with his son his next steps during their alone time.

"Martín, you know that since your birth I have been a widower, as my wife before God, Catalina Suárez Marcaida, died months before you were born. Thanks to the arrangements my father made before he passed away, I now have the opportunity to marry a Castilian woman, Juana de Zúñiga, niece of the Duke of Béjar, who is the Prince Felipe's godfather."

"I understand, Father. So, where will you live?"

"My intention is to return to New Spain. I have settled my situation with His Majesty, and I cannot neglect the rest of the family, my business, and my encomiendas. Additionally, I wish to continue my explorations of the South Sea[10]."

---

[10] Pacific Ocean.

Death of the Empress. May 1539.

Martín and the other pages had been in Toledo for five days, staying in the chambers of the Palace of the Counts of Fuensalida. In the upper part of the palace, since her last childbirth three days earlier, was Empress Isabel.

The pages of the Empress's House had accompanied her on her journey to Toledo, where she had gone into labor a few days ago. The pages did not hear the Empress's cries during labor, as she was a strong woman. It was rumored that during her previous births, no one had heard her scream. But this time, the labor had been difficult, and the child she bore was stillborn. Since then, the fevers had been consuming her.

In the Palace of Fuensalida, alongside the Empress, were King Carlos and their son, Prince Felipe. The king had not left his wife's bedside since the fateful childbirth. The pages had accompanied Prince Felipe twice a day to the nearby Church of Santo Tomé to pray for his mother's recovery. Processions were held in Toledo, and in all the churches and chapels, masses were offered for the Empress's health. It was all in vain.

On May 1, 1539, Empress Isabel passed away. From the ground floor of the Palace of Fuensalida, Martín could hear the king's mournful cry, followed by great sobbing.

"Leave me, for I have lost everything dear to me!" Martín heard the king shout, perhaps resisting the attempts of some nobles who were trying to make him release his dead wife's body.

The pages did not dare to approach the monarch, who had locked himself in his chamber. With great respect, they approached Prince Felipe and offered their condolences one by one.

"Thank you, Martín," Prince Felipe responded upon hearing his condolence. "I ask you to pray to God for her soul."

"Every day of my life, I will do so, Your Highness," replied Martín, who felt grateful to the Empress for the kindness she had always shown toward the pages of her house, especially toward him.

Prince Felipe lifted his gaze and looked at Martín; he knew that the Mestizo would fulfill what he had said. He was known for his honesty and loyalty.

Before the birth of her first child, the Empress had ordered that in the event of her death, she did not want her body embalmed. Among the pages, word spread that the marchioness and the chief lady-in-waiting were preparing the body with myrrh and aloe balm. Afterward, her body was wrapped in a Franciscan habit and placed in a lead coffin, inside another wooden one. The space between the coffins was filled with cotton, musk, and other fragrant herbs.

The pages received the clothes they were to wear for the Empress's funeral from the Royal House. After washing and grooming himself with his companions, Martín dressed in mourning attire.

In front of a mirror, he shaved and trimmed the fine dark brown mustache he had been growing since his facial hair first appeared. His dark hair, styled in the fashion of the time, slightly covered his ears. Martín saw his reflection in the mirror and, although he did not consider himself vain, acknowledged his good looks, which had brought him some success with maidens when he lived with them or attended dances. At sixteen, he knew he was attractive in the eyes of women; his almond-shaped honey-colored eyes elicited sighs from them. His wheat-colored skin from childhood had turned bronze over the years. His body, though slender, was not weak at all. He had toned it with physical exercises, beyond those marked by his tutor of games, skills, and swordsmanship.

He dressed in solemn black, as was natural in such a situation. On his velvet doublet, the red cross of the Order of Santiago was embroidered on the left side. Between the cross and his heart, there was a small inner button that he had sewn onto all his doublets and shirts, where he always fastened the fine leather case that held his mother's handkerchief. The gold cross that his father had given him when they left New Spain always hung around his neck.

He adjusted his ruff to hide the scars left by the Court physician two years ago when the doctor lanced the glands on his neck after he fell ill with scrofula.

He recalled that when he started feeling ill, Licentiate Antonio de Toledo had ordered him to leave the Royal House and go somewhere else until he recovered. He stayed at the home of his guardian, Diego Pérez de Vargas, and there he spent several months recuperating. One day, when he was starting to get better, he heard the voice of Licentiate Francisco Núñez, shouting at his guardian.

"Señor Pérez de Vargas, why did you send a letter to the Marquis of the Valley with the note of the expenses incurred due to Martín's illness?" the angry Licentiate Núñez asked angrily. "I received a letter from the Marquis yesterday, in which he expresses concern and distress about what is happening with his son, whom he says he loves as much as the one he has with his wife, Doña Juana."

"I wanted him to know that, in addition to my fees, the additional expenses for the doctor and his treatment needed to be reimbursed," the guardian defended himself.

"You have acted improperly and dishonestly. Either that, or you wanted to worry the Marquis about his son's condition. I am here to bear any expenses incurred by young Martín for any reason. Do I not pay your fees every month?" the representative of Hernán Cortés inquired.

"That you do, Licentiate. Without delays," the guardian tried to placate him with his response.

"Well, say goodbye to that money. That payment will cease shortly. The Marquis of the Valley has ordered me to find a guardian to replace you in Martín's care," Licentiate Núñez concluded. "Now I will visit the young man. I must report on his health in my next letter to the Marquis."

Since Martín left the home of Diego Pérez de Vargas, who had been his guardian for several years, he had been tutored by Juan de Avellaneda.

All the pages lined up in the small square in front of the facade of the Palace of Fuensalida. They were dressed in black doublets and wore dark hoods over their heads; each page carried a lit torch. The Empress's coffin was carried out of the palace on the shoulders of six nobles, including the Duke of Béjar, who was the uncle of Doña Juana, Hernán Cortés's current wife. When they exited the building with the coffin, Martín saw the king looking out from one of the windows. It seemed to Martín that His Majesty had aged several years in just two nights. Later that same day, a rumor spread that after the Empress's coffin was taken out, King Carlos retreated, inconsolable, to the Hieronymite Monastery of Santa María de Sisla.

A solemn procession moved through the streets of Toledo, accompanying the Empress's body, which would soon be taken to Granada, guarded by soldiers and pages, to rest alongside the Catholic Monarchs, Isabel and Fernando, as she had always wished.

Four macebearers led the parade, followed by the group of pages including Martín. A company of Spanish and German soldiers surrounded the coffin. Behind the casket walked the Bishop of Badajoz and Bishop Campo, followed by the grieving Prince Felipe, tearful and as pale as if his skin were covered in ash. Several cardinals, prelates, ambassadors, officials of the

Royal Household, stewards, and ministers walked behind the prince.

Road to Granada. May 1539.

As they passed through the streets of Toledo, the townspeople came out to bid farewell to their queen with tears, shouts, and commotion. Upon leaving the city, only the pages, a few nobles and knights, and a squadron of soldiers continued with the procession. The Marquis of Llombay and his wife, along with Prince Felipe, accompanied Empress Isabel on the road to Granada. They marched toward Orgaz, where they would take their first rest.

Martín thought that with Empress Isabel's death, a chapter in his life had ended. He saw the decision to leave the Royal House as imminent. It was possible that Prince Felipe might call him to join the knights of his household, but it was uncertain. Martín pondered this as they walked the dusty roads of Castile until they reached Orgaz, where masses were held for the soul of the Empress.

The next day they departed for Los Yébenes, where they rested at the Castle of Guadalerzas. From there, the procession continued toward Granada, making stops in several towns over the next few days: Castle of Malagón, Sanctuary of Our Lady of the Incarnation in Calatrava la Vieja, Carrión de Calatrava, Sanctuary of the Virgin of the Saints in Pozuelo, and in Calzada de Calatrava.

They rested for a couple of nights in Viso del Marqués, a town that the king had sold that same year to Don Álvaro de Bazán y Solís, who welcomed the Empress's procession along with his son, Álvaro de Bazán y Guzmán, courteously attending to them. From Viso, they headed to Navas de Tolosa, where they stayed at the castle. They then passed through Linares, Baeza, Jaén, and finally reached Granada.

During those days, Martín constantly reminisced about the years he had spent in Spain. Eleven years had passed since his father had taken him from New Spain, the same eleven years since he learned of his mother's death. Since then, many things had happened to his father, certainly more than Martín knew.

He learned that in 1530, his beloved grandmother Catalina had traveled with his father to New Spain. Due to illness during the voyage, Catalina Pizarro had to rest for several months in Santo Domingo until she recovered somewhat and was able to continue the journey, though still weak. Upon arriving in New Spain, his grandmother passed away and was buried in the Convent of San Francisco in Texcoco. Learning of her death caused Martín profound melancholy that lasted for months.

Martín also learned of the birth of a half-brother who bore his same name, the son of his father and his wife, Juana de Zúñiga. He felt hurt when he found out that this child would be the heir to the title of Marquis of the Valley of Oaxaca, instead of him, Hernán Cortés's firstborn son. Over the weeks, conversations with Licentiate Antonio de Toledo at the Royal House, helped him understand that his father had done this to be more closely connected with Spanish nobility. Naming the heir to the marquisate a son born within the marriage to a Castilian noblewoman made court relations more direct and beneficial agreements more achievable.

He had been informed by others, not by his father, as rumors among the nobility were frequent, about the variety of lawsuits Hernán Cortés had faced upon his arrival in New Spain. Among other things, he learned of the judicial review that began as soon as Cortés returned from Spain, as well as another lawsuit filed by his former mother-in-law, María Marcaida, who claimed half of the assets from his marriage to her deceased daughter. Martín learned of a lawsuit against the Audiencia governing New Spain, regarding the census of the twenty-three thousand vassals granted to him by His Majesty, since the Audiencia calculated the vassals in a way that significantly increased the amount of tribute he had to pay.

In 1535, his father had formalized his entail in the city of Colima, New Spain. Martín knew of the continuous failures and problems he had encountered with the explorations of the South Sea, as well as with the encomiendas. It seemed that since he had taken the city of Tenochtitlan, none of Hernán Cortés's enterprises had been successful.

Because of all this, Martín had decided to return to New Spain when possible. He wished to reunite with the family he had lived with before leaving and to meet his new siblings. He intended to offer his assistance to help alleviate his father's burdens.

Upon the arrival of the funeral procession in Granada, they were received by the Marquis of Mondéjar, Don Luis Hurtado de Mendoza, who at the time was Viceroy and Captain General of the Kingdom of Granada. With him were the judges of the Chancery and a large number of knights and soldiers from the city, all in mourning, carrying lit torches.

They proceeded to the Royal Chapel, where they formally delivered the Empress's coffin. From his position, Martín could see the Marquis of Llombay opening the coffin in the presence of the archbishop, the bishop of Osma, the Marquis of Villena, and Captain General of Granada. Upon removing the lids and revealing the body for identification, Don Francisco de Borja, Marquis of Llombay, had a fainting spell and nearly collapsed onto the ground.

"Cover her again, I beg you," he said in a faint voice, while his wife, the Countess of Faro, and Doña Guiomar de Melo hurried to cover the Empress's body once more.

A penetrating, unpleasant odor of putrefying flesh spread through the great hall. Undoubtedly, the journey under the sun, the intense heat, and the lack of embalming had caused the body to decay.

"Your Grace must swear that the received corpse is that of Empress Isabel, wife of King Carlos," the archbishop said to the Marquis of Llombay, who was still being fanned with palm fronds.

"I cannot swear that this is the Empress, but I do swear that it must be her corpse that we place here," he responded, regaining his composure. "I also swear to serve no lord who might die on me," he added, making it clear to those present the strong impression the sight of the corpse had made on him.

After the final mass, Martín Cortés, accompanied by three others, carried the Empress's coffin to the vault, alongside the remains of the Catholic Monarchs.

Decisions. July 1539.

Despite still being unaware of what would happen to the pages who depended on the Empress's household, they continued their studies and routines for weeks after returning from the burial in Granada. At the end of June, rumors began to circulate among the pages and some teachers. It wasn't long before they received news of their fate.

"Mestizo, we're going to be part of Prince Felipe's household!" exclaimed Botijo with glee.

"It seems the prince himself has drawn up a list of the pages he wants in his household. We three are included," added Algarrobo, the illegitimate son of the Duke of Medina Sidonia.

"Without a doubt, this is good news. How did the news come? Is it reliable?" asked Martín, doubting its veracity as rumors were common at court and among the servants.

"A scribe from the Prince's household is my father's cousin. He himself sent the list of pages here to the Royal House," replied Algarrobo.

At that moment, a scribe entered the dormitory and, on a wooden board hanging on the wall, pinned some sheets. Once he left, the boys went to the board to read the announcement.

One of the sheets confirmed the names of the pages who would join Prince Felipe's household, and listed those who, upon joining, would receive the title of *Gentilhombre de boca*. Martín saw the list of the three who would change rank. The second on the list was him, Martín Cortés Malintzin.

"From now on, we'll have to serve stew to the prince," Martín commented quietly, disappointed by what seemed to him a humiliating position.

"Don't forget, Mestizo, we'll also accompany him to war when needed."

"That's true," replied Martín, showing a smile, although deep down he knew it was a second or even third-tier position at court.

The other sheet the scribe had pinned up contained the new subjects and the times they would be taught:

Monday
- 10 a.m. Castilian Grammar. Orthology and Calligraphy.
- 5 p.m. Latin.

Tuesday
- 10 a.m. Syntax.
- 5 p.m. Rhetoric and Poetics.

Wednesday
- 10 a.m. Algebra.
- 5 p.m. Geometry.

Thursday
- 10 a.m. Plane Trigonometry.
- 5 p.m. Analytical Geometry, Dynamics, Hydrostatics.

Friday
- 10 a.m. French Language.
- 5 p.m. English Language.

Saturday
- 10 a.m. Fortification and Military Drawing.
- 5 p.m. Geography.

Sunday
- 10 a.m. Military Instruction. Infantry Regulations.
- 5 p.m. Fencing.

Martín considered himself a good student. He had been diligent and received praise from his teachers since joining the Royal House of Pages. It was common for him to help other classmates who struggled, whether with letters or numbers, although what he enjoyed most was anything related to the art of war. He relished the lessons from the defense and fencing master, as well as the athletic exercises. He felt that physical effort freed him from worries and alleviated the feelings of loneliness and abandonment he suffered.

The journey accompanying the Empress to her final resting place had made him reflect. He had already made his decision. He did not wish to continue in the Royal House. He was tired of the court's ballroom dances and the hypocrisy of the nobles and hidalgos, who sought to advance at anyone's expense. Although he was well-known and esteemed among his peers, Martín did not consider any of them true friends. He knew that various families were always plotting intrigues, often using their children in the Royal House as tools for their palace conspiracies.

On July 18, as had been his custom for several years, Martín walked to the Church of San Pedro el Real, near the Royal House. This time he was accompanied by Botijo and Algarrobo. It was the feast day of Saint Marina, and in memory of his mother, he used to attend a mass for her soul.

"Friends, I appreciate you joining me for the mass for my mother," Martín said as they walked.

"There's nothing to thank, Mestizo. You also join us for our own masses and services," Algarrobo replied.

"Yesterday I saw that your tutor came to visit you," Botijo remarked. "Is everything alright?"

"He told me that my father has left us some mines in Taxco, in New Spain, to my brothers Luis and Martín, the younger one. The three of us in equal parts," Martín commented, remembering that along with the mine, his father had also given them a hundred slaves branded with the iron of King Carlos, so that the three of them would have resources to serve His Majesty.

"Is he giving the same to the bastards as to the little marquis?" Botijo asked, turning red as he realized he had called Mestizo a bastard.

"No, Botijo. We're only sharing those mines," Martín responded, biting his tongue, as he disliked anyone disparaging his family, including his half-brother Martín. "Well, he's also left me a couple of encomiendas, in Tlapa and Atacaxtla, two small villages I don't know where they are."

"You'd better have someone trustworthy manage that, Mestizo. It's the only way to keep an eye on your assets, especially when sharing property with your family, like the mine you mentioned."

"I'll manage it myself. I plan to return to New Spain soon, but not to take more from my father's inheritance. What I want is to assist him in any way I can. It's time to thank him and try to give back some of what he's given me. I've been here all these years thanks to him."

"As we all have, Mestizo. Our fathers are the nobles and the ones with money. We're the illegitimate children they support," said Botijo, laughing, as dim-witted as a sheep.

"My situation is different. I don't feel comfortable being kept, and even though my father is a marquis, he doesn't really belong to the nobility. I know Hernán Cortés is considered an upstart, even though he has done more for Spain and the Crown than many nobles at court. Certainly more than all of them. Don't lump me in with your lot," Martín snapped, irritated.

"Botijo didn't mean to offend you," interceded Algarrobo. "Now you also have the opportunity to establish a relationship of trust with Prince Felipe; we will be *gentilhombres de boca*. You will be close to the future king of Spain. Even if you don't have a title, you will be a hidalgo, in addition to being a knight of the Order of Santiago."

70

"I already told you, I'm not at court to serve beans to the prince, nor to add more stew to his plate; that's what being a *gentilhombre de boca* implies. I'll always be beside the king and the prince, but I want to do it in war, not in the palace dining room. I'm not a man to gossip like maidens, or like some of the noble sons you know, who think spreading rumors about other knights is also a type of battle. I want to honor my father, the Order of Santiago, and the king, but not in the way that's expected," Martín replied, ending the conversation as they arrived at the church.

Sisters. April 1540.

It was his second voyage across the ocean, and once again, it was a challenging journey. Martín had departed from Seville at the beginning of the year, and as with his previous trip, the ship was battered by a severe storm near the Lucayan Islands, causing him to curse that place. The pilot tried to steer the vessel into the port of Havana, but the storm prevented it, leading the ship to run aground on some shallows near the shore. From the coast, small boats approached the ship when the waves allowed, and they were able to take the passengers to the city. After resting for a week in Cuba, Martín was able to resume his journey, embarking for Veracruz.

Arriving in the first Spanish city, founded by his father in New Spain, and the last one Martín had visited, brought back childhood memories. It had been twelve years since he had left that port, being only six years old at the time. New constructions of buildings by the sea, such as shipyards, renovated fortifications, and docks, made the place almost unrecognizable from when he had spent a couple of days there before traveling to Spain.

He quickly found a group of travelers heading to Mexico City, the capital of New Spain, and joined them after paying a handful of coins to the guide organizing the caravan and the muleteers. In Veracruz, he bought an old piebald mare for a small sum, which would save him from making the journey on foot, although, seeing the poor condition of the animal, Martín thought he would likely end up walking.

During the journey, he preferred not to share his name and let the other travelers think he was a merchant seeking goods to trade in Spain. He listened to their opinions about Hernán Cortés. He learned how respected his father was, both by the Indians and the Spaniards. He sensed a desire among the people for the marquis, as they called him, to be governor or viceroy to better defend the interests of those living in New Spain.

The journey to Mexico was slow, as they had to travel in a group and share the route with several merchants with carts loaded with goods, preventing them from making good progress. They had just crossed a particularly cold section called the Paso de Cortés, located between the snow-capped peaks of the Popocatépetl volcano and the summit of Iztaccíhuatl, when Martín could see Mexico City from the heights. It was no longer surrounded by a large lake as he had heard in many stories, though there was a lagoon on one side.

Martín separated from the caravan heading to Mexico City, as he wanted to make a stop in Texcoco, where he headed to the Convent of San Francisco. Once there, he asked to see the abbot. He begged the cleric to grant him permission to enter and pray at the tomb of his grandmother, Catalina Pizarro. Upon learning Martín Cortés's identity, the Franciscan opened not only the doors of the chapel where his grandmother was buried beside the altar but also offered him an unoccupied cell to rest from his journey. Everyone at the convent was grateful for the numerous donations his father had made over the years. The abbot informed him of the burial places of two of his half-siblings, children of Doña Juana de Zúñiga and Hernán Cortés, who had been born and died shortly after arriving in New Spain. He prayed for all of them, as well as for Marina, his mother, whom he never forgot in his prayers.

His tutor, Juan de Avellaneda, had told him before leaving Spain that his father lived in the palace he had built in Cuernavaca, along with his wife and children, both natural and legitimate. From Texcoco, Martín took the road to that city. He was astonished upon arrival by the fabulous vegetation of the city and its cool temperature. It was not hard to find his father's palace.

He was impressed by the grandeur of the residence Hernán Cortés had built on the outskirts of Cuernavaca, at the foot of a hill. It was a pleasant place, surrounded by lush plants and trees. The palace had two levels and was at least sixty feet high, with arcades in the central third of its facade, while the other two ends were stone walls with a few scattered windows. To Martín, it looked more like a fortress than a palace.

"To whom should I announce you?" asked an Indian servant who attended to him after opening the palace door.

"Tell the marquis that his son, Martín Cortés, is here." Noting the servant's surprise, he remembered that his father had another son by that name from his wife. "Excuse me, my name is Martín Cortés Malintzin, and I am the marquis's firstborn. I have come from Spain."

The servant made him wait over an hour outside the palace. When the first drops of rain began to fall, the servant opened the door and asked him to come inside. Leading him to a small, well-lit parlor, the servant indicated that he should take a seat. Martín preferred to remain standing and look out the window. In the distance, through the light rain, he could see a high hill covered with dense forest. Its peak was clear of trees, which must have been felled. Martín thought he saw a large cross erected on the summit.

"They call it the Marquis's Cross. Beyond that point are the domains of my husband, Hernán Cortés, the Marquis of the Valley of Oaxaca," said a woman's voice behind Martín as he looked at the small mountain.

Martín turned and found himself facing a woman of simple beauty. She wore a fine cloth dress and had short hair, which was unusual for a noblewoman. Her pale skin gave the impression of someone sickly, but when Martín saw the vitality in her movements, he realized his first impression was false.

"Your Grace must be Doña Juana," said Martín, making a small bow. "Thank you for receiving me. My name is…"

"Martín. Your name is Martín," Doña Juana de Zúñiga interrupted, "just like my son and your grandfather. Please, I ask you to take a seat. We have much to discuss."

"I wouldn't want to inconvenience you, Doña Juana. The reason for my visit is to see and speak with my father, if it's not a problem," Martín excused himself.

"That conversation will be difficult. The marquis left for Spain last January with our son Martín and Luis, another natural son of the marquis," Doña Juana said, sitting next to the chair she had offered moments before. "At least your father has had the decency not to bring more illegitimate children to the palace since our marriage," she added with a cold smile.

Martín felt faint. He had not expected his father to return to Spain in the same season he was crossing the same ocean. Neither Francisco Núñez nor his tutor, Juan de Avellaneda, had informed him when Martín told them of his journey. Perhaps some of the letters Hernán Cortés sent to Spain announcing his return had been lost. Or maybe some pirate had attacked the ship carrying them, as such attacks were becoming more and more common.

He let himself fall into the armchair, tired, ashamed, and confused. It had been a costly journey for him, both financially and because of the risk due to storms. He had traveled with the intention of serving his father and supporting him in any need he might have, but now he saw that he would not be able to do so.

"I understand you may feel affected by not finding your father after such an arduous journey. I myself lost my twin sons shortly after arriving, undoubtedly due to the hardships endured during the crossing. I beg you to rest in our house for as long as you need. Here you can meet some of your family and reunite with your other sisters, who also live in our residence."

"Thank you very much, Doña Juana," Martín said, bowing to her and taking her hands. "You are very kind. I was at the

Texcoco convent and prayed before the crypt of your sons," he commented, eliciting a timid smile of gratitude from the woman.

The following days were joyful for Martín, despite the unfortunate journey and the disappointment of not being able to meet his father. He saw Leonor Cortés again, who had been born a few months before Martín left for Spain. He also met his father's three daughters with Doña Juana: María, Catalina, and Juana. But the reunion he enjoyed the most, and that brought him the greatest joy, was seeing his older sister, Catalina Pizarro, again. He spent the entire week in Cuernavaca with her.

Catalina had lived in Hernán Cortés' palace since it was built. Martín had last seen her twelve years ago, when he left for Spain with his father. She had been only twelve or thirteen back then and had been like a second mother to Martín during his early childhood in Marina's absence.

"I have a surprise for you, Martín. I'm sure it will make you very happy," she told him one day while they walked through the palace courtyard after the second rain of the day and before the third arrived, as always happened in that season.

"Nothing could make me happier than seeing you again, Catalina," Martín replied, unable to hide his emotion at being with her once more.

"Don't be silly. Come with me. There is something that will make you happier than seeing an old maid," she said, taking his hand and dragging him inside the palace.

Martín followed his sister up to her room, which was at one end of the upper floor. Catalina's bedroom, spacious and well-lit, had a table and two chairs by the window, along with several books placed on it.

"When I return to Spain, I hope you will use that pen to write to me, Catalina. I don't want to be without news of you for so long," he said, noticing the inkwell and the pen beside it.

"Sit down, Martín," his sister asked him while she bent down beside her bed and pulled a wooden box from underneath. "I brought this small chest from the palace where we grew up in Coyoacán. I don't know if you remember it."

"I think I do," Martín replied, without taking his eyes off what his sister was holding in her hands. "Could it be the box where my mother kept her clothes?"

"That's right, brother."

Martín felt a deep emotion rising from his chest. His sister embraced him.

"I never understood how you could be so attached to her, having spent so little time together, Martín. I didn't want this to be lost. I knew you would return one day, and it would make you happy to have it. I remember you always carried one of her handkerchiefs with you."

"Yes, I remember that too," Martín responded, avoiding mentioning that he carried that same handkerchief with him every day in a case.

"Do you want to open it?"

Martín lifted the wooden lid. Inside were some folded huipiles. He did not want to take out his mother's clothes and disturb them. Martín thanked his sister for the gift.

"Catalina, I'll be leaving Cuernavaca in the next few days. I plan to go to Mexico City and resolve a matter. Once I do that, I'll return to Spain," Martín said, determined to follow in his father's footsteps.

"Take me with you, brother. I don't want to continue living in this palace. When father is not here, Doña Juana treats me differently. I am not her daughter, and I understand that seeing me only brings her bitterness. Luis has already gone to Spain with father."

"But Leonor lives here too; she's also our half-sister."

"Leonor was only two years old when father returned from Spain already married, and it hasn't been difficult for her because

78

she raised her from a young age. I was already a young woman when I met Doña Juana."

"I can't take you with me this time," Martín said after thinking for a moment. "I must return to Spain. I plan to join the king's army, but I promise to meet with our father when I return and ask him to prepare for your journey to Spain. I'll request that he arranges a marriage that will allow you to live there."

Catalina embraced him, thanking him for interceding with Hernán Cortés and seeking a husband who could take her away from living in the Cuernavaca palace with her stepmother.

"Do you want me to keep the chest with your mother's clothes until you return?" Catalina asked, glancing at the small trunk on the floor.

"No, sister. Instead of leaving you as the guardian of my mother's clothes, I've thought it would be better to take it with me," Martín replied, smiling, already knowing what he planned to do with his mother's clothes.

Ten days after his arrival in Cuernavaca, Martín said goodbye to Doña Juana and all the girls in the house. Emotionally, he embraced his sister as they parted. Catalina reminded him of his promise.

"I beg you to intercede with father to arrange a marriage for me. Make sure the one he chooses is a good man, Martín," she whispered in his ear as she said goodbye. "I trust you."

"I will, sister," Martín replied. Then he mounted the horse that Doña Juana had given him instead of the old, dappled mare he had arrived on. With a gentle tap of his heels, the horse set off from Hernán Cortés's property.

By the end of the day, Martín had reached Mexico City. He asked some gentlemen he saw in the main square about the man he was looking for, and they not only gave him directions but also accompanied him to the man's house on Medinas Street. With a slight bow, they bid Martín farewell. He had no doubt that, given the man's name and position, everyone would know where he lived.

In front of Martín stood a two-story building with numerous windows and balconies framed in gray stone. The blood-red facade stood out against the other buildings painted in softer colors. He remembered that the palace in Coyoacán, where he had spent his early years, also had a similarly colored exterior. There was a strong resemblance between the two houses. Undoubtedly, the bold red color of both residences had been requested by the same person in the past.

After introducing himself, the maid who opened the heavy door with large metal rivets asked him to enter the vestibule. She closed the thick wooden door once horse and rider had crossed the threshold. A servant took Martín's horse, which was laden with saddlebags and a bulky bundle on the rump, to the stables. Martín rested on a cold stone bench until he was shown into a sitting room on the ground floor, adjacent to the vestibule where he had waited.

While filling a glass of water, the maid informed him that the master of the house had not yet returned from his errands.

"The lady of the house moved a few days ago to a retreat in the Chapultepec woods, so you will have to wait for the master in the sitting room," said the maid.

"Is his daughter at home by any chance?"

The maid looked him over from head to toe, noting that he was well-dressed, polite, and unarmed.

"Yes, the young lady is at home, but you must understand, sir, that you must first be received by her father."

"I understand," Martín commented, taking a seat, and waiting for the master of the house to appear.

It was already dusk. Martín had been waiting in the sitting room for two hours when he saw through the curtains some horses stopping in front of the main door of the residence. The young

80

man on horseback dismounted and helped the older gentleman, who was on the other horse, to dismount. It was clear that he did not need help to dismount, but Martín saw that it was a gesture of chivalry and not of support.

He heard the doors open wide and the sound of the horses' hooves as they entered the vestibule. Voices were heard outside the room where Martín was waiting, undoubtedly informing the master of the house of the visit of a man who called himself Martín Cortés, but who was not the young son of the Marquis of the Valley.

The door to the room opened, and a thin man with scant gray hair and a well-trimmed gray beard entered. He stopped, observing the young visitor, and closed the door behind him. He approached Martín to get a better look at him in the dim light coming through the window. He stopped in front of him.

"Without a doubt, you are Martín Cortés Malintzin," said the master of the house, nodding his head to affirm his statement.

"That is my name. Juan Jaramillo is your name, and you are the mayor of Mexico," Martín replied.

After shaking hands, Juan Jaramillo lost his initial shyness and embraced Martín, who returned the man's heartfelt hug, and they patted each other's backs. As they parted, Martín saw Juan Jaramillo blushing with the emotion of the encounter.

"The last time I saw you, you were only four or five years old. I had returned from Las Hibueras with your father and with Marina, your mother."

"If I'm not mistaken, you and my mother got married on that trip."

"That's right. I married Marina on the outbound journey, and on the return trip, on the ship that brought us back, our daughter María was born. It's a pity that Marina passed away a little more than a year later. What a great woman she was!" said Juan Jaramillo, his face saddened.

"I regret being the cause that made you remember and relive the sorrow of that loss. I do not intend my visit to cause any inconvenience or distress. I would like, if it's not too much trouble for you, to meet my half-sister, María," Martín commented.

"Your visit is no trouble at all. In fact, I will have a room prepared for you right away," he said as he approached a small silver bell on the table and rang it. "I hope you can enjoy a few days in our company and get to know my daughter María, your half-sister, better."

The young man who had helped Juan Jaramillo dismount when they arrived at the house entered immediately. Jaramillo informed him that the guest would be staying for a few days and that he should notify the staff to prepare a bedroom. He also asked him to call his daughter to the room.

"Martín, please sit down," Jaramillo said, indicating an armchair and sitting down himself.

"From what I've heard, the trip to Las Hibueras must have been arduous and very difficult," Martín commented.

"Almost as terrible as the siege and capture of this city, and believe me, that was something horrible," Jaramillo replied. "Hernán Cortés always had soldiers and captains around him who thought of betraying him, but your father knew how to assert himself over all of them. I never thought that Captain Cristóbal de Olid, who had proven to be an excellent warrior, brave and honorable, would turn out to be a traitor. He was deceived by the governor of Cuba, Diego Velázquez, the true enemy of Hernán Cortés. Velázquez offered him the governorship of Honduras and convinced him, which was a betrayal of your father. That was the reason for the expedition to Las Hibueras, to punish Cristóbal de Olid."

"At least you returned with a wife and a daughter from that expedition," Martín responded.

"That's true; every time I see my daughter, I am filled with pride. She has many of Marina's traits, la Malinche, as some called her. I hear María's footsteps coming," he said as the door to the room opened and a young woman with olive skin, similar to Martín's, entered.

"Daughter, let me introduce you to your half-brother, Martín Cortés Malintzin," Juan Jaramillo said, rising from his chair.

María Jaramillo approached Martín and hugged him with emotion, which moved her father, who shed a few tears at witnessing their reunion.

"Martín will stay with us for a few days," said Juan Jaramillo.

"Brother, I have prayed many times for God to give me the opportunity to see you again. We met when I was little, but I don't remember it. Father remarried and had no more children with his new wife, so you, Martín, along with my father, are my only family," said María Jaramillo in a sweet voice, taking Martín's hands and squeezing them.

Dinner that night extended into the early morning hours. The siblings could not stop sharing their lives, asking each other questions, interrupting, laughing at their experiences, and getting emotional over the losses, illnesses, and difficulties each had faced. Juan Jaramillo watched them in silence, not daring to interrupt. It was a conversation between siblings that felt as if they had only been apart since the previous day, considering how well they spoke and understood each other.

Juan noticed the similarities in their features. Brother and sister had bronze-colored skin, fine, straight dark brown hair. Their gazes were similar, with eyes a soft brown, like rosemary honey. Both had a good bearing. Martín was slender but strong; tall, more so than was common for young men his age. María had long hair and, at fourteen, she was beginning to show the lines of the woman she would soon become.

Martín observed his sister as she spoke, noticing something familiar in her features and expressions, though he couldn't quite identify it. Occasionally, as she told him something, Martín would get lost in thought, trying to figure out who his half-sister reminded him of. He convinced himself that the resemblance was because they shared the same mother.

"I would like to give you something I brought, María. A gift, but I need you to show me where my room is, as my belongings must have been taken there."

The maid escorted Martín to the upper floor of the house and led him through a hallway overlooking an interior courtyard, to his room. Hanging over the back of a chair was his saddlebag with his clothes, and on the bed was the bundle his horse had carried. He picked it up, left the room, and headed back to the living room where Juan Jaramillo and his daughter were waiting.

"I believe you are the person who should have this," Martín said, entering the room where they had dined a few hours earlier and continued their conversation. "It wouldn't be fitting for a gentleman to be carrying this," he said, placing the chest on the table in front of María Jaramillo.

The young woman opened the box, intrigued. She did not understand what she was seeing inside. They looked like traditional Aztec clothes. She took one of the folded garments on top and unfolded it.

"It's a huipil," she said, not understanding what her brother intended by giving her this.

Juan Jaramillo immediately remembered who these clothes belonged to. La Malinche had always loved that attire and never wore Castilian clothes.

"Is it a huipil…?" repeated María. "From our mother?"

"Yes, it's a huipil from our mother."

María took out the garments one by one from the chest. She spread out four huipiles and five handkerchiefs over the chairs.

84

"I don't wear traditional Aztec clothes, and even if I did, I prefer to keep these as a treasure," she said, smiling. "Thank you, brother. I never would have expected her clothes to be preserved. She left none at home when she went to Xilotepec."

"Do you remember her?" Martín asked.

"I was two years old when she left," replied María, implying that she had no memory of her.

"She went to Xilotepec, near Santiago de Querétaro. She wanted to organize an encomienda that Hernán Cortés gave her as a dowry. In a nearby village, before arriving, she fell ill with smallpox and passed away," Juan Jaramillo informed.

"Yes, I learned that from my father. I remember something of her face, her hair, and her clothing," commented Martín, looking at La Malinche's clothes on the chair.

"After our return from Las Hibueras, she visited you several times at Luis Altamirano's house. I accompanied her on some of those visits. She carried María, who was a baby then. You played with your mother while your sister slept. She loved you very much. She affectionately called you 'my tiger.'"

"I remember our farewell before I left with my father for Spain," said Martín, avoiding mentioning that what he remembered most was her scent. "My grandmother Catalina showed me a letter where my father also referred to me as a little tiger," he commented, smiling at the memory.

"It's time to rest. Martín, you can stay with us as long as you need," said Juan Jaramillo, rising from his chair.

"I'll stay just a few days. I came to New Spain to reunite with my father, but by a terrible coincidence, we both crossed the sea without knowing the other was heading in the opposite direction."

The two siblings enjoyed each other's company all week. They walked through the streets of the city center. María, holding

Martín's arm, pointed out the owners of some of the largest palaces and residences in Mexico City.

The mestizo siblings approached to see the old shipyards on the shores of the lagoon that still existed on one side of the city. Inside, some of the brigantines Hernán Cortés had ordered built in Tlaxcala to besiege Tenochtitlan by water were preserved.

"One of those brigantines was captained by my father," María said.

"It's incredible that they're still in good condition. Did you know they were built in Tlaxcala and brought disassembled to Texcoco?"

"Yes, my father told me that with those small ships, they captured Cuauhtémoc when he tried to flee Tenochtitlan, the same day Hernán Cortés entered with his troops and settled in Tlatelolco."

Martín was amazed at the length, width, and straightness of the streets. From María, he learned that before the Spanish conquest, the ancient city of Tenochtitlan had only a third of its streets on land, and the rest were mostly navigable canals, some still in use, with a small strip of land for walking like a causeway. The city center, where the main square called the Zócalo was located, had all its nearby streets on solid ground, as the old waterways had been filled in.

"This square was built over the largest sacred precinct of Tenochtitlan, brother. There, where your father's residence is," she said, pointing to a large building on one side of the square, "was the palace of Moctezuma II. The church you see was built with the same stones that once formed the Great Temple, dedicated to Huitzilopochtli and Tláloc."

Martín was mesmerized by his sister's expressions as she spoke, her gestures as she explained things, and even her way of walking. Everything seemed, somehow, familiar. He kept

86

thinking that what he saw in her were his own gestures, since they shared the same mother. It was not until he focused on her smile that another person came to mind. A woman he had not seen in twelve years, who had long since passed away. Watching María, Martín remembered his grandmother, Catalina Pizarro.

At that moment, everything made sense to Martín. The expressions on María's face, her gestures, her way of smiling, talking, and even walking—all reminded him of his grandmother Catalina, with whom he had lived when he arrived in Spain and whom he had loved dearly.

How could it be?

He closed his eyes for a moment and stopped walking. How foolish he had been. Yes, a true idiot. Martín realized the obvious. Martín finally understood. His father had given his mother, La Malinche, to Juan Jaramillo, and they had married. But the passion between La Malinche and Hernán Cortés had not ceased, despite her being married to another man. Without a doubt, they had passionate encounters, resulting in his mother becoming pregnant with Hernán Cortés's child once more.

"Martín, brother. Are you alright?" María Jaramillo asked, frightened, noticing that her brother had stopped with a lost look and a pale face.

"Yes, María. Sorry. I felt a slight dizziness," Martín replied, looking at her closely again. There was no doubt. She might be mestiza, like him, but the expressions on her face were the same as those of his grandmother, Catalina, Hernán Cortés's mother. Now that he looked closely, even the shape of her nose was the same. María had inherited her grandmother's features.

"Father…" Martín murmured, shaking his head as he stared at the cobblestone pavement of the main square.

"Brother, you're scaring me. Let's go have a cacao drink under the arches of the building. They say many Spaniards suffer from dizziness when they arrive in this city. They claim they lack air and breath. I think that's what's happened to you."

She took his arm and led him to a cantina where they served drinks, cookies, and sweet cakes. Sitting at a table under the arches of the building, Martín watched the people walking by. He saw Spaniards in elegant clothes with their wives and children, but he also saw Indians dressed in the Castilian style. Occasionally, he observed numerous brown-skinned children playing in the Zócalo.

"They are mestizos, Martín, like us," his sister commented while they sat by the square, drinking cacao. "The Spaniards paired up with Indian women from the moment they arrived. Also, Aztec nobles, the ones you see dressed in the Castilian style, have taken Spanish wives. The children of these couples are the ones you see with skin darker than the Spaniards but lighter than the Indians."

Martín listened, his mind still reeling from his realization. As he sipped his cacao, he looked at María, feeling a deep connection and a newfound understanding of their shared heritage.

Martín could not shake from his thoughts the revelation he had discovered just an hour earlier, a few steps from where they were now. Juan Jaramillo was a good man and did not deserve to know what Martín had realized about María's parentage. Maybe someday, he would tell his sister, but only when Juan Jaramillo was no longer in this world.

"Does everyone live in the city?" he asked, trying to distract himself from the discovery he had made about his sister's lineage.

"Yes, although there are areas where more Spaniards live and others where more Indians reside. In the center, where we are now, more Spaniards or descendants of the conquistadors tend to live, though some Aztec nobles have their new houses here as well," María informed her brother, who looked at her affectionately.

"Tell me, María. Don't you have any other siblings? Has your father not had more children with his second wife?"

"No, I don't have any other siblings. I believe I mentioned it when we first met. Despite being married for over ten years, my father hasn't had children with Beatriz, my stepmother. Maybe she has a barren womb."

Martín thought that this could be a possibility, or perhaps Juan Jaramillo was impotent or sterile, which would confirm his suspicion that María was indeed his blood sister.

"You don't have any suitors yet, being so beautiful?" Martín asked, hoping to steer the conversation away from his unsettling thoughts.

María blushed at the question. After taking a sip of her cacao drink, she looked out toward the main square in front of them.

"I do have a suitor, but my father says I'm still young and should wait a few more years. He has already asked for my hand. Father has told him that he will grant it if he waits and behaves honorably during this time."

"Who is the lucky man to have you as his wife?"

"You are very curious, sir," María replied, laughing. "His name is Luis de Quesada, a gentleman born in Spain, in Granada. He has an encomienda in Santiago de Querétaro. He is a serious and honorable man."

What she didn't tell Martín was that her father had nearly imprisoned her suitor for organizing a fake abduction with his friends. Juan Jaramillo had stopped them from taking her from the house. Reluctantly, and to avoid the scandal of anything happening between them before marriage, her father granted Luis de Quesada her hand.

In one of the frequent conversations Juan Jaramillo and Martín had during those days, Martín learned that after the return from the expedition to Las Hibueras in 1526, Hernán Cortés had appointed Jaramillo as mayor. A year ago, Juan Jaramillo had been appointed again as Mayor of Mexico and was now the Mayor of Mesta. He was not ashamed to tell Martín that, in 1530, he refused to raise the banner during the feast of San Hipólito, a date commemorating the Spanish triumph in the capture of the ancient Tenochtitlan. He was reprimanded by the Mexico City council for that refusal, but it did not escalate further.

"Why did you do it, Juan? Why did you refuse to raise the banner?" Martín asked.

"Martín, I stood beside Hernán Cortés in every battle since our arrival in the Indies. I fought in Cempoala, Tlaxcala, and Cholula, as well as other minor skirmishes. I escaped Tenochtitlan on that fateful night," Juan Jaramillo recounted, his gaze drifting out the window. "Nearby is Tacuba Street, which was once the Tacuba causeway. Right there, at the Toltecs channel, we lived through our hell on earth. We trampled over our companions and allies to survive while the Aztecs slaughtered us. After escaping the city, I fought in the Battle of Otumba, where God spared our lives."

"I remember Gonzalo de Sandoval told me about Otumba when I was a child during our journey to Spain," Martín said.

"What a great man, captain and friend Gonzalo de Sandoval was!" Jaramillo exclaimed, turning his gaze to Martín. "Later, I returned to Tenochtitlan with your father and captained one of the brigantines that besieged this city."

"María told me. But I don't understand. All of that is reason for celebration and remembrance," said Martín.

"Indeed, it is; but the majority of the population here is Indian. It would be different if it were celebrated in Spain, where few would be offended by the victory. On the contrary, there are plenty of reasons to celebrate it. But to hold such commemorations in New Spain is to remind the vanquished of the humiliation of their defeat. Moreover, Marina had recently passed away at that time, and such a manifestation seemed offensive to me."

90

"Even though she participated in the victory."

"She didn't just participate—your mother was crucial to the conquest of Mexico," Jaramillo reminded him. "Without her, it wouldn't have been possible. Or perhaps it would have taken longer. And many more lives."

During the days Martín stayed at Jaramillo's house, Doña Beatriz de Andrade, Jaramillo's second wife, returned from the resting house. They had married three years after Marina's death. She had been staying at the resting house the Mexico City council had allocated to Jaramillo and Marina on a plot near the Chapultepec forest, where they had built a house with a garden and a small farm.

Martín said goodbye to everyone before his departure, thanking them for their hospitality, kindness, and affection.

In a private moment with Martín that morning, Juan Jaramillo handed him a small leather sack.

"Martín, I know you rely on your father's allowance and that you made this journey expecting to find him. Ocean crossings are expensive, so I wish to give you this money to help you," Jaramillo said, handing him the small bag of coins.

"I cannot accept it, my dear Juan. You have already done so much for me. You have hosted me in your home and treated me like a son," Martín replied, declining the offer.

"Alright. Don't take it as a gift. Let's both think of it as a loan to be repaid when it's convenient for you," Jaramillo said with a smile, seeking a dignified way for Martín to accept.

"I'll accept it then, with every intention of repaying you."

Illustration #2

Hernán Cortés' Palace in Cuernavaca, as it must have been in XVI century

Brothers. May 1541.

Martín Cortés spotted the sands of Seville from the ship that had carried him across the ocean from Veracruz to the Andalusian capital. The journey had been swift, free of storms, unlike the previous two voyages, and untroubled by English or French pirates. They managed to complete the ocean crossing in forty-five days.

Leaning over the ship's rail, he observed the approach maneuver against the current of the Guadalquivir River. The sandy shore was bustling with people, goods, livestock, a few fires where fish were being roasted on spits, stalls covered with awnings, small shipyards, and above all, a cacophony of voices and activity.

Upon disembarking, he had to register, like all travelers, at a table set up near the wooden plank used for passengers to disembark from the ship.

"Your full name. Place of birth. Destination," demanded one of the scribes filling out the arrival logbook, without looking up.

"Martín Cortés. Born in Coyoacán, New Spain," he responded, raising his voice to be heard over the clamor.

"Destination?" asked the scribe after noting his details in the book.

"Destination?" Martín hesitated for a moment, unsure where to go to meet his father. He thought it best to head to the town of Madrid and inquire about him with Juan de Avellaneda, his tutor, or Francisco Núñez, his father's representative.

"Toledo!" someone behind him said. "Don Martín Cortés will go to Toledo."

The scribe noted Toledo in his book and asked Martín to step aside so he could continue with the rest of the passengers.

"Don Martín," the man said once the young man had stepped away from the desk and approached him. "I see you've grown into a man. If I hadn't heard your name, I wouldn't have realized it was you. Quite the gentleman, indeed." The man observed Martín up and down with pride.

"Juan de Lepe, how could I forget! You looked after me since I left Mexico at just six years old and accompanied me during our journey. When we arrived in Seville, I lost track of you and never heard from you again," Martín said, moving closer to the aged Juan to embrace him.

"Your father, the marquis, sent me a message. An acquaintance of his sent him a letter from Cuba when you arrived after nearly shipwrecking on your way to New Spain," Juan de Lepe said, almost breathless, smiling. "Three or four months ago, the marquis sent me a notice. I left Lepe, my village, and came to Seville, where I have rented a place near the Puerta del Arenal. From there, I could watch the ships arriving from New Spain. When people disembarked, I listened closely to the scribes keeping the register."

"And today you heard my name," Martín said, smiling.

"Thank the Lord I did, because, as I said, I wouldn't have recognized you; you've changed so much."

Martín rested for a couple of days at an inn near the Giralda, the same tower that had left him speechless at six years old. Before leaving Seville, he rode his horse to Juan de Lepe's house and bid him farewell with another embrace.

"Take care, Juan. You can return to your family in Lepe now," Martín said as he mounted his horse.

"Thank you, sir. I will always keep you in my prayers."

Before going to the residence of Juan de Castilla in Madrid, where his father was staying, Martín wanted to stop in Toledo, and visit the Fuensalida Palace, where Empress Isabel had passed away two years earlier. He recalled the moments of mourning shared with his fellow pages. He seized the opportunity to enter the Church of Santo Tomé and prayed for the empress's soul.

96

There was not a day when he did not remember her in his prayers, as he had promised Prince Felipe when his mother died.

"Father!" Martín exclaimed as he entered the room where his father sat at a table, writing. He had told Lucas, his father's old servant, not to announce his arrival, as he wanted to surprise the Marquis of the Valley.

"Martín, my son! Is it really you?" Hernán Cortés exclaimed, rising from his chair, moving toward his son. "I didn't know you had arrived in Seville."

"I asked good Juan not to inform you. I would reach you faster than any letter he could send," Martín replied, embracing his father warmly.

"Good Lord, so many years have passed," Hernán Cortés said, placing his hands on his son's shoulders and looking him in the face. Martín was taller than him, with tanned skin and a dark mustache above his lip. His straight, dark hair reached his neck.

"Twelve years have passed, father. I was about seven years old when I was left at the Royal House of Pages. Now I am nearly nineteen."

"And you are a man. Strong," he said, squeezing his arms, "intelligent, as confirmed by Licentiate Antonio de Toledo, and loyal, as one of your companions told me when he saw me visiting the Royal House. Now that I see you, I am not ashamed to say you are also handsome. Without a doubt, you got that from your mother," Hernán Cortés laughed. "You have her same look," he said emotionally, embracing his eldest son again.

"You are also strong and look healthy, father," Martín replied, returning the compliment.

"They told me you were honest, son. Don't start lying now," Hernán Cortés replied with a smile. "These past years have aged me more due to the lawsuits I've faced than the battles I've fought."

Father and son moved to the armchairs beside the desk. Martín noticed his father was writing a letter. He recalled that his father's writing was always full of flourishes and pen strokes, making it somewhat difficult to read.

"I was writing to the king," Hernán Cortés commented, realizing his son had seen the pages on the table.

"I regret not writing to you to inform you of my journey to New Spain, father. I wanted to arrive to be at your service. I knew about the problems you had in the South Sea, as well as the numerous unjust lawsuits you were facing."

"Son, as far as I know, the letter announcing my imminent arrival in Spain never reached its destination. I don't know what happened. It's not the first time one of my ships hasn't arrived," he said, recalling when French pirates intercepted a shipment of gold he was sending to the king. "It was an unfortunate coincidence that we both undertook the journey at nearly the same time."

"I visited your palace in Cuernavaca, father. I met your wife, Doña Juana. She seemed like a wonderful woman—elegant and a good household manager. I also met your daughters and was able to reunite with Leonor and Catalina."

"Yes, I have been fortunate with Juana. She has brought me peace in such difficult times in New Spain," he paused thoughtfully, "and she is a good woman. Since your mother, Juana is the only woman I can say I have loved."

"I also went to Mexico City. There I met my sister María," Martín mentioned, hoping for some reaction from his father that would confirm what he had discovered.

"The daughter of Juan Jaramillo? I hope good Juan is in good health. I have always had special esteem for him. I appointed him mayor of Mexico," Hernán Cortés recalled. "I saw his daughter, your half-sister, a couple of times when she was still small. She could barely walk."

Martín was tempted to tell his father that María was not his half-sister. To reveal that she was his blood sister; and the daughter of Malinche and Hernán Cortés. The thought flashed through his mind like lightning, but as quickly as it came, it left. He would have liked his father to know that María was just like her grandmother Catalina, retaining the same features, expressions, and even mannerisms as her grandmother, except for the color of her skin.

But Martín would not do it. He would not reproach his father for being unable to stay away from Marina, even though she was married to Juan Jaramillo. Nor could she avoid the attraction and love she felt for him.

"Is everything alright, son? You fell silent," Hernán Cortés commented, his gaze sharp.

"Yes, father, I was just distracted. I'm a bit tired from the journey."

"Before you retire to rest, I want you to meet Martín Cortés, your younger brother. You will also see Luis, who is already a man, like you."

Hernán Cortés asked Lucas, the servant, to call his sons without informing them of their older brother's arrival.

Martín heard footsteps running down the hallway. The door burst open, and a boy of about seven years old ran in.

"Who are you?" he asked boldly, leaving Martín astonished by the boy's audacity.

"Martín, that is no way to enter a room or address a stranger," Hernán Cortés reprimanded.

"Don't worry, father. Hello, I'm Martín Cortés, and I'm your older brother," Martín said, extending his hand to greet his namesake.

"Oh, you're the mestizo. Yes, I've heard about you," the boy said, shaking the offered hand. "I am Martín Cortés de Zúñiga. One day I will be the Marquis of the Valley."

"I know. Nice to meet you," Martín replied, surprised by the boy's boldness. "I'm Martín the Mestizo, that's true, and you are Martín the Creole."

"Hello," said a voice from the doorway.

"Hello, you must be Luis," Martín said, addressing the young man who had entered.

"And you, Martín, my older brother," said the other, giving him a vigorous hug.

Luis Cortés, three years younger, must have been around sixteen. He was slender and had a sparse goatee under his chin. He was slightly shorter than Martín but had a lot of energy and strength, which Martín felt when he hugged him. Hernán Cortés, seated by his desk, looked at his three sons with pride. He knew that his eldest would always look after the other two; he was the most responsible and noble. Luis was loyal in his own way, though he was raised differently, with a haughty temperament and more independence. Young Martín was, without a doubt, the most spoiled of all the children. He had been raised with utmost care, as Doña Juana had lost the twins, a boy and a girl, during her first childbirth. Therefore, young Martín had received all their attention and had been pampered as if he were an only child, which had given him a somewhat selfish and demanding nature.

Several months went by in Madrid. Hernán Cortés and Martín the Mestizo visited the court on several occasions. During these visits, Martín had the opportunity to greet Prince Felipe again, who remembered him fondly. He recalled the brief time they had spent together when he served in the Prince's House as a page. Martín conveyed the affection he had for the prince's mother, and the prince thanked him for remembering her.

King Carlos was planning an expedition against the pirates who frequently raided Spanish coastal towns, boarding ships carrying goods in the Mediterranean. On one occasion, the king's troops attacked Tunis, the city taken by the pirate Barbarossa the previous year. The Tunis Expedition, as it was known, was a great success for the monarch, and now he wished to repeat the operation in Algiers, the base of the Moorish pirates threatening Mediterranean trade, causing great harm to the people, heavy losses to merchants, and significant damage to the crown itself.

Hernán Cortés gathered his sons in their Madrid residence. He had decided to join the fleet being assembled to attack the Moors and pirates.

"Sons, I will take charge of gathering a group of soldiers to join us in the campaign the king is organizing to punish the Moors in Algiers. Martín, you are the youngest, and you will continue your training at the Royal House of Pages in the House of Prince Felipe, just as Martín the elder did before."

"I will, father," young Martín responded politely.

"The three of us will march to Málaga, where the fleet led by the Duke of Alba de Tormes, Don Fernando Álvarez de Toledo y Pimentel, is being assembled. As soon as we are ready, we will join the rest of the fleet in the bay of the city of Mallorca," Hernán Cortés said to Martín and Luis. "I have ordered your weapons, armor, and clothing to be prepared for the campaign. I know you both are brave and daring. I trust in your grace to further ennoble our family."

The day before they were to depart for the port where the troops would gather, Martín the Mestizo was summoned by his father.

"Close the door, son. I don't want anyone to interrupt us now."

Martín closed the door and slid the bolt to ensure no one could enter. He approached the table where his father was sitting and took a seat across from him.

"What I'm about to show you, Martín, has caused me more than a few headaches. Even with the king himself and his wife, Empress Isabel, may she rest in peace."

Hernán Cortés took out a robust cedarwood case, decorated with restrained elegance.

"You know that, although much gold was lost during the fateful night when we retreated from Tenochtitlan, some of it was recovered after the city fell."

"I've heard the stories, father."

"Well. This case has never left my side since those years. It contains five large, exquisitely cut emeralds. They were part of Moctezuma's treasure, and he given to me uncut shortly after we met. Somehow, Empress Isabel learned of their existence and asked to see them, even requesting that I sell them to her, promising the king would pay their value. I showed them to her but refused to sell them, explaining that they were a gift for Doña Juana on our wedding day," Hernán Cortés confided.

"But they weren't given as part of the dowry," Martín commented.

"No, they weren't. And that was the cause of the king and his wife's displeasure with me. Fortunately, that is in the past now. At least, I hope their displeasure is only temporary."

Hernán Cortés turned the case toward his son.

"Open it, please."

Martín unlatched the small clasp and lifted the lid. Inside, on a black velvet lining, lay five intricately cut emeralds, each casting greenish glints as they caught the sunlight streaming through the window.

"They are valued at over a hundred thousand ducats, son."

Martín carefully lifted each emerald from its velvet bed. The first, the largest, was shaped like a partially opened rose. The second was sculpted to resemble a hunter's horn. The one in the center was a fish with gold inlaid eyes. The fourth had the shape of a bell with a large pearl as its clapper and bore an inscription on the bell's body that read "Blessed be the one who raised you." The fifth and final emerald was a cup with a gold base and a large pearl embedded in it. The rim of the cup had the inscription: *inter natos mulierum non surrexit maior.*[11]

"Saint Matthew?" Martín asked after reading the phrase.

"That's right, son. I see Licentiate Toledo was right when he praised your talent."

"Father, you don't intend to take this great treasure to the campaign in Algiers, do you?" Martín asked, placing the jewels back in their case and closing it.

"Son, this could be our safeguard. If we are captured by the Moors, they will only release us for a good ransom. I have shown you these jewels so you know they exist and that I will carry them with me. If I die, you must pass them on to your brother Martín; he will inherit a large part of my estate," Hernán Cortés said, a hint of shame in his voice. "But you need not worry, I will not leave you destitute. I don't want you to think that."

"Father, I will fulfill your will, and there's no need to justify your decisions to me."

"Remember that if I die, the emeralds are to be used solely for paying any of our ransoms," Hernán Cortés said, taking the case and placing it back in a drawer.

---

[11] Of those born of women, there arose no one greater.

The Algiers Expedition. October 1541.

"That's our galley, Martín: La Esperanza,[12]" said Hernán Cortés.

"A good name for a ship, no doubt. Do we know who will command it?"

"The captain will be Enrique Enríquez, an excellent sailor with experience in several naval battles. I've heard good things about him," Hernán Cortés replied, satisfied.

In front of them at the port of Málaga was part of the fleet that would attack Algiers. There were around two hundred large ships, such as galleons, galleys, caravels, and urcas, along with about a hundred smaller vessels, like tafureas and escorchapines. On the dock, there was a great deal of activity as horses were being loaded on board via long gangplanks. All the ships were being loaded with culverins, falconets, and arquebuses.

"A message has been sent to the king for Admiral Andrea Doria's fleet in Mallorca to set sail as soon as possible. We had planned to meet them there, but due to bad weather, we will meet the rest of the navy west of Algiers at Cape Cajina," Captain Enrique Enríquez said to Hernán Cortés and his sons.

"Captain, are there many men and ships?" Martín asked.

"The largest fleet ever assembled. If my numbers are correct, we'll have around four hundred fifty war and transport ships, and sixty-five galleys. For the landing, there will be nearly twenty-four thousand men from your ranks and about twelve thousand sailors from mine. The majority of the troops are Spanish, though there are also Italians and Germans."

Martín saw a man in religious garb approaching them. He was slightly older than Martín, with a bald head. Taking advantage of the moment when his father had finished speaking with Captain Enríquez and the captain had moved toward his

---

[12] The Hope.

galley moored at the dock, the man seized the opportunity to approach Hernán Cortés.

"Captain Cortés? I've finally found you," Hernán Cortés turned and observed the religious man. "Forgive me for calling you captain, I forgot that you are now the Marquis of the Valley. I heard you received that well-deserved title after our last meeting," he commented flatteringly.

"Friar López de Gómara, I'm glad to see you again!" exclaimed the conquistador, shaking the friar's hand. "If I'm not mistaken, the last time we saw each other was in 1529, when I came to Spain with my son Martín," he said, pointing to his son.

The two men continued talking on the dock. Luis took the opportunity to visit a nearby brothel, while Martín oversaw the loading of their weapons and supplies on board. He inspected his father's small cabin, where the two brothers would sleep alongside Captain Enríquez. Space on the galleys was limited, as they were overloaded with soldiers, artillery, and animals. The galley slaves, who rowed beneath the deck, also reduced the usable space, unlike on sailing ships which used only sails and not oars.

On October 18, the fleet assembled in Málaga set sail for Algiers. During the voyage, they endured a storm, which fortunately did not damage the ships, and there were no casualties. By October 21, they had Algiers in sight, but an easterly wind and rough seas prevented the ships from landing troops, as the waves near the shore made it impossible.

Martín felt the energy of the imminent battle against the pirates. He could see them from the deck, patrolling the coast on their horses. The distance was so short that he could see the glint of their curved swords and the long beards some of them wore.

On October 23, seeing that the storm had somewhat abated and the waves near the coast were less intense, various troops landed between Larach and Hamma, locations near Algiers. The men jumped into the water from the boats, which reached up to their waists. They carried arquebuses, gunpowder, and provisions for three days above their heads. Unfortunately, the landing could not be completed, as the storm intensified again by midday, preventing the rest of the soldiers from reaching the shore and leaving the horses and heavy artillery on the ships.

Martín heard rumors that King Carlos had sent a messenger to Hassan-Aga, the Sardinian eunuch who commanded Algiers—known as "the well-guarded" due to its privileged position and fortifications. The messenger never returned with a response. Martín also caught wind of gossip about a witch, who protected the city with her dark arts, while cursing the armies attempting to take it.

The few troops that had managed to disembark advanced toward the city on three fronts. The main and leading front was composed of Spaniards, followed by Germans, and Italians in the rear. Hernán Cortés and his two sons watched from the stern of La Esperanza as the king's soldiers were harassed on the coast by Moorish horsemen armed with crossbows and some muskets.

During the night, the storm that had begun at dusk increased in force and violence. The coast was invisible from the ships, and the sailors were occupied with ensuring the wind did not drive them against the rocks or cause collisions between the ships.

On October 24, the first light of dawn illuminated the place where the soldiers had camped late the previous day. Everyone on board the ships were appalled. The violent storm had devastated the camp, and the ground where the men had camped was muddy. The Moors within the city walls emerged at dawn and attacked the weak forces that had disembarked and had spent a sleepless night due to the storm. Despite being soaked by the night's rain and chilled by the cold, they bravely defended themselves against the Moors and managed to repel them, inflicting many casualties.

Taking advantage of a brief calm in the weather, the ships moved closer to the coast again and unloaded more horses and artillery. The plan was to attack the city of Algiers the following day.

Seeing that the coastal undertow had diminished, troops began landing one league from Algiers, between the Khemir and Harrach torrents. The galleys received the order, and approached the shore, starting to lower a large number of skiffs and boats filled to the brim with soldiers. The galleons protected the men approaching the beach, sweeping the coast with their cannons, and clearing it of the Moorish squads waiting for His Majesty's troops. The first to reach the shore engaged in skirmishes with some enemies who had not retreated. The Spaniards were surprised that some of their opponents were Spanish Moors, traitors from major cities like Mallorca or Valencia. They killed several Moors during these brief fights on the beach and drove the rest into flight without suffering any casualties among the king's troops.

Once the captives were interrogated to learn about the forces inside Algiers, they confessed that only eight hundred Turks and about five thousand native Moors defended it. It seemed that the capture of Algiers was assured.

Martín overheard some veteran sailors speaking with Captain Enríquez. Seeing that Hernán Cortés and his son had heard what was being said, Enríquez decided to inform them of the situation.

"Marquis, my most experienced men and I, as well as some captains from other ships I've spoken to, believe a strong storm is approaching. We would do well to move away from the coast and seek a nearby bay for shelter," said Enríquez, concerned.

"I believe you, Captain; you know the sea. But we have orders to disembark as much as we can. We will try to do so before the storm hits. Rest assured, with God's help, it will be done," Hernán Cortés replied, as eager as his sons Martín and

Luis to set foot on land and fight the infidel, something father and son had sworn to do on the Bible when they received the habit of the Order of Santiago.

The storm arrived sooner than anyone anticipated. On the night of October 24 to 25, a strong northeasterly wind dragged the ships, even with anchors and chains in the depths. The sea began to swell as if it were starting to boil. Waves tossed the ships in all directions. Black clouds covered the sky after sunset, unleashing torrential rain.

"I'll try to get closer to the coast so you can disembark!" Captain Enríquez shouted over the roar of the storm to Hernán Cortés.

La Esperanza approached the coastline as much as it could, before the waves broke. Skiffs were lowered, and Martín Cortés jumped onto one, helping his father and his brother Luis down. Before boarding the small boat, Hernán Cortés wrapped a cloth around his arm and tied it with a knot.

"The emeralds are here, Martín," he said, raising his voice to be heard over the storm.

The skiffs neared the beach. Martín turned and, through the night's shadows, saw the nearest ships being thrown against the rocky shore, some stranded and others half-sunken. From the boat, he could hear the wood of the ships splintering against the rocks and the sailors' cries for help. The galleys were the only ones spared from being wrecked on the reefs, thanks to the strength of the rowers who rowed for their lives. Thus, most of the galleys were saved.

As they neared the shore, a large wave capsized the boats still far from the beach. Martín was plunged into the cold, dark water, feeling limbs thrashing against him. He felt a blow from the overturned skiff against his back and clung to it. He managed to lift his head above the water to see where he was. He could hear the waves crashing against the sand not far away, so he let go and swam toward the beach.

"Father! Luis!" Martín shouted from the shore into the sea, barely visible in the darkness and incessant rain.

"Here I am, brother!" he heard Luis's voice nearby.

"Come closer, Luis. Father! Father! If you can hear me, please call out!" he shouted as his brother reached him.

Luis and Martín called out for several minutes, searching for their father on the beach. Other men were also shouting, calling for comrades or family members, just as they were.

"Sons! Over here," Martín heard, followed by coughing.

The two brothers ran toward the voice. They saw Hernán Cortés on his knees on the beach, his hands buried in the muddy sand, digging as if searching for something.

"Father, get up. The Moors are upon us. We can already hear the swords clashing," said Martín, lifting his father by the armpits.

"I've lost them, Martín!" Hernán Cortés lamented, sobbing. "The cloth I had tied around my arm came undone when the wave hit us."

"What's important now is to live and defeat the infidel, father. If we survive this, you'll have time to search for them or obtain others," Martín said, hugging him.

Some men who had survived the more than one hundred fifty shipwrecks swam ashore or clung to floating debris. Others also reached the sand but were dragged by the current, drowned. The Moors on land, seeing the weakened survivors reaching the shore, began approaching to slaughter them with their scimitars.

Martín Cortés, along with his father and brother, walked with the rest of the soldiers toward the city of Algiers. Hundreds of bodies littered the sands, drowned from the shipwreck, or beheaded by the Moors upon reaching land. Hernán Cortés was despondent; the loss of his greatest treasure, the coveted emeralds, had left him without the will to fight.

The king's troops regrouped outside Algiers, awaiting orders from His Majesty for the attack. Seeing another city siege before him, as he had once experienced in Tenochtitlan, restored Hernán Cortés's resolve, momentarily forgetting the economic loss he had suffered hours earlier.

Admiral Andrea Doria, witnessing the naval disaster caused by the storm, ordered the ships to head to the shelter of Cape Matefu. The situation on land was dire. Captains alerted the king about another approaching storm.

Concerned about defeat at the hands of nature, the monarch decided to hold a council on land to determine whether to continue the attack or retreat. He summoned the captains and certain nobles who had managed to disembark. The general recommendation to the king was to lift the siege of Algiers and withdraw the troops to Cape Matefu, where Admiral Andrea Doria's fleet awaited.

Almost without food or water, the troops marched away from the outskirts of Algiers. The Spanish soldiers guarded the rear during the retreat.

"This retreat is a disgrace!" Hernán Cortés shouted angrily to his sons and other captains nearby. "King Carlos has been advised by cowardly or inexperienced men. We, those of us here in the rear guard, could conquer Algiers if given the chance. I accomplished more in Mexico with fewer men, without as many weapons or resources, against enemies a hundred times more numerous and powerful."

The Count of Alcaudete, Don Martín de Córdoba y Velasco, shared the Marquis of the Valley's opinion. Many of the men present supported Hernán Cortés's comment, although the most enthusiastic about the capture of Algiers was Martín. The Mestizo had fought three or four Moors the previous day, killing two of them. He had sworn to fight the infidel as a member of the Order of Santiago, and now he was being ordered not to. If he ultimately retreated from Algiers, he decided it would not be his last battle; he would continue fighting on other fronts, as the king was always at war. However, what he lamented most was that his father, the great Hernán Cortés, the greatest conqueror Spain had ever known, had not been considered by the monarch when deciding what to do in Algiers.

Martín accompanied his father to see King Carlos before he boarded the skiff that would take him to his galley.

"Your Majesty," said Hernán Cortés, accompanied by Martín, bowing before the king. "I beg you to grant me permission, with some soldiers, captains, and my sons, to return to Algiers. I will personally bear the cost of this campaign I am requesting."

"The decision is final, Hernán," the king responded informally. "I know you are a brave and daring man. I have also heard reports of your son, the Mestizo, being a capable man," he said, glancing at Martín, with whom he had shared moments in his life when Martín was a page knight. "But the decision is made. We must consider the greater good in this case. The order is given and is unchangeable."

At that moment, a count approached to inform the king that the boat was ready to return to the galley.

The re-embarkation of the troops was chaotic. Under a new storm and the constant attack of the Moors, the soldiers had to board the small boats and approach the galleys anchored away from the beach. With so many ships sunk or stranded, the survivors had to crowd into fewer vessels, making space insufficient. On the ships, sailors threw overboard the horses that had not been unloaded, as well as the heavy artillery, to lighten the load and make room for the troops.

Martín, along with his father and brother, managed to return to La Esperanza, on which they had arrived. Upon boarding, they found Friar López de Gómara, who quickly went to greet Hernán Cortés. Martín thought this cleric had too much interest in staying close to his father, as if seeking some favor or

112

advantageous deal. He did not give it much thought and set about helping the sailors who were working to get the soldiers aboard quickly.

The ships dispersed in different directions, with some heading to Spain and others to Italy or Sardinia. Two more ships crashed against the coast after boarding the soldiers. The men who managed to swim to shore were surrounded by the Moors, but the valiant soldiers of the king faced them bravely, refusing to be killed. After negotiating the surrender the next day, they were escorted to Algiers as prisoners.

Some galleys had to tow by rowing smaller and overloaded vessels. The ship carrying the king was damaged in the storm and lost its masts. Protected by other ships, including La Esperanza with Martín on board, they headed to Bougie, a town east of Algiers, to repair it in the shelter of the storm. They remained there until the storm cleared on November 23, almost a month after the initial landing.

On December 1, La Esperanza, carrying Martín Cortés, his father and his brother, arrived at the port of Cartagena. No one counted the men who died in the Algiers Expedition, but the ships that did not return were numbered at one hundred sixty. During the journey to Cartagena, a young gypsy on La Esperanza played a guitar and sang a song:

> Who can, with good words,
> without a note of error,
> recount such a sad fate,
> whether they are more or less.
> Those the sea has swallowed?
> No mind can say,
> without a note of shame,
> those missing from the count,
> only that Lord knows

who sent the storm.

On the return trip, Hernán Cortés had the opportunity to speak with his sons. He informed them that he would go to Valladolid. He intended to find a way to regain the king's favor for his projects, as he felt His Majesty no longer desired his advice and conversations.

Martín decided to accompany his father. He saw how deeply affected his father was by the financial loss of funding the Algiers Expedition and the loss of his jewels. Martín believed that what weighed most on his father was falling out of the king's grace, having once enjoyed his favor, and being sidelined from important matters at court.

Luis Cortés stayed in Toledo, living in the house of a friend of Hernán Cortés. Martín and his father arrived at the palace of Comendador Rodrigo Enríquez in Valladolid, though by then it belonged to Jerónimo de Padilla.

Martín spent a few months in Valladolid, keeping his father company, who learned to enjoy the tranquility of not being involved in explorations, conquests, battles, or legal disputes. In Padilla's palace, the conquistador felt somewhat close to the court, where nobles, hidalgos, merchants, and other gentlemen came hoping to advance in his circle. Martín met interesting people who came to visit his father for conversations in which the young man, with good taste, participated.

In the Cortés Academy, as those gatherings at the palace were known, Martín met and conversed with Cardinal Paggio, Archbishop of Cagliari, Juan de Vega, Friar Dominico de Pico, Juan de Zúñiga, and the Marquis of Falces, Antonio de Peralta, among others. All came to speak with Hernán Cortés, the Marquis of the Valley of Oaxaca, and those who did not yet know him took the opportunity to do so.

The guests quickly saw that Martín the Mestizo was an educated man with great culture, possessing extensive academic knowledge and fluency in French, Italian, and German. Everyone was interested in his mestizo origins. They asked Hernán Cortés to speak about the role of Doña Marina in the conquest of Mexico, to which the Marquis of the Valley eagerly obliged, recalling numerous battles he fought and some negotiations he conducted through her.

Friar López de Gómara had begun living with Martín and his father in Valladolid. This friar was also a regular at the Cortés Academy, where he took notes whenever the Marquis recounted experiences from the conquest of Mexico. When his father was visited by former companions who had accompanied him, Friar López de Gómara enjoyed asking them for permission to spend time alone with them, during which he inquired about details or events that occurred during the conquest.

However, not everything was happiness and rest in Valladolid. Problems persisted both in New Spain and at court, where the king refused to respond to the frequent letters Hernán Cortés sent him, reminding him of all he had done for his glory in the Indies. Another concern for Hernán Cortés was the lack of liquidity; despite having many resources and assets in New Spain, he lacked ready money due to the lengthy process of transferring it from the Indies to Valladolid. Consequently, he had to turn to the court's usual bankers, such as Leonardo Lomelin, Domingo de Lizarraras, and Jacome Boti. To secure the three loans, Martín Cortés negotiated and formalized the agreements with the bankers to ensure his father received funds until the necessary money arrived from New Spain.

Illustration #3

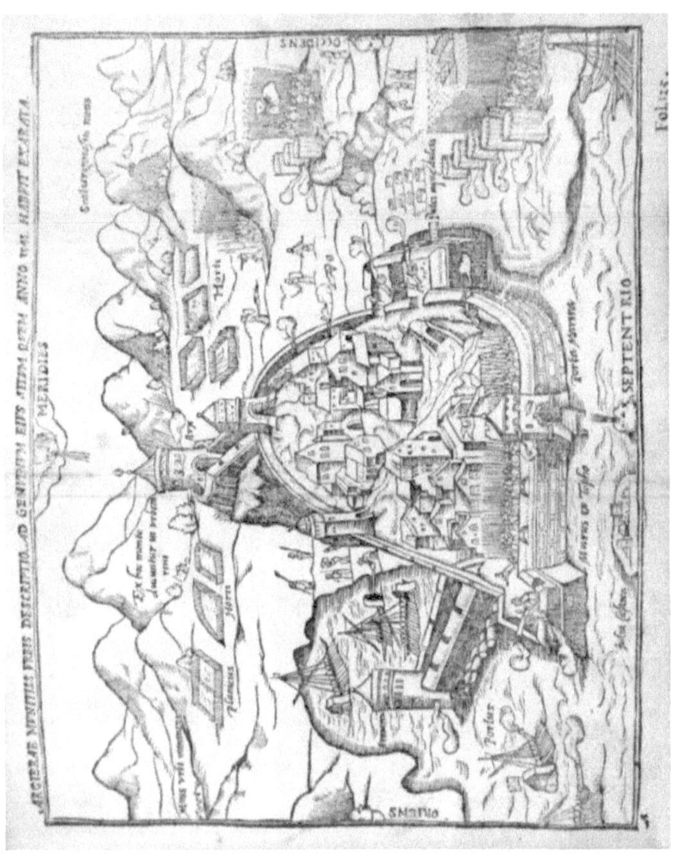

Siege of Algiers, according to an engraving from 1555

Battle of Ceresole. April 1544.

Martín Cortés was exhausted. He had been walking under the rain in Piedmont for four days. He had arrived in Italy toward the end of 1543 to support the war King Carlos was waging against Francis I, who had allied himself with Christianity's greatest enemy, the Ottoman Empire. The infidel Turk.

Incorporated into the army of the Marquis of Vasto, Martín had participated in the siege and capture of the city of Mondovì the previous September, alongside two thousand Spanish infantrymen, seven thousand Italians, and three thousand Germans. After the surrender of the Frenchman Charles de Dros, they had entered the city and sacked it. Due to Martín Cortés' valor and effort in the siege and capture of the city, the Marquis of Vasto had appointed him captain of the infantry.

They had crossed the Po River toward Turin and now found themselves in the Piedmontese town of Ceresole, a settlement taken by His Majesty's imperial troops. Martín commanded the Spanish infantry, serving under Raimundo de Cardona, who led the two thousand Spanish infantrymen, the six thousand Italian landsknechts, and a large number of arquebusiers.

The Marquis of Vasto had ordered the troops to form on a plateau outside Ceresole. The advance of a large French army, led by Count Enghien, had been detected. During the French approach to the imperial army's position, a skirmish occurred between some squadrons, resulting in only a few wounded. The French troops chose to occupy a hill opposite the imperial army. Between the two forces, a small valley formed, separating the two plateaus.

"Have your weapons ready, your steel polished, and your armor complete!" Martín commanded his men. "At my order, everyone be alert and maintain perfect formation. I want no slackers or lazybones. Anyone I catch slacking off, I'll cut an ear off right then and there. No questions asked."

The men respected Captain Mestizo, as they called him among themselves, though no one dared to call him that to his face. He had demonstrated bravery and daring in the skirmishes they had engaged in, as well as in the capture of Mondovì. The Mestizo was a captain who did not stay behind when it was time to fight; on the contrary, he led his men from the front in battle. He had rescued soldiers who were in great distress or wounded when no one else would approach them. It was said he had inherited his bravery on the battlefield from his father, the great Hernán Cortés.

"I don't want anyone left behind. We rescue our wounded comrades, risking our lives if necessary. To the arquebusiers: no wild shots. We need every shot to wound or kill the enemy," he said, addressing the few gunmen who accompanied them.

Alongside the Spanish infantry were two thousand German infantrymen. A short distance from Martín were nearly six thousand Italian landsknechts, armed with their long pikes of almost five yards. It was a battle-hardened troop that knew how to combine arquebus fire with their formidable long lances. When infantry armed with swords intended to fight them, they first had to overcome the hedgehog-like formation of long pikes. Martín was glad to have them on his side, certainly better than facing them in battle.

Dawn broke on April 14, Easter Sunday. After a brief mass conducted by accompanying priests, the imperial armies formed on the plateau. Martín, at the head of the Spanish infantry, shared the position with the Germans. To his right, on the far-right flank of the imperial army, was the Neapolitan light cavalry with three hundred horsemen. To Martín's left, there were two hundred more mounted riders.

120

"We have few horses on our flanks," Martín Cortés commented to Raimundo de Cardona, the captain leading the Spanish and German infantry.

"I believe the landsknechts will perform well in battle," Raimundo de Cardona replied. "The danger we face is being outmatched by the French cavalry. Luckily, they aren't in abundance either."

In the center of the imperial army were seven thousand Italian landsknechts with their long pikes and a few hundred arquebusiers. Next to them, on the left flank, were six thousand Italian infantrymen and, on the farthest edge, three hundred Florentine horsemen.

Martín surveyed the Holy Roman Empire's army of King Carlos, occupying the entire length of the plateau.

Opposite them, on the other elevation and just beyond the small valley that separated them, was the French army under the command of Francis of Bourbon. The left wing of their formation, directly facing Martín, comprised about four hundred light horsemen, two thousand Italian infantrymen, three thousand French infantrymen, and around four or five hundred heavy cavalry. In the center of the enemy army, four thousand Swiss infantry were positioned on a rise in the middle of the plateau. This same rise prevented Martín from seeing the right wing of the French army, but he assumed it would be similar to what was in front of him.

The arquebusiers of King Carlos' troops were ordered to advance, and the French army responded with the same maneuver, moving their arquebusiers forward. Both battalions descended the gentle slope leading to the valley and began firing their artillery as soon as they were within range.

From his position, Martín saw the smoke produced by the arquebuses and heard their sound, occasionally punctuated by a louder one from the heavy artillery. They shot at each other with rigor, methodically loading their arquebuses while praying to

God that a ball fired by the enemy wouldn't strike them. When the smoke thickened, obscuring the men and their weapons, flashes of the detonations helped locate them amidst the haze. After an hour of the artillery exchange, the Marquis of Vasto ordered the imperial army to advance.

"To battle, gentlemen!" Martín shouted to his men. "Leave none alive! For Spain! For the King!"

The two armies descended into the valley that separated them. Martín noticed the landsknechts advancing on his left until they reached the center of the battlefield. The pikes were raised and being lowered as the French army approached, resembling a giant hedgehog bristling with quills. From the flanks, the arquebusiers provided covering fire for the landsknechts. In front of the troops Martín commanded, the imperial horsemen surged ahead at a gallop but were soon outmatched and defeated by the French.

From that moment on, Martín was engulfed in a brutal slaughter. The battlefield began to fill with the dead and wounded, with blood and entrails, with screams and laments. Captain Mestizo urged his men to keep fighting. Several times, he narrowly escaped death, but each time he spotted his enemy first and fended off the attack.

After several hours of battle, the trumpets sounded, signaling the imperial army's surrender. The French army, instead of capturing the enemies who laid down their arms, continued massacring hundreds of unarmed men.

Martín retraced his steps, ascending the slope until he reached the plateau where the day had begun. From above, he could see that of the large imperial army he had been part of at dawn, only about four thousand remained alive. Surrender was never an option for Martín. Of the nineteen thousand men who had entered the battle on the imperial side, Martín estimated that fourteen thousand had perished. From a distance, he saw the French had captured around three thousand soldiers. Around fifteen hundred who neither surrendered nor died were retreating from the battlefield.

Baron Seisneck fled on horseback, with the surviving German infantry trailing behind. Martín regrouped the surviving Spanish infantry. A battalion of four hundred Spaniards followed him on the long march to Asti, twenty-five leagues away. He believed they could regroup with His Majesty's troops from there.

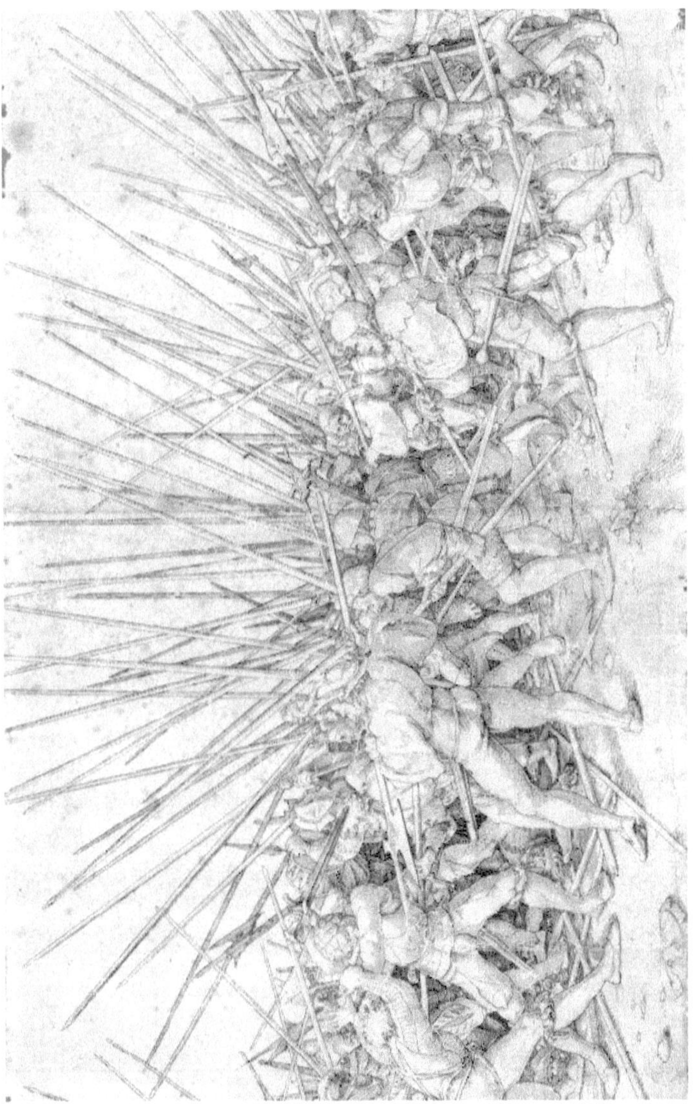

Encounter between two troops of pikemen and arquebusiers. XVI cent.

Way to Compostela. March 1545.

After the Battle of Ceresole, Martín had been incorporated into several armies and participated in minor battles. King Carlos was negotiating an agreement with Francis I, so some troops were withdrawn from Italy. Among the soldiers returning to Spain was Captain Mestizo.

Upon his landing at the port of Barcelona, he decided to make a pilgrimage to Compostela. It was one of the vows he had made when he joined the Order of Santiago, and he thought it was time to fulfill it. He was twenty-three years old and had already participated in numerous skirmishes. He did not wish to die without having kept the promise he made the day he had taken the habit of the Order. He had returned to Spain poorer than when he had left to fight in Italy two years earlier. Numerous wounds covered his skin; some were healed, while others were still covered with poultices and bandages. His body had no trace of fat; he was strong and spirited. He was filled with the anticipation of making the pilgrimage to the tomb of the Apostle Santiago, to whom he had entrusted his life many times in battle. He decided to find a moneylender to pawn his armor and weapons. It was a journey he needed to make with as light a burden as possible.

He arrived at the old Jewish quarter of Barcelona, where moneylenders and guarantors could be found. Although of Jewish origin and declared converts several years ago, it was well known that, in private, the conversos continued to observe Hebrew traditions, customs, and rites.

He found a place that seemed more respectable than the others he had seen that morning. He intended to return to redeem his belongings eventually and did not want to leave them with someone who might disappear, losing his possessions. Martín presented his armor, sword, and some clothing to the elderly Jew who attended to him. He would only take with him a few changes of clothes, a large waxed cloak in case of rain, and the doublet with the cross of the Order of Santiago. As always, he wore his mother's handkerchief inside his shirt.

"Sir, for all this I offer you two hundred pesos," said the moneylender after a quick glance. "That's the most I can provide at this moment. Many soldiers are returning from the war, and we are full of swords, shields, morions, and other items. They don't come back for them, and it's hard to make a profit," he remarked, feigning little interest in what Martín was offering, though Mestizo knew it was just a tactic to pay less.

"Excuse me, sir, but I believe you have not properly inspected what I'm offering and are confusing it with the usual trinkets soldiers bring. This armor is fine workmanship, made from the best steel. Notice it only has a few scratches and two dents, barely marking the metal. This Toledo steel saved my life on several occasions. Other iron would have deformed and injured the wearer," Martín said, hoping to get more than the two hundred pesos the miserly moneylender offered. In reality, the value of what he was trying to pawn exceeded fifteen hundred pesos.

"I'll give you a bit more for that cross around your neck."

The old moneylender's eyes had lit up upon seeing the gold cross that Hernán Cortés had given his son.

"I regret I cannot leave it with you," Martín replied, tucking the cross inside his shirt. "It is a gift from my father, and I intend to enter the cathedral of Compostela with it around my neck."

"You are going to Compostela on pilgrimage?" the moneylender asked, alarmed. "In that case, I'll return your

Biscayan sword[13], and only keep the Toledo one[14]. It's not worth dying on the way before the apostle pardons your sins."

"Is it that dangerous?" Martín asked in astonishment.

"As dangerous as a war. Look, sir, I propose this: I'll give you the Biscayan sword to carry with you and fifty pesos more. In total, two hundred and fifty. That's all I can pay. Believe me, I'm losing money. I'd prefer you not be killed on the pilgrimage and be able to return to redeem your belongings. Paying the interest, of course."

Martín agreed. Though not satisfied with the deal, he did not want to go from moneylender to moneylender, hoping someone would pay fifty pesos more. Moreover, he had also heard rumors about the insecurity of the pilgrimage to Compostela and appreciated the Jewish moneylender's warning. He took his Biscayan sword and sheathed it by his side.

"Tell me your name so I can record it in the pawn register. If you come back before the end of August, you can recover your belongings," the old man said as he opened the book to make the entry.

"My name is Martín Cortés, captain of the imperial army, born in Coyoacán, in New Spain."

The old man stopped writing midway, the quill still in his hand. He lifted his head and observed the young dark-skinned man before him.

"Are you the son of Hernán Cortés, the conqueror?"

"Hernán Cortés is my father, that's correct."

"Now I understand. You're the Mestizo. Seeing the color of your skin, I thought I was speaking with some descendant of the Moors, but now I see. I'll add a hundred pesos more to the pawn. I made good money trading with people coming and going from

---

[13] Medium-sized dagger used as a support for the sword.
[14] Long sword, made of Toledo steel, hence its name.

the Indies years ago. Since pirates started attacking ships, I decided to leave that business. Too risky."

The moneylender finished noting the details in the register and handed Martín three hundred pesos.

"Sir, you are mistaken," Martín said. "You were offering me two hundred and fifty pesos, then added a hundred more when you learned of my father."

"True," the moneylender admitted reluctantly as he placed the missing fifty pesos on the table.

Martín loaded his bundle onto his back, put a straw hat on his head, the Biscayan sword at his side, and on the other side, a gourd with water. He departed from Barcelona for the sanctuary of Montserrat, where he rested and prayed for three days in the company of the Benedictine friars. From there, he walked to Lérida, reaching Fuentes, and taking the road toward Zaragoza. He was surprised to see the path frequented by a multitude of idlers, vagabonds, vagrants, and cripples, both genuine and fake. It was common for him to sleep in stables or outdoors under a tree. The few inns and houses that accepted pilgrims quickly filled their cots. In some towns, he even found proclamations at the entrance announcing that lodging was prohibited for *Santiago beggars*.

He had left the city of Zaragoza behind several days ago and was now nearing Logroño when Martín heard the voices of men seemingly arguing. He could not see who it was, but he knew from the sound that they were behind the large rock that formed a narrow curve in the path.

"I swear to God, if you resist, I'll slit your throat right here," said a rough male voice. "Search him well, Pelao; they told me he came from Lodosa after making a good sale."

"Hand over the purse!" shouted another man. "I said hand over the purse, you son of a bitch! Hand it over now, Francisco, or you won't see your wife and daughter again."

"How do you know my name?" Martín heard a third man stammer.

Martín took his cloak from his bundle and put it on. As he rounded the curve, he nearly stumbled upon them. One man was searching another, who was being held from behind with a knife to his throat. A horse lay struggling on the ground nearby; it had been stabbed twice in the belly with long poles and was dying.

"Stop right there, sir!" said the man holding the victim from behind with the knife at his neck. "Don't come any closer. Move along," he ordered, gesturing with his head for Martín to continue walking. His accomplice watched silently as he searched the victim's clothing for money.

"Here it is!" he exclaimed, pulling a tied black leather pouch from the man's sash.

"I will give you some coins, but let that man go," Martín said, putting his left hand inside his doublet while his other hand remained hidden under the cloak.

The man with the knife observed Martín's gesture. He released the man he had just robbed and pushed him to the ground. The thief then advanced toward Mestizo, intending to rob him as well. He did not notice that under the cloak, Martín had his hand on the hilt of the Biscayan sword at his belt. The robber reached into Martín's doublet, mistaking the case where Martín kept his mother's handkerchief for a money bag, and tore it away. Quickly, Martín drew his Biscayan sword and stabbed the bandit twice in the belly. Before falling to the ground, the criminal managed to stab Martín in the arm with his knife.

"Son of a bitch," the robber spat, curling up in front of Martín, blood dripping from his mouth as he died. Martín stepped forward and finished him off by stabbing him in the heart. Then he pried open the thief's hand, retrieved the case with the handkerchief, and put it back in his doublet.

"Compadre!" the other man yelled, terrified as he saw his partner being killed.

"If you don't want to end up like your friend, return this man's belongings and get out of here," Martín ordered.

The bandit did not hesitate; he dropped the bag, scattering coins across the ground, and ran off, disappearing into a small grove beside the path. Martín looked at his arm wound and saw that the thief had made a deep cut in his doublet and flesh before dying. The blood was flowing slowly, which was a relief—it was much better than if it had been gushing. Some things were quickly learned in battles.

"Good God!" exclaimed the man who had been assaulted. "You'd better come with me to my home so they can tend to that wound. We're less than a league from my village."

"That would be best," Martín replied. "The wound isn't too deep, but it's better to clean and bandage it."

"Poor Cejudo, he was a good horse, though already old," said the man, looking at the animal, which had stopped twitching on the ground. "I only used him to go to Lodosa two or three times a year for business."

"Be careful with whom you deal from now on. Someone had a loose tongue and told those two what you were carrying," Martín commented as he pressed his arm, trying to stop the bleeding.

Martín helped the man hide the saddle among the bushes. As he said, when they reached the village, he would send a boy to retrieve it and deal with the dead bandit.

"It's better my boy takes care of this than informing the constable in Logroño."

Don Francisco de Porras y Ordoriz, turned out to be the man Martín had saved. He was the lord of Agoncillo, a small village near Logroño, close to the path from Zaragoza to Compostela.

While they walked, Francisco de Porras spoke about the good farming lands he owned and the livestock he raised. A couple of times a year, he went to Lodosa to sell part of his harvest or some livestock. When Martín encountered him, he was returning from a sale, carrying money that, as he confided, would support his family and servants for a year.

Don Francisco had a fine house in Agoncillo, next to the church and across from the small castle of Aguas Mansas. At his residence, Martín was attended by María de Balboa, Francisco's wife, and a village barber who claimed to have experience with wounds and whom Francisco had called upon as soon as they arrived. Realizing that the barber was doing more harm than good, Martín decided to clean his wound himself with some of Francisco's brandy and bandage it with clean cloths. That was another thing one learned in wars.

Once his wound was tended to, they brought him into a large kitchen with a solid oak table in the center, near the hearth where the wood was burning. A maid served Francisco and Martín steaming garlic soup with chunks of bacon. During the meal, the lord of Agoncillo, curious about his origin, asked Martín about his life, something he was used to due to his unusual skin tone. Martín spoke about his life, his background, his family, and the places he had been. María de Balboa, Francisco's wife, stood in the kitchen with the maid, listening to the story without missing a detail of the life Martín was recounting to her husband. They were astonished to meet someone who had lived alongside Prince Felipe, his mother Empress Isabel, and King Carlos himself.

"I beg you to stay in our humble home for a few days until your wound heals. Then you can continue your pilgrimage, feeling better and stronger," offered Don Francisco. "In this house, there are only women, and I appreciate the conversation with a man who has seen so much of the world."

"I truly appreciate your hospitality, Don Francisco. I will rest tonight if you permit, but tomorrow I must continue my journey. It is important that I complete the path and visit the tomb of the Apostle Santiago."

At that moment, a beautiful young woman appeared in the doorway, catching Martín's attention. She entered silently, observing the mysterious guest who was speaking with Don Francisco. She approached María de Balboa and whispered something in her ear.

"Sir, this is my eldest daughter, Bernardina," said the proud master of the house.

Don Francisco was pleased to see how Martín looked at his daughter, unable to take his eyes off the young woman. Don Francisco had quickly realized, after just a few hours of conversation, that this mestizo was a good man. He seemed honorable and courageous, as had been demonstrated by the attack he had endured and the death he had dealt to the thief. He knew that his daughter had had several suitors. He and his wife had never wanted to impose any marriage on her, and Bernardina had dismissed the options presented by her parents. Now, Don Francisco saw that she too was giving Martín looks that she had never exchanged with other suitors.

"Don Francisco, you are right. It would be best if I stayed a few days, taking advantage of your invitation. I feel somewhat weak and dizzy, surely due to the blood I have lost," Martín said, finding an excuse to stay in Agoncillo.

"No more words. You are in your home," replied Don Francisco cheerfully, seeing that his daughter and Martín could not take their eyes off each other. "María, have the room next to Maruja's chamber prepared."

Don Francisco thought it better for the young man to be near the old maid Maruja's chamber rather than his daughter Bernardina's. After all, he wasn't about to serve her on a silver platter.

Martín spent several very pleasant days in Agoncillo. Don Francisco proudly showed him the extensive crops he cultivated in the area, well-watered by two nearby rivers. After a week,

Martín asked Don Francisco for permission to walk alone with Bernardina, promising to respect her. Don Francisco gave his consent. The next day, and for another week, the two young people walked along the paths of Agoncillo, sometimes having picnics by the banks of the Leza River and other times by the Ebro River, which flowed by the village.

Bernardina de Porras was a well-formed young woman. She had a thick mane of jet-black hair, fair but not pale skin, and large brown eyes with long lashes. Bernardina was three years younger than Martín, who had just turned twenty-three. When they were alone under the shade of the poplars by the rivers, they grew close and playfully intimate, though Bernardina made it clear she reserved herself for her future husband. Martín had had lovers throughout his life, but he had never felt the feelings of love that he felt for Bernardina.

A day before leaving Agoncillo, Martín asked for Bernardina's hand from Don Francisco de Porras and his wife, Doña María de Balboa. The parents, after consulting with their daughter and seeing Bernardina's smiling nod, granted Martín her hand.

"As you know, I must complete my pilgrimage, having made a vow to the Order of Santiago when I joined as a member," Martín explained to Bernardina's parents, who already knew how important it was for him to keep his word or promise something. "When I finish, I must return to my father and inform him of my marriage to your daughter. I do not require his approval; I only wish to tell him in person. If he has already returned to New Spain, I will send a letter to inform him, and then I will return to celebrate our marriage."

"I believe you to be a man of your word and honorable. I trust that you will keep your promise. You have my blessing to continue to Compostela and proceed with your plans. My daughter will remain in our care until you return to marry her,"

Don Francisco said, shaking hands with Martín to seal the commitment.

The Wedding of the Mestizo. January 1546.

"I would be pleased if you could attend my wedding, father," Martín said after informing him of his upcoming marriage.

"I feel weak, son, but you have my blessing for your commitment. You mentioned that they are not of nobility, and I think you are right to marry the one your heart chooses. Don't make the same mistake I did by not marrying Marina," Hernán Cortés confessed. " Please, don't misunderstand me. I love Doña Juana, but not with the same feeling I had for your mother. Perhaps it's old age that makes me say this. Who knows? I find myself moved by things I had never even considered before. I even cry when I remember certain moments of my life: the deaths of comrades, the tragedy of betrayal, Marina..."

"Don't worry, father. Your blessing is enough for me to marry Bernardina," Martín responded happily. "I will ask my brothers to accompany me. I wish for someone from my family to be with me and to be my witnesses on that day."

"Martín, I must ask you a favor."

"Tell me, Father, how can I serve you?"

"Once you are married, it is important to me that you join His Majesty's troops. In a few months, the imperial army will gather in Barcelona to depart for Germany, where they will fight against the Schmalkaldic League," Hernán Cortés said, hoping that continuing to support the monarchy would be well regarded by King Carlos, who still rejected his company.

"The Schmalkaldic League is the league of the Lutherans?"

"Yes, son. You know well that this war against the Lutherans is not just about religion. We are not foolish enough to believe certain things at this point, right?" he asked, not expecting an answer. "It is also about territories and, above all, business."

It had been more than two years since Martín said goodbye to his father to go to Italy, where he had been fighting against the troops of Francis I. He had planned to stay with Bernardina and start a family. His future father-in-law had offered a generous dowry that would allow them to live with dignity. Now his father was asking him to return to war against foreigners in distant lands. Martín's sense of honor toward his father and the king compelled him to agree.

"Of course, father. I will present myself in Barcelona and place myself at His Majesty's orders for the campaign against the Lutherans. Will any of my brothers accompany me?"

"No, Martín!" Hernán Cortés responded, agitated. "I don't want two of my sons fighting in any war or campaign at the same time. It was foolish for the three of us to go on the Algiers expedition together. Now I know. I risked too much on that venture. Fortunately, only the emeralds were lost, and we did not have to mourn any deaths in our family. Promise me, Martín, as my firstborn, that you will not allow your brothers to fight simultaneously in any war. The family cannot be left without its men. We must keep the family name alive," Hernán Cortés said, gripping his son's hand tightly.

"I will do so, father. Don't worry."

Martín was surprised that his father now cared so much about the survival of the family when he himself had risked his life for so many years. Old age, as his father had mentioned moments ago, was beginning to show in a man who had always been daring in his decisions.

Knowing that he would have to travel to Barcelona in the coming months to join King Carlos's troops, Martín wrote to the Jewish moneylender where he had pawned his weapons and armor before starting his pilgrimage to Compostela. He begged him to extend the deadlines so he could retrieve his belongings, committing to pay the stipulated interest to redeem them. He trusted that the moneylender would receive his request and be reasonable.

Luis was delighted when he heard of Martín's upcoming marriage and offered to be a witness and godfather. He ordered his belongings to be prepared for the trip to Logroño, where the wedding would take place in the city's cathedral.

"Later, I will join you in Barcelona, brother. I know the king is gathering the imperial troops to go against the Schmalkaldic League," Luis said, excited to participate in another battle.

"You can't, brother. You must stay with our father. I have seen him weak and a bit disoriented," Martín lied, using their father as an excuse to prevent his brother from joining the war. "Our younger brother, Martín, is still at the Royal House of Pages. We can't take him out to care for our father. Besides, you know our younger brother's temperament. He would be at galas and banquets with his noble friends every day."

"Alright, brother. I think you're right," Luis responded, though not entirely convinced.

When the younger Martín met with his elder brother at the Royal House, where he studied, he excused himself from attending the wedding.

"Brother, don't take it personally, but I will not leave the Court for even a day to attend a wedding in a God-forsaken village. It's not even for someone of nobility or the daughter of a nobleman," the younger Martín said, disdainfully declining the invitation.

"It's in Logroño, brother, not a God-forsaken village. And it's my wedding. I am your older brother."

"I wish you the best in your marriage to Fernandina, Mestizo."

"Bernardina," Martín corrected, irritated.

"Whatever. Don't take it personally, but I don't think the son of the Marquis of the Valley of Oaxaca should lower himself to attend that ceremony. I would outshine you with my presence, and no one would notice you. In any case, it's good that our brother Luis will accompany you."

With that, the younger Martín, the heir to the marquisate, approached his mestizo half-brother and, after embracing him, he left.

Battle of Mühlberg. April 1547.

The fog had covered everything Martín could see. A thick, milky white mist blurred the end of the arquebus he held. He lay behind a mound of earth, peering toward the Elbe River, which he knew was just a few yards ahead. Although invisible in the fog, its gentle waters could be heard flowing by. The previous evening, he had observed it before nightfall. It was about a hundred yards wide where they were stationed. To his left, although he could not see it, there was a pontoon bridge, well-guarded by Protestant troops.

This time he was in command of a squad of musketeers within the Spanish Tercio. Martín preferred fighting with his Toledo sword, which he still carried sheathed at his side, but since his arrival in Germany, they had been given an arquebus. He had to practice and improve his marksmanship with it. More and more, firearms were prevailing over swords, spears, or crossbows in battles. Martín considered musket warfare less honorable than traditional sword fighting, but he accepted it as the current way of war.

The troops of the Holy Roman Empire under King Carlos were superior to those of the Schmalkaldic League on this occasion. Martín was part of the Spanish Tercios, composed of eight thousand veterans, along with Belgian, Flemish, German, Hungarian, and Italian soldiers, and horsemen. In total, they numbered nearly forty-four thousand men. It was a true Tower of Babel, with soldiers from various nations, all under the reign of Carlos I of Spain and V of Germany. On the other shore, it was estimated that about twelve thousand infantrymen and three thousand horsemen awaited them. The numbers favored the Spanish monarch, but Martín knew all too well that this did not always guarantee victory.

For a moment, he escaped from Mühlberg and the small mound of earth that hid him from the enemy. He recalled the few months he spent with Bernardina after their wedding. It was a time of peace in his life. They had moved to a village near his parents.' There, Martín learned to raise animals and to plant and harvest cereals. Peaceful months spent in the company of a woman he loved and who loved him in return. He remembered the day Bernardina told him she had missed her period, and the joy he felt when her belly began to show. Unfortunately, by Christmas, he had received a letter from his father informing him of the army's upcoming departure from Barcelona in January. They had been delayed longer than expected, but the time had come to join them.

By now, Martín thought, Bernardina must have been giving birth. They had agreed that if it was a girl, she would choose the name, but if it was a boy, he would be named Fernando, after Martín's father.[15]

Captain Mestizo gathered a group of ten men who had distinguished themselves in several skirmishes for their bravery and valor: Alonso de la Cueva, Jerónimo de Sierra, Francisco Centeno, Juan de Artés, Pedro Ollero, Francisco de Salinas, Gómez de Robledo, Juan de Bolena, Francisco Gregorio, and Diego de Mallorca.

"Gentlemen, in a few moments we will launch a surprise attack on the enemy," Martín said quietly to the ten men who formed a semicircle before him. "Yesterday, when I asked if you knew how to swim, you all said yes," they all nodded silently. "Let's strip down now. Leave only your breeches to cover your modesty and keep your sword at your belt."

---

[15] Hernán Cortés was baptized as Hernando. Throughout his life, he used the names Fernando, Ferdinando, Fernán, Hernando, and Hernán.

142

The men undressed in silence, each one placing their clothes, weapons, and bundles in small piles. Martín entrusted the care of their clothes and weapons to a boy who accompanied them and helped with the supplies and rations.

"Let's go get them," Martín Cortés whispered, confident that this maneuver would surprise the Protestants. He knew that in front of them, the Elbe River widened and formed a shallow area that could be crossed on foot. At least, that was what he understood from a local Catholic German from Mühlberg who had approached them the day before. After speaking with the man and understanding him, Martín devised a plan that he believed could succeed. He requested an audience with the Duke of Alba and shared the information he had obtained from the German. He explained the plan he had devised, and the Duke of Alba took some time with King Carlos. The Duke returned and granted Martín permission to execute the attack.

Accompanied by his ten men and a hundred arquebusiers, he approached the bank of the Elbe River. They felt the water at their feet before they could see it. Martín ordered the ten almost naked men accompanying him to cover their faces, arms, and chests with mud. Once they were smeared with the mud, he gave the order for everyone to enter the stream.

Along with his group of ten men, the hundred arquebusiers followed, slowly submerging themselves to avoid making any strange noises in the water. When the water reached their waists, Martín ordered them to spread out as much as they could, as long as they could still stand. It was crucial not to bunch up and be shot like ducks in a hunt.

"At my signal, start sweeping the shore with your arquebuses, gentlemen," Martín whispered to his nearest men so they could pass the order along.

With their arquebuses raised above their heads, they advanced through the river, with the water reaching their chests. Martín estimated that the enemy shore was within range of the musketeers and gave the signal to halt. He could not see the shore because of the fog, but he knew it was there, right in front of them.

"For Spain! For the Empire!" Martín shouted into the fog.

All the Spanish arquebusiers, as if in echo, began firing on the enemy shore. They heard some screams ahead, indicating that Martín had not miscalculated the distance.

The musketeers continued firing, trying to keep their gunpowder dry, which hung from their necks. Martín and his ten men began to swim. Without splashing, they swam toward the pontoon occupied by enemy troops. He knew it was ahead of them, hidden in the fog, even though he could not see it yet.

With their comrades' gunfire covering them, they headed for the enemy-held bridge. They heard bullets whizzing overhead from both sides. If anyone dared to stand up, they faced certain death.

They reached the pontoon bridge and climbed aboard, catching the Protestant soldiers by surprise. The enemy did not react when they saw a dozen naked men, covered in mud, armed with swords and daggers, climb onto the pontoon. Some of the soldiers managed to flee, but the rest were killed on the barges forming the pontoon as they desperately tried to dismantle it, to prevent King Carlos's troops from crossing the river.

With the bridge taken by Martín's advance party, the imperial army was able to cross over it. The cavalry traversed the Elbe River, via the shallow area used by the arquebusiers moments before.

The fighting on the shore occupied by the Lutheran army was brutal. Soon, an order was given to cease fire, as the fog, though dissipating, still made it difficult to distinguish friend from foe at a distance. Martín fought fiercely. Nearly naked, he held the Toledo sword in his right hand and wielded the Biscayan dagger in his left, using it for support when he was too close to maneuver the sword.

By mid-morning, the sun had completely cleared away the fog, within which they had fought for three hours since dawn. Almost eight thousand dead from the Schmalkaldic League covered the ground on the shore of the Elbe River. Imperial casualties totaled two hundred men.

"It has been a great victory, no doubt, thanks to the courage and bravery of your men, who managed to open a space for the rest of the army to penetrate," said King Carlos to Captain Álvaro de Sande, who commanded the Spanish Tercio.

"Your face is familiar to me," the king said, observing Martín Cortés, who was still dressed in his breeches with his face smudged with gunpowder, sweat, and the mud that still clung to him.

"Your Majesty, I am Captain Martín Cortés, knight of the Order of Santiago. I served in the household of Empress Isabel, as well as in the household of Prince Felipe," he replied, bowing before him.

"Now I remember you. You are the Mestizo. The son of Hernán Cortés, the Marquis of the Valley, correct?" said King Carlos, smiling as he identified Martín.

"Hernán Cortés is my father, Your Majesty, that is true."

"Like father, like son," he said with a laugh. "Only a son of Hernán Cortés could have led this daring and valiant maneuver that has granted us such a great victory." King Carlos noticed that Martín was bleeding from a slash on his arm, holding it with the other hand, as the bone had been broken by a sword blow. "De Sande, order the Tercio's physician to attend to Captain Cortés's wound and broken bone before it worsens."

When the doctor cleaned Martín's wound and stopped the bleeding, he bandaged the arm with clean cloths. The physician set the broken bone using several splints and bandages. Martín's boy, who had stayed on the other shore, brought his clothes and bundle. The boy helped him dress, as the wound caused him pain with any movement.

"Captain Cortés?" asked a young man dressed as a knight's page.

"That's right. Who is summoning me?" Martín asked while the boy helped him put on his hose.

"His Majesty requests that you present yourself, along with the ten brave men who helped you take the pontoon."

"In an hour we will be before His Majesty. I need to regroup them; they're all over the place right now," Martín replied. He watched the page walk away, recalling when he himself had worn a similar uniform in the Royal House.

He decided to wear his doublet with the embroidered cross of the Order of Santiago, but unable to fit his broken arm through the sleeve, he had the left one torn off. When he gathered his men, he advised them to dress in their finest and cleanest clothes, as they had been summoned before His Majesty.

Using a piece of an enemy flag, he fashioned a sling to support his splinted arm. Once they were all ready, they approached the king's tent and waited in formation outside. It was not long before the monarch emerged from the tent, accompanied by the Duke of Alba.

"Soldiers of the Tercios," the king said in a grave voice, standing before them, "Captain Martín Cortés. You have shown unprecedented bravery, beyond what could be expected. You risked your lives so that your comrades and the rest of my men could achieve this victory. I wish to reward the ten soldiers who took part in this incursion with a scarlet velvet suit trimmed in silver." The soldiers smiled at the reward, knowing they could sell the garments for a good price to those who wore such finery. "As well as a reward of one hundred escudos for each of you." At the mention of the amount, they could not hide their joy. It was a sum equivalent to five years of wages.

"Captain Martín Cortés will be rewarded with two velvet suits, one black and one scarlet, and two hundred escudos," the king said, then approached Martín and shook his hand.

146

The imperial victory dissolved the Schmalkaldic League, and its leaders, Felipe I of Hesse and John Frederick I of Saxony, were imprisoned in Halle Castle rather than executed.

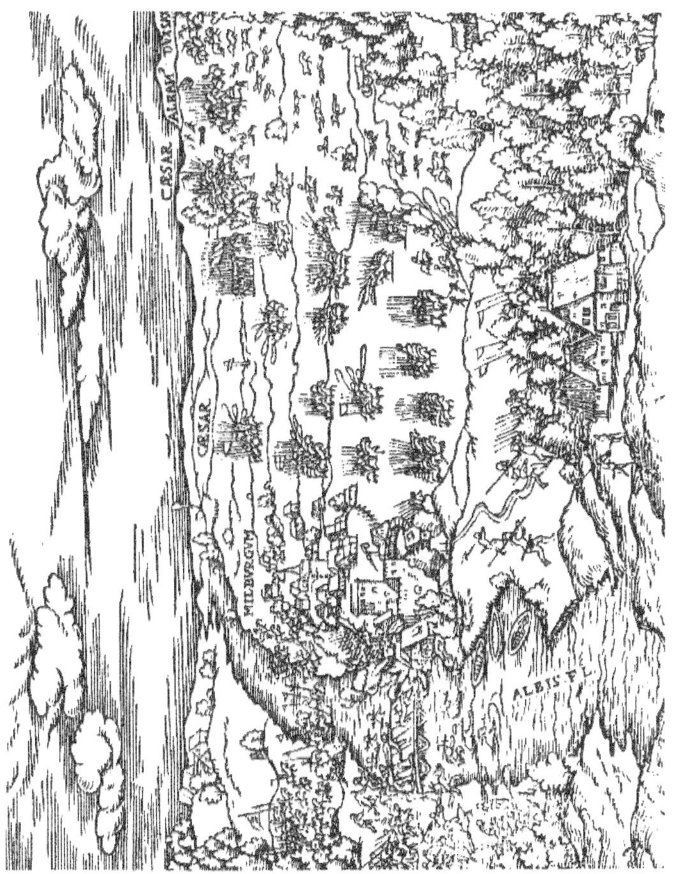

Battle of Mühlberg, woodcut by Luis de Ávila y Zúñiga, 1550.

The Death of the Father. August 1547.

Martín was riding toward Seville, where he had been told his father was living at that time. He felt great joy and excitement, as before heading south, he had spent a couple of months in Agoncillo where he finally met his daughter, whom Bernardina had refused to baptize despite her parents' complaints, until Martín returned from the war. On the last day of June, she was baptized as Ana, the name Bernardina liked. The bad news had come from the midwife who assisted in the birth, as it was complicated. The midwife, based on her experience, recommended that Bernardina shouldn't have more children, or she might die.

He learned through a letter from his brother Luis that their father had weakened over the past few months and had moved to Castilleja de la Cuesta, a small village near Seville. After saying goodbye to his wife and daughter, he headed there.

In Castilleja de la Cuesta, he found his father living in the grand house of Alonso Rodríguez, a judge in Seville. Although Hernán Cortés still had a bright and a sharp mind, Martín noticed his father had limited mobility and complained a lot about his pains. Nevertheless, Hernán Cortés received many visitors every day, just as he used to do years ago in Valladolid with the so-called Cortés Academy.

A scribe finished collecting some documents signed by Hernán Cortés and left the room. Martín stood by the window, looking at the house's inner courtyard, where there was a garden with a tree growing in the center that seemed familiar to him.

"It's a papaya tree, Martín," said Hernán Cortés, approaching the window next to his son and resolving the doubt that seemed to be in his gaze. "During our trip in 1528, I brought seedlings of various trees. I gave one of them to Judge Rodríguez, the owner of this house. I like to eat some of its papayas from time to time. Their smell and taste remind me of New Spain. Besides, I'm missing a few teeth and appreciate eating a fruit that almost doesn't need to be chewed."

Martín had learned that Friar Francisco López de Gómara, who was living with Hernán Cortés, had not left his father's side since they departed from Valladolid. From what Martín gathered, Friar Francisco was writing Hernán Cortés's memoirs, listening to the Marquis's stories, and asking many visitors about their experiences with him.

Hernán Cortés asked his son to sit. He was once again feeling fatigued from breathing when walking or standing.

"Son, I have finally arranged the marriage between your sister María Cortés and the son of the Marquis of Astorga, Don Alvar Pérez Osorio."

Martín smiled and squeezed his hand, resting it on his own.

"I'm glad, father. I like to see how you always care for all your children."

"Always do the same. Family is all we have. Do not betray them. You can deceive anyone you want, but not your own. Without them, we are nothing. You have proven to be loyal, honest, and brave. Unlike some of your brothers…" murmured Hernán Cortés so that only Martín could hear. "Swear to me by your mother's handkerchief, which I imagine you still carry under your clothes, that you will always take care of your family."

Martín placed his hand on his heart and felt under his shirt the small pouch where he always kept the handkerchief. He promised his father he would take care of the family.

That promise, which he did not intend to break, would bring Martín many problems in the future.

His father's condition worsened each week, but the final blow to his health came from two pieces of news, both related to marriages.

The first was about the engagement of María Cortés Zúñiga to Alvar Pérez Osorio, the son of the Marquis of Astorga. Don Alvar Pérez had decided to cancel the arranged marriage. Grieved by the news, Hernán Cortés sent Martín to Seville to bring the scribe Tomás del Río, who had previously drafted his will. His father wished to change it.

The scribe spent the morning locked in with the conqueror, while Martín and his younger brother, of the same name, wandered around the house.

"What do you think father is doing with the new will?" young Martín asked anxiously, constantly peeking to see if the scribe had come out yet.

"Our father knows what he must do, we must trust him. We can only pray for his recovery. I have seen him dejected these last few days," Mestizo replied, trying to calm him.

"He promised me I would inherit the marquisate. He never said he would leave it to you, even though you are the firstborn. It would be frowned upon for a mestizo to inherit the title."

Martín observed him. He was always surprised by his younger brother's lack of respect. He would have slapped anyone else for the insolence he had just shown.

"Brother, watch your tongue. I know you're upset, but we all have to accept whatever father decides to put in his will. If he already promised you the marquisate, you can be sure it will be yours," he replied, annoyed.

The door opened, and the scribe emerged, laden with sheets tied with a satin ribbon. He passed by the two heirs, acknowledging them with a nod. Young Martín ran after him, intending to find out the changes Hernán Cortés had made to the will. Mestizo entered his father's room and approached him. He found him weak. When his father saw him, he asked for a chamomile tea. Martín moved to the table where the jug was and poured a glass.

"Where is your younger brother?" Hernán Cortés asked in a low voice, gasping for air.

"He's outside, father. He was praying for you," he replied, while placing some pillows under his back, to help him recline and breathe more easily.

"Don't lie to me, son. Knowing him, he's probably gone after the scribe to see if he could extract any information."

Martín did not respond to his father. He picked up the glass of chamomile tea and set it on the small table beside the bed.

"He will inherit the title, Martín," his father reminded him. "I promised Doña Juana that our first male child would inherit the marquisate that His Majesty granted me when I married her."

"Don't worry. You have nothing to fear from me. It's your wish, and that's enough for me."

"Now I regret it, but it's the promise I made," he said, taking his son's hands. "Promise me you will watch over him. That you will serve, obey, and treat him properly."

"If it is your wish, so it shall be," Martín replied, somewhat annoyed by the promise to care for someone he considered ill-mannered, selfish, and despotic.

The second blow to Hernán Cortés's health came from another messenger. No one knew the contents of the letter he received, but his father asked the Mestizo again to bring the scribe Tomás del Río back to Castilleja.

"I must add a codicil to the will from two days ago," the two brothers heard their father say when the scribe entered his room. Martín almost had to push his younger brother out of their father's room and close the door behind him.

"What happened now?" young Martín shouted outside the room. "That messenger brought a letter from Luis. Why call the scribe back so urgently to draft a codicil?"

154

"I don't know, brother. I'm worried something has happened to Luis. We haven't heard from him in a long time."

The door opened an hour later, and the scribe came out, looking scared.

"It is important that you attend to the marquis. I see him in a bad state. I drafted the codicil, but he doesn't even have the strength to sign it," the scribe said, alarmed.

"What did the marquis tell you?" young Martín asked impatiently.

"I cannot disclose the content of the codicil or the will, as you understand," the scribe replied, annoyed. "What I can tell you is that your brother, Don Luis Cortés, has informed his father of his engagement to Guiomar Vázquez de Escobar."

"Who is she?" young Martín asked his older brother.

"She is the niece of Bernardino Vázquez de Tapia. You should know this, brother. He was one of the accusers against Pedro de Alvarado and our father during his trial of residence," Mestizo replied. "I will find a witness who is not family to sign the codicil."

Two hours later, among others, Friar Pedro de Zaldívar and accountant Melchor de Mójica entered Hernán Cortés's room. Along with Friar Diego de Altamirano and Licentiate Infante, they signed as witnesses to the codicil presented by the scribe. Francisco López de Gómara, always carrying sheets of paper, a quill, and an inkwell, joined them to record what transpired around Hernán Cortés.

"My father can no longer speak. I ask you to proceed with the anointing of the sick," Mestizo said with great sorrow to Friar Pedro de Zaldívar.

Sitting by his bedside, Mestizo prayed for his father, who was already beginning to struggle for breath. Young Martín paced like a caged animal, agitated, casting furtive glances at his father and older brother.

"*Per istam sanctam Unctionem et suam piissimam misericordiam adiuvet te Dominus gratia Spiritus Sancti. Amen,*" murmured Friar Pedro de Zaldívar over Hernán Cortés's body. "*Ut a peccatis liberatum te salvet atque propitius allevet. Amen.*"[16]

Taking his last breath, Hernán Cortés spoke, and all could hear his final words.

"Mendoza... no... no... emperor... I... I... promise... November eleventh... fifteen forty-four..."

Hernán Cortés closed his eyes for the last time.

On November 2, 1547, the greatest Spanish conqueror passed away. On All Souls' Day, when prayers are said for the deceased in Purgatory, Captain Hernán Cortés, Marquis of the Valley of Oaxaca, died at the age of sixty-two in an upstairs bed in the house of Judge Rodríguez de Medina in Castilleja de la Cuesta. He left this world accompanied by his son Martín Cortés, heir to the marquisate, and his firstborn son, Mestizo Martín Cortés, who held his father's hand and prayed beside him at the moment of his death.

"Never did any captain achieve such feats with so small an army, nor win so many victories, nor subjugate such a vast empire," said Mestizo, standing up after having closed his father's eyelids.

Beside him, Friar López de Gómara tirelessly took notes on the events and conversations in the room.

The next day, Hernán Cortés's sons, Martín Cortés Malintzin and Martín Cortés Zúñiga, along with Judge Rodríguez, the owner of the house, Friar Pedro de Zaldívar, Francisco López de Gómara, the Duke of Medina Sidonia, Friar Diego Altamirano, and other

---

[16] Rite of Extreme Unction: Through this holy Anointing, and through his kind mercy, may the Lord help you with the grace of the Holy Spirit. Amen. So that, free from your sins, he may grant you salvation and comfort you in your illness. Amen.

156

noblemen gathered in the main hall of the house in Castilleja de la Cuesta.

After opening his leather folder, the scribe, Tomás del Río, proceeded to read aloud the lengthy will that Hernán Cortés had dictated to him a few days before.

The first clause of the will required his children to transport his body to New Spain to be buried in Coyoacán. The following clauses dealt with various instructions, such as offering one thousand masses for the souls in purgatory, two thousand for those who died in his company during the conquest of Mexico, and another two thousand masses for the souls of people with whom Hernán Cortés had unresolved matters. However, these were not the most surprising clauses.

He left a good dowry to all his daughters, but especially to his eldest daughter, Catalina Pizarro, who lived in his palace in Cuernavaca. Undoubtedly, Catalina was the daughter Hernán Cortés loved the most, and in addition to the largest financial dowry, he bequeathed her several encomiendas, including Chinantla, Matalacingo, and Tlaltizapán.

The marquisate was inherited by Martín Cortés Zúñiga, as promised. However, he was obligated to pay his brothers, Martín Cortés Malintzin and Luis Cortés Altamirano, one thousand gold ducats annually, a sum that would allow them to live comfortably.

He required Martín Cortés Malintzin and Luis Cortés to serve and obey their brother Martín Cortés Zúñiga, treat him with respect, and not disobey him or the king. Should they disobey or fail in their duties to their brother the marquis, they would be disinherited. Likewise, any sons or daughters who married an enemy of Hernán Cortés would be disinherited.

The will also instructed the heir to the marquisate to build hospitals, a monastery, and a school in New Spain.

"What is the content of the codicil?" asked Martín, the new Marquis of the Valley, nervously when the scribe finished reading the will, prompting disapproving glances from everyone.

The scribe proceeded to read the codicil, which announced that Don Luis Cortés Altamirano was disinherited due to his engagement to the niece of Bernardino Vázquez de Tapia.

Martín Cortés, the marquis, sighed with relief.

During the reading of the will, a letter containing the last wishes of Grandmother Catalina Pizarro was also read. In the document, Hernán Cortés's mother bequeathed some properties in Soria to her grandson Martín Cortés.

"To avoid confusion and disputes, I want it to be clear that my grandmother, Catalina Pizarro, left those lands to me,' said Martín Cortés, the marquis, before the assembled company. His boundless greed was evident, even after inheriting the marquisate and much of his father's assets in New Spain.

The Mestizo did not protest. He had lost his voice upon hearing his younger brother, the marquis, make this recent declaration. Rage welled up from his stomach, clouding his vision. He breathed heavily. He heard others speaking in the room, but he could not understand what they were saying. He rose from his chair and took a few steps, silencing those who had been talking. He approached the scribe, Tomás del Río, who still had the letter from Grandmother Catalina on the table. Silently, he picked up the brief document and read it carefully. When he handed it back to the scribe, he simply pointed to the date on it.

The scribe's eyes widened as he grasped what the Mestizo had pointed out. He asked Judge Rodríguez and the Duke of Medina Sidonia to come closer. The three of them reviewed the documents in the scribe's possession while murmuring among themselves.

"What's the matter with you all?" asked Martín, the marquis, arrogantly. "Another last-minute surprise from my father?"

Judge Rodríguez glared at him with disdain.

"No, marquis. Your father's will and codicil are correct," he replied, scrutinizing him. "We were verifying your grandmother Catalina's letter."

"What's wrong with it?"

"It is signed in the year 1529, four years before you were born. It was undoubtedly written before your grandmother even departed for New Spain, where she passed away. In 1529, Catalina Pizarro had only known the firstborn of her son Hernán, her grandson Martín Cortés Malintzin. Your grace hadn't even been conceived," Judge Rodríguez explained to the marquis, making it clear that he could not possibly be the heir to those lands.

Martín, the marquis, made a futile attempt to protest, but the Duke of Medina Sidonia took him by the arm and led him to a corner of the room, where they spoke quietly for a few moments. After a while, they returned to the table where Judge Rodríguez and Scribe del Río stood.

"Whatever," said Martín, the marquis, condescendingly, "let my mestizo brother have those barren lands in Soria."

On November 4, the funeral procession of Hernán Cortés, consisting of his two sons, Martín Cortés Malintzin and Martín Cortés Zúñiga, along with clergymen, nobles, hidalgos, and fifty poor men carrying lit torches, walked behind the coffin. They made their way to the Monastery of San Isidro del Campo, in the town of Santiponce. The Duke of Medina Sidonia had offered his own crypt for Hernán Cortés's burial until his remains could be transported, as Hernán had wished, to Coyoacán in New Spain.

"A burial fit for a prince," Mestizo murmured to his brother the marquis, noting how respected and loved their father had been.

"A prince who doesn't even have his own grave, and has to rest in a borrowed crypt," the marquis remarked.

"'Do not delay in taking him to New Spain and burying his remains in Coyoacán. That was the first clause of his will,' Mestizo reminded his brother, emphasizing that the benefits of their father's inheritance came with obligations.

When they arrived at the monastery, the prior, Friar Pedro de Zaldívar, verified that it was indeed Hernán Cortés who was to be laid in the crypt. After the confirmation, they laid him in the tomb, beneath the steps of the main altar.

Surprising everyone, and perhaps attempting to echo his brother's words after their father's death, Martín, the marquis, stood before the tomb and recited a clumsy verse he had composed:

Father, whose fate improperly
this lowly world possessed:
Valor that enriched our age,
Rest now in peace eternally.

Less than a week had passed since Hernán Cortés's death when the Mestizo received word that his brother wished to see him. Martín went to his father's chamber, knowing his brother had taken it for himself.

"I'm going to auction off his belongings in Seville."

The Mestizo was shocked to hear his brother's intentions. Their father's body was still warm, and the new marquis was already planning to dispose of part of his inheritance.

"But our father never sold his belongings, and there's no reason for you to do so, brother. He left you enough money to cover the debts. If you allow me, I can approach the lenders and negotiate an extension or reduction of the interest rates."

"I am the owner of everything now, Mestizo. Better let me make the appropriate decisions."

"Of course, brother, but you are barely fifteen years old, and you have an agreement with your future father-in-law, Don Pedro de Arellano, the Count of Aguilar. Father signed the marriage agreement for you and your sister, María Cortés. I was a witness to the agreement, and you've already committed a significant amount of money. People will surround you only to benefit from the fortune father has left you."

"I repeat, brother, that I do not need your help to manage my assets," the marquis replied.

The brothers never spoke of it again. The auction of Hernán Cortés's belongings was organized in Seville, including his furniture, clothing, linens, mattresses, crockery, weapons, armor, and a collection of books. Martín the Mestizo could not bear to see his father's possessions displayed on the steps of the cathedral beneath the Giralda, so he chose not to attend the auction.

Ana and Fernando. August 1554.

In early 1548, Martín traveled to Berlanga, in the lands of Soria, where his grandmother had left him some fields. His wife Bernardina went there with Ana, their daughter. Martín put the fields in order and began to sow some and harvest others, as his father-in-law had taught him the year before. The couple lived a peaceful life in that small village of barely two thousand inhabitants. The lands inherited from his grandmother were vast and fertile. Everything indicated that they could live well off it, though without luxuries.

In the middle of the year, a cart arrived in Berlanga and headed to Martín's house. An older woman, caring for a baby, was traveling in it. The carter stopped in front of the Mestizo's house and handed him a letter. As Martín read it, he learned that the child the woman carried was, in fact, his son. According to the letter, the maid he had lain with while in Seville caring for his father had become pregnant. The girl's father, being from a good Sevillian family, had sent her to another city when he had learned of her pregnancy. There she had given birth to the baby now brought to Martín, who was said to be the father. In the letter, the girl's father explained that his daughter was unmarried and deserved to live her life without it being tainted by an illegitimate child. The Mestizo took charge of the situation and, taking the basket where the baby lay, carried him into his home. The carter, without waiting for any response, left Berlanga.

"I will take in this baby because he is your son, Martín. I will care for him as if he were my own, but do not bring me another bastard," said Bernardina, removing the shawl covering the baby in the basket.

"You certainly cannot deny he is your son. He has the same skin tone as Ana," she added coldly.

Martín did not reply to his wife. He had never thought that maid, or anything related to her, would cross his path again, but here was the proof that it had not turned out that way. Just as his own father had taken responsibility to care for, educate, and support any natural child, Martín also committed to it. After all, he was a bastard child himself.

In the church of Berlanga, the Mestizo's son was baptized. In the registry of the small church, the child was recorded, noting the names of his parents, Martín Cortés and Bernardina de Porras, and the name with which he was baptized, Fernando Cortés de Porras, in honor of his father.

Years passed, and Martín enjoyed the life he led with Bernardina and their children, Ana and Fernando. Martín accompanied his laborers when they went to work in the fields. He liked to feel the warmth on his back or the cool of the mornings when they picked grapes, pruned the vines, or the almond trees.

Ana and Fernando grew up in a peaceful village. Martín gladly paid for a good teacher for his children, so both could learn letters and numbers. Bernardina kept her promise to raise Fernando as her own son. She treated him with the same affection and love she had for Ana. If anyone in Berlanga knew that the baby was not theirs, they never mentioned it. They were the largest landowners in the village and were well-regarded by their neighbors. They appreciated that Martín always went to help the men in the fields and paid better wages than other lords in the region.

During those years, Martín wrote several letters to New Spain addressed to his sisters, Catalina Pizarro, the eldest of his half-sisters, and María Jaramillo, the daughter of Juan Jaramillo and La Malinche, his mother.

He lost contact with his sister Catalina in 1550, when he received her last letter. In it, she complained about the behavior of Doña Juana de Zúñiga, the widow of Hernán Cortés. Catalina told him that she was being pressured by Doña Juana and Juan Altamirano to cede to her stepmother the properties near Cuernavaca that she had inherited from her father.

In 1553, he received a letter and a package from his brother, the heir to the marquisate. In the letter, his brother informed him that he was living at the Court alongside Prince Felipe, and that the prince had become engaged to Mary Tudor, daughter of the English king Henry VIII and Catherine of Aragon. Martín opened the package from his younger brother. Inside was a book: *The Conquest of Mexico* by Francisco López de Gómara. His younger brother warned in the letter that the king would soon likely ban the book, with severe penalties for anyone who published or even possessed it.

"It displeases King Carlos and his son, Prince Felipe, that some, like our father, should outshine them in fame and honor. They will prevent our father and the Marquisate of the Valley from receiving the recognition and honor they deserve. It is their common practice to behead anyone who stands out too much," Martín read his brother the Marquis's words, smiling as he thought that even his younger brother disliked being overshadowed.

It was then that the Mestizo understood why López de Gómara had been constantly by Hernán Cortés's side during the final stage of his life. He had gathered information from his father's years of conquest and taken testimony from the many visitors who had accompanied him. He was surprised by the dedication in the book. He had expected it to be dedicated to his father, Hernán Cortés, but López de Gómara dedicated it to his brother, Martín Cortés Zúñiga:

To the most illustrious Lord Don Martín Cortés, Marquis of the Valley. To no one else should I dedicate, most illustrious Lord, the Conquest of Mexico, but to your lordship, who is the son of the one who conquered it, so that, just as you inherited the estate, you may also inherit the history...[17]

Martín had always thought that López de Gómara had been a flatterer of his father, but judging by the dedication, in recent years he had also been dedicated to exalting and glorifying the figure of his younger brother, the Marquis.

In the following weeks, Martín enjoyed reading the book. Far from the prejudice with which he had begun reading it, he found it a faithful account of his father's past, consistent with all the stories Martín had heard from various people throughout his life. He had always had great affection and respect for his father, but reading the book helped him better understand certain attitudes and behaviors of Hernán Cortés. He learned much about New Spain and ancient Mexico through its pages. This helped him better appreciate the land of his birth and even take pride in his mestizo heritage, especially with such illustrious parents, Hernán Cortés, and Doña Marina, La Malinche.

Thanks to a few letters, Martín had not lost touch with his sister, María Jaramillo. He learned that in 1546, after several miscarriages, she had a son named Pedro. In her most recent letter, she informed him that her husband, Luis de Quesada, would be taking young Pedro to Spain to continue his studies. Afterward, her husband would join the entourage accompanying the Spanish prince to England to celebrate his second marriage, following his widowhood in 1553.

Martín himself had also received a letter from the prince's household, with orders to join the entourage that was to go to England for the marriage between Felipe and Mary Tudor.

---

[17] Extract from the book by López de Gómara.

166

The Prince's Wedding. July 1554.

In La Coruña, nearly four thousand attendees gathered, including servants, soldiers, knights, and nobles. There, Martín met his brother, the Marquis, whom he had not seen since their father's death. The Marquis greeted him coldly, almost as if he did not know him, which contrasted with the affectionate greeting Prince Felipe gave him upon recognizing him.

"Mestizo, I am glad to see you. I had lost sight of you for a while. I believe the last time we met was after the battle in Piedmont," recalled the prince.

"Your Highness, you have an excellent memory," replied Martín the Mestizo, bowing. "After that battle, I participated in the Mühlberg campaign, where, alongside your father, we achieved a beautiful victory against the Schmalkaldic League."

"I know, Mestizo, and I have not forgotten that thanks to your bravery in surprising the enemy, by the Elbe River, the rest of the army could cross. I believe my father rewarded you for that."

"Indeed, Your Highness. My men and I received a splendid gift from His Majesty and a handsome reward."

His younger brother watched the conversation between them with some annoyance. He had not been able—or willing—to participate in any battle that would allow him to demonstrate his valor and manhood. Although he lived every day with Prince Felipe, he saw that the closeness the prince shared with his brother, the Mestizo, was not the same as with him.

"I also remember that you made me a promise when my mother, Empress Isabel, passed away," commented Prince Felipe, without clarifying what promise Martín had made, testing whether they had been mere empty words or if he still remembered.

"I promised Your Highness that I would pray for the soul of your mother every day of my life. I have fulfilled this every morning in my prayers. For Empress Isabel and for my mother, Doña Marina... and for my father, in recent years," he replied to the prince's question, and the prince was satisfied with his response and bid Martín farewell.

During the voyage to England, the guards on board were vigilant, fearing an attack from the French navy, as that country opposed the union between the English and Spanish monarchies.

"Your Grace must be Martín Cortés," a man remarked to the Mestizo during the journey while he contemplated the large fleet heading to England.

"I am Martín Cortés but permit me to say that if you are looking for my brother, the Marquis of the Valley, you have boarded the wrong ship. He is on another vessel, traveling with Prince Felipe," Martín replied, observing the stranger who had approached to greet him and who had an accent similar to many he had heard from New Spain.

"I am not mistaken. It is you I seek. I am..."

"Luis de Quesada," Martín replied, smiling. "You must be Don Luis de Quesada, who is married to my sister, María Jaramillo."

"The very same. I am pleased to meet you," the man responded kindly, extending his hand for a handshake. Martín disregarded the hand and embraced his brother-in-law.

The voyage allowed the two men to form a good friendship. Luis de Quesada was about five years older than Martín, so he must have been around 37 years old. They updated each other on their families and lives. Martín learned from him that, after the death of Juan Jaramillo, he bequeathed a third of his inheritance to María, and the rest to his wife, whom Martín had met when he visited Jaramillo's house.

Martín thought he had done well not to tell anyone about the discovery regarding María's paternity. Juan Jaramillo did not deserve to learn that his daughter resembled Hernán Cortés's mother during his lifetime. María Jaramillo would also have been affected by the knowledge that the father she had always respected and loved was not truly her father, but merely her mother's husband. Moreover, Martín's suspicion could not be confirmed.

"Better to take the secret to the grave or let it be known once I am dead, when it can no longer affect anyone," Martín thought, unaware that years later, he would recall it when speaking about his life to Inca Garcilaso de la Vega.

Luis de Quesada encouraged Martín to return to New Spain, offering help if needed. He had several estates with sugar mills and various plantations. He said he could use someone to help manage them. Martín appreciated his brother-in-law's offer but informed him that he also had fields in Soria, which, although not making him rich, provided good returns.

After eight days of sailing, they arrived at the port of Southampton. Once Prince Felipe's large entourage disembarked, they marched in a long caravan to Winchester, following the eight ambassadors who had gone to greet them at the port.

Martín Cortés witnessed the meeting between Mary and Felipe. The English queen, besides being older, was quite unattractive. In fact, she had a terrible mouth with crooked and rotten teeth, as it was said she spent her days eating sweets. Mary Tudor covered Prince Felipe with a large black velvet cloak, and then conferred upon the Spanish prince the Order of the Garter; this gesture was reciprocated by Prince Felipe, who pinned a gold brooch with a huge diamond and a large ruby on her bodice.

The celebrations after the wedding lasted nine days, during which nobles from various nations held horse exhibitions and reenactments of battles. Martín the Marquis enjoyed participating in almost all of them, aligning himself as a companion to Prince Felipe when he wished to join in. Martín the Mestizo watched from the stands with Luis de Quesada, observing the displays of chivalry, tournaments, horseback battle reenactments, and sword duels held in the arena.

"Do you not participate in the tournaments?" asked Luis de Quesada, as they watched a joust between English and Castilian nobles.

"I have fought in many places, my dear Luis. Without displays or flowery battles. By blood and fire. This is theater. I hope you never have to fight for your life or the lives of others, knowing it could be the last time you wield your sword," Martín replied, feeling a certain embarrassment at the spectacle his brother was making in front of the crowd. "Among those seated, I recognize certain captains and nobles I have seen truly fight. They watch these tournaments as if it were an insult to the effort they demonstrated on the battlefield, along with their companions. As if mocking those who offered their lives for the Crown."

As if it were not enough to endure the embarrassment of seeing his brother groveling to the prince, Martín also had to bear the insults and belches from the English, drunk on their vile beer, shouting from the stands. More than once, Martín's hand went to the hilt of his Biscayan dagger, and Luis de Quesada had to restrain him.

Martín found in his future brother-in-law a trustworthy man, someone close to whom he could delegate his affairs in New Spain. He entrusted him with reviewing the state and accounts of the two encomiendas of Tlapa and Atacaxtla, which his father had gifted him years before his death, and also with reviewing the accounts of the Taxco mine, which Hernán Cortés had left to his three sons, and from which Martín had yet to see a peso.

"I have never received from my brother the thousand ducats annually that my father obligated him to provide in his will," Martín confessed to Luis. "I ask you to see if it is possible to claim it without going to court. I would prefer not to have to file a lawsuit against the Marquis over it."

"If your brother is unwilling to pay what he is obligated to by your father's wishes, you will have to file a complaint against the Marquis. But don't worry, Martín. I will try to resolve it through mediation, to avoid a lawsuit. We all find them unpleasant," replied Luis de Quesada.

As if it were not enough shame for Martín to see his brother the Marquis participating in the jousts, he had to witness the moment when the queen awarded him a prize for his luxurious and elegant clothing and his beautiful armor.

"The little Marquis has brought more trunks of clothes than Prince Felipe himself," Martín heard one of the Spanish dukes attending the wedding say behind him, amid laughter.

Unexpected Visit. November 1561.

The cold had arrived early that year, affecting Martín more than the rest of the men who had accompanied him to prune that week. His kidneys and all his bones ached. Painful chilblains appeared on his ears and hands. He noticed that the men who went to work in the fields with him suffered fewer hardships due to the cold. He thought it might be because his Mexican heritage made him more accustomed to warm climates than to the cold Extremaduran winters.

They had started pruning early, with frost still on the gnarled vine branches they had to cut. They ate some roasted sausage over the embers of a fire one of the men had lit early in the morning, which helped warm their bodies a little at the start of the day. By mid-afternoon, they finished pruning and returned to the village, walking behind a mule loaded with their tools. In a few days, Martín would return to gather the cut vine shoots into bundles, which were always useful at home for starting fires.

Upon arriving in Berlanga, he was surprised to see two beautiful horses tied to the bars of his house's windows. He had never seen such fine horses in those lands. As he approached, he saw his son come out of the house and take the reins of one of the animals, the finer one, to lead it to the back of the house where the stable was.

"Fernando!" Martín called to his son, who had not seen him arrive, being so captivated by the ornate saddle.

"Father, I didn't see you. I was going to take your brother the Marquis's horse to the stable."

"Is my brother Martín in the house?" he asked in surprise, turning toward the front door.

"Yes, father. He just arrived accompanied by Luis, your other brother. That's his other horse tied up here. I'll take it to the stable next to this one. I'll give them water and barley," Fernando replied, stroking the neck of Martín the Marquis's horse.

"Good, son. When you remove the saddle, don't leave it out there. Bring it inside. We don't want to leave any temptations in sight."

Martín watched Fernando walk away and lost sight of him as he turned the corner of the house. He never tired of watching his children. Both had the same bronzed skin tone, a bit lighter than Martín's. Fernando, a tall and lanky lad of fourteen, was always willing to help in the fields, but Martín preferred that he stay home with the tutor he had brought years ago from Salamanca to teach his two children equally, as they were almost the same age.

He reached the door of the house and, while tying the mule to the grille, observed Luis's horse. A good animal, although of lesser stature than his brother the Marquis's. It had a beautiful saddle, though it did not match the fine craftsmanship of wood, leather, and silver rivets he had seen on the Marquis's saddle.

The Mestizo put his hand on the handle and, after a deep sigh, opened the door and entered the vestibule.

He heard the voices of two men, unable to distinguish what they were talking about but recognizing the tones of his two brothers. When he closed the door, Bernardina soon appeared, emerging from the kitchen, drying her hands on her apron and still flustered by the unexpected visit.

"Martín, your brothers arrived a while ago. You didn't tell me they were coming," Bernardina whispered as soon as she reached him, avoiding being overheard by the guests.

"I haven't heard from them in years, Bernardina, as you well know," the Mestizo replied, rubbing his hands to warm up, trying not to touch the painful chilblains. "I haven't seen Luis since shortly after father died, and Martín since the wedding of King Felipe II."

"Could their visit have anything to do with the lawsuit you filed against Martín in New Spain over the Taxco mine?"

"We'll soon find out, Bernardina. I'll go and see what they've come for," he said, making a move to head to see his brothers waiting in the room.

"No, Martín. I don't want them to see you just back from working in the field. Go upstairs and freshen up. Good heavens, look at your hands!" she exclaimed, noticing the irritated skin from the chilblains. "I've left the lemon oil by the washbasin. I figured you'd be suffering from the cold today. After you wash and dry your hands, rub the oil on them. It will help."

"Thank you, dear," Martín replied, kissing her on the lips and taking the opportunity to squeeze her waist playfully.

"Go on, wash up and tidy yourself a bit. I see you're not as cold as you seem," she said, laughing softly. "I'll bring your brothers some wine and the aniseed biscuits I made this morning."

In his bedroom, the Mestizo applied the oil to his hands after washing them and felt the itchiness subside. He dressed in the simple, clean clothes his daughter had left on the bed. He went downstairs and entered the room where his brothers were waiting. Two pine logs crackled lively in the fireplace, warming the room. Each brother held a glass of wine in hand.

"Martín!" Luis exclaimed upon seeing him. He set down his wine glass and went to him, embracing him tightly. "I've been longing to see you again!"

"Luis, what have I done that you haven't written me even once in all this time?" Martín said, smiling.

"I tried, but I lost track of you both and didn't know how to reach either of you. It wasn't until recently that our younger brother found me in Barcelona," Luis responded, his voice thick with emotion at reuniting with his elder brother.

The sound of a glass being set down on the table was heard. Turning, the two brothers saw the Marquis approaching them.

"I have nothing to reproach you for, Mestizo. You filed a lawsuit, because you thought you had the right to claim something from me, and you won," the Marquis said, raising his hands to show his palms, indicating he had nothing to hide.

"We wouldn't have reached that point if you had fulfilled our father's will. You knew the three of us were to share the profits from the Taxco mine, but you never distributed them. Luis was disinherited, unfortunately, from the thousand ducats a year father charged you with. But I was not disinherited, and you never gave me any money from it either. I don't hold any grudge against you, brother; I just claimed what was rightfully mine."

"I agree with you that it was father's wish for the three of us to own the Taxco mine, but you know he never signed it. Besides, our father supported you for much of your life with money, servants, horses, weapons, and he even left you two towns in encomienda in New Spain," the Marquis replied, trying to find some balance between them.

"Are you going to put a price on what he gave me in life?" Martín asked, irritated.

"Let's forget what happened, Mestizo. Let's start our relationship anew," said the Marquis, extending his hand. "I have grand plans, and nothing would make me happier than for my two brothers to be a part of them."

"We can talk about whatever you like. Do you already know about our brother's plans?" the Mestizo asked Luis after shaking the Marquis's hand.

"He didn't want to tell me what it was about until we were all together," Luis excused himself.

When Martín's brothers arrived, Bernardina had instructed the maid who helped them at home to kill and roast a piglet and bake more loaves of bread for the guests. When dinner was ready,

176

his wife prepared the table in the room where the three men were and served them the roast piglet.

That night, Bernardina dined in the kitchen with her children. Although Ana and Fernando talked about the mysterious visit of their father's brothers, their mother did not share with them the snippet of conversation she had overheard in the room when she went in to set the table where they would dine. Bernardina prayed to the Virgin of Hope that what she had heard was just a misunderstanding and that they were not insisting her husband return to New Spain.

"Brothers, there is no problem between us that we cannot resolve," the Marquis commented diplomatically after having eaten the roast piglet. "For my part, I recommend, Mestizo, that you drop that lawyer you empowered in New Spain to represent you. That bastard has given me enough headaches."

"Watch your tongue, brother. Remember you are speaking to two bastards," Martín responded, also recalling his son Fernando, a bastard like himself.

"It's just a manner of speaking, brother," the Marquis excused himself. "That Quesada has been relentlessly hounding me."

"The Quesada you refer to is my brother-in-law," Martín clarified, leaving the Marquis astonished, as he was unaware of their relationship. "Yes, brother. Don Luis de Quesada is married to my sister María Jaramillo."

"Actually, your half-sister," the Marquis commented ironically.

"María Jaramillo is my sister... my half-sister, sorry. Just as you two are as well," Martín replied, correcting himself. "Luis de Quesada, her husband, has only defended my legitimate interests."

"I acknowledge that I owe you money, Martín, but now we have the opportunity for the three sons of Hernán Cortés to return to New Spain. I have lands, encomiendas, and vassals. What I owe you, I will repay when we get to Mexico."

"But as far as I know, the matter of the vassals has not been resolved by the Crown," added Luis to the conversation.

"King Felipe II authorized over a year ago, in 1560, that one could enjoy towns in encomienda without a limit on the number of vassals. That issue, brothers, has already been resolved," the marquis proudly remarked. "There is no doubt that my closeness with the king helped him understand the problem New Spain had with the encomiendas, and the vassals we had."

"What do you intend with your return, Martín? I thought you were enjoying your wealth and resources here. You've always liked mingling with the nobility and the court," questioned the Mestizo.

"With my return... our return, I intend for us to be regarded as we deserve. Our father was denigrated in the last years of his life. That was because he was in Spain, and did not have at his disposal the power he had gained in New Spain. Here he was just another marquis. In Mexico, he was the great Hernán Cortés. His title didn't matter; he was respected by all," the marquis commented, his eyes shining.

"But you mustn't forget that we are all subjects and vassals of Felipe II. I wouldn't want you to fill your head with dreams, brother," replied the Mestizo, which was a harsh blow to his brother, the marquis.

"I would never pretend to overshadow His Majesty, brother. What I want... what we need to do, is to continue what our father started. To put his estates and businesses in order, to involve ourselves in the administration of New Spain, to obtain positions, and for the Crown to trust a Cortés again, as a sign of loyalty and fidelity."

"I will go with you," responded Luis.

"Mestizo? Don't you wish to return to your homeland, the very place where you were born?" asked the marquis, trying to flatter him.

"Let me remind you, brother, that all of our father's children are Novohispanic. You included, whether you like it or not. Besides, here in Berlanga, I live well with my wife and children. I am happy and for the first time in my life, the years pass without having to go to battles or wars. Nowadays, I have no ties to New Spain, except for my sisters."

"Very well. I understand your stance and your reluctance to return. I didn't want to do this, but you've left me no choice," the marquis commented seriously, looking into the Mestizo's eyes. "Our father stated in his will that you both are obligated to obey me and support me in whatever I need. If you do not heed my request, I could disinherit both of you from what you have."

"I have received nothing from you over these years, Martín!" the Mestizo reproached, standing up from the table, enraged. "Not even after winning the lawsuits have you deigned to pay me a single peso. Now you come to my house to threaten me so that I accompany you forcibly to New Spain? Are you not man enough to carry out your plans without needing Luis or me by your side, as if we were your squires?!" the Mestizo shouted, red with anger.

"Just remember, dear brother, that the inheritance does not only refer to what our father left you, and to which I already responded that I would pay you. When I mention that I can disinherit you, I am also referring to this house and these lands that our grandmother bequeathed to you," the marquis responded calmly, taking a sip of wine.

"You said it, brother. Our grandmother left them to me. To me," said the Mestizo, jabbing his finger into his chest.

"That's true, but they were part of our father's inheritance. Whether you are right or not, the lawsuit that would arise between us could drag on for years, during which none of us would enjoy our grandmother's assets until a court resolved it," the marquis remarked, with the satisfaction of having cornered his older brother. "I might not have the money right now to pay your thousand ducats a year, but I do have enough money to pay lawyers to prolong the lawsuit."

Martín the Mestizo took a deep breath. He felt dizzy. He drank his half glass of wine and moved closer to the fire. He had lost all warmth in his body. His skin, which had been flushed from the fury of shouting at his brother, now appeared pale. He breathed deeply, staring at the fire, with the pine logs almost consumed. He could not tell if the heat was from the fire, the wine, or the simmering rage within him. Behind him, he heard his brothers' breathing, the sound of glasses being set on the table, wine being poured. A dog barked outside the house in response to a nearby owl that had hooted moments before.

It had been more than an hour since he heard his wife and children go up the wooden stairs. Their bedroom was above the room they were in, so Martín had no doubt that Bernardina had heard everything discussed among the brothers.

He thought about the promise he made to his father. He had promised to respect, defend, and obey Martín the marquis. He knew his brother was right, that a lawsuit over the property rights of their grandmother's assets could drag on for years, during which they could not be used because they were in dispute. On the other hand, his brother promised to compensate him for the debts if he accompanied him to New Spain.

"Brother, should I throw more logs on the fire, or have you made a decision?" asked the marquis in a mocking tone. "Today, we traveled several hours to reach this village and now we want to rest. Tomorrow, I will leave, and I wish to know if I should settle my affairs and acquire passage in Seville for us to travel to New Spain, or if I should go to Toledo to file a lawsuit against you for breach of testament."

180

The Mestizo turned slowly and looked at the marquis, illuminated by the multi-branched candelabrum on the table. His heart urged him to defy his brother and choke him with his own hands. Kill the dog and the rabies will end. Fortunately, his mind prevailed over his anger.

"I will go with you, brother," Martín responded, smiling, surprising the marquis with this unexpected gesture.

"I expected nothing less from your nobility."

"But we are going to sign an agreement between gentlemen," added the Mestizo. "In this agreement, you will allow me to lease the assets that our grandmother Catalina Pizarro bequeathed to me and that I have worked on these years while I am in New Spain."

"Of course, it's reasonable," responded the marquis.

"Additionally, against the debt you owe me, you will support my family and me when we arrive in New Spain and during our stay."

"That's fair. You will live in the residence I have next to the main square in Mexico. You will enjoy a part of the palace for yourselves," the marquis commented, standing up and approaching his older brother to seal the commitment.

Both embraced by the fireplace. Martín the Mestizo held his brother tightly, preventing him from pulling away, using the opportunity to bring his mouth close to the marquis's ear. The marquis, already terrified, tried to break free from the Mestizo's grip.

"And I swear by my mother, La Malinche, that if you ever threaten me again like you did tonight, I will end your life, brother. It will be no effort for me. Unlike you, I have killed many men in my life, some for less reason. I will accept the consequences of your death," the marquis tried to break free from his older brother's embrace but could not until the Mestizo loosened his arms.

The marquis straightened his clothes and reshaped his face from the panic that had taken over upon hearing his older brother's threat. Luis didn't fully understand what had passed between them, but the tension in the room gave him enough of a clue.

"Perfect, let's toast, brothers, to our return to New Spain," said the marquis, approaching the table and pouring more wine into the glasses.

Arrival in New Spain. December 1562.

In August of 1562, the ship carrying the three brothers was struck by a hurricane. The winds tore the sails and damaged the vessel they had sailed on from Spain. After five days of being battered by violent waves, torrential rains, and strong winds, the storm finally calmed, but the pilot had lost his bearings. No land was visible on the horizon, and fresh water and food were starting to run low. Martín, the marquis, spent hours praying in his small cabin below deck with his wife, Ana Ramírez de Arellano, who was about to give birth. Luis and Martín the Mestizo traveled in a shared space with other men.

With effort, and after three days adrift, they managed to repair some torn sails and hoisted them on the damaged masts, which allowed the ship to move again. They sailed west, knowing that they would see land at any moment. After a week of blind navigation, they sighted the coast on the horizon.

Dark clouds gathered as they approached land. Before being hit by a second hurricane, the pilot identified the coastline ahead as being south of their destination. They were in the Gulf of Honduras. The second hurricane once again destroyed all the sails and toppled one of the masts, killing three men working on deck. Luckily, this time the hurricane only lasted two days, followed by four more days of heavy rain.

The rainwater helped quench the thirst of everyone on board. Anchored in a cove, they lowered several boats and reached the shore. Martín and Luis disembarked, armed with a few arquebuses. Hours later, they returned to the ship with some game, which provided small rations for the sailors and passengers.

The ship was repaired using cloth provided by some merchants, which they fashioned into new sails. They weighed anchor and sailed north for many leagues, always navigating along the coast, as they did not want to stray far in case the sails failed, or another storm struck them.

On September 20, 1562, they arrived at the port of San Francisco de Campeche, where the Cortés brothers disembarked. The small population there had already heard of the delays suffered by the ship carrying the Cortés family and had presumed the vessel lost at sea. Their arrival at the port was met with joyous celebration.

The marquis's wife, Ana Ramírez de Arellano, who was also his niece, gave birth to a son in Campeche. The Mestizo stood as godfather as the child, Jerónimo Cortés, was baptized in the small church that had been built in the town. A month after their arrival in Campeche, they continued their journey to Veracruz.

On the way to that great city, the ship passed the mouth of the Coatzacoalcos River. Martín the Mestizo leaned over the port side, gazing at the enormous river meeting the sea. He knew that his mother, Marina, was from this area, from a town called Olutla. He was tempted to visit that province upon reaching Veracruz, but he knew he could not on this occasion. He had committed to traveling with his younger brother, as had Luis. The marquis had not yet revealed his plans, but knowing his pretentious and vain character, Martín was certain he would cause some sort of conflict with the authorities in New Spain.

Only three months had passed since he left Bernardina and their children in Berlanga, promising to send for them once he was settled in Mexico. The passage for the three of them had been paid before he departed from Seville, giving them a year to make the journey to New Spain. As soon as Martín arrived in Mexico City and settled in his brother's palace, he would send a letter to Bernardina.

In Veracruz, they joined a caravan heading to Mexico City, just as Martín had done twenty-two years earlier when he traveled to New Spain to reunite with his father, only to discover that Hernán Cortés had simultaneously departed for Spain.

The Welcome. January 1563.

The Mestizo always thought of his sisters María Jaramillo and Catalina Pizarro, and longed to see them both again. He stayed connected with María and her husband, Luis, and informed them of his upcoming arrival in Mexico. He had certain fears regarding Catalina Pizarro, his older sister. In 1550, their sporadic communication had ceased. He asked his brother, the marquis, who responded evasively, claiming ignorance, as his relationship with his mother, Doña Juana, had also deteriorated due to disputes over Hernán Cortés's will and inheritance. Doña Juana had filed lawsuits in New Spain against her own son.

They were only a day's journey away from Mexico City. They were resting in Texcoco, where the three brothers went to pray at their grandmother Catalina Pizarro's tomb in the Monastery of San Francisco. After a mass was offered for her soul, Martín was surprised to encounter a group of noblemen and principal men who had come seeking his brother, the marquis.

"I notified certain nobles and friends of our arrival in Mexico before leaving Veracruz," he explained, seeing the puzzled look on his older brother's face at the men who had come to visit him. "They are very glad to see me return and wish to celebrate."

The next day, as they approached Mexico City, a reception of nobles and lords awaited them in Coyoacán, a city founded by their father and where Martín was born. The Cortés brothers bid farewell to the caravan they had traveled with from Veracruz, stopping at an area where tents, tables, and chairs had been set up.

Principal men came to greet the marquis, bowing to him in a manner that embarrassed his brother, the Mestizo, as such reverence, which was typically reserved for high nobles and royalty. The brothers were offered a magnificent banquet, with roasted game and turkeys. After the feast, a display of battle and a tournament took place, where more than three hundred men clad in armor and bearing weapons performed before the marquis, who was seated on a large chair on a raised platform.

"Brother, I think there's something we don't know or are missing," Luis whispered to the Mestizo. "This reception is more fitting for a viceroy than for our brother, even if he is the Marquis of the Valley of Oaxaca."

"I agree, Luis. Not even if our father were the one returning to Mexico would I understand this," Martín replied.

After the various tournaments on horseback and on foot, as well as the parade of the cavalry, the arrival into Mexico City had been carefully organized. Night had just fallen when they entered the capital with a procession of over two thousand horsemen, all wearing black velvet capes and carrying lit torches. At the center of the procession, riding a magnificent black stallion, was Martín Cortés Zúñiga, the Marquis of the Valley of Oaxaca.

Hundreds of women leaned out from the balconies and windows of the houses, resting their arms on richly embroidered shawls draped over the sills and railings. As the marquis passed by, they threw flower petals, and he greeted them all from his horse. The procession concluded in the main square, where the viceroy himself, Luis de Velasco, was waiting at the entrance of the palace, accompanied by his son. The marquis dismounted and approached the viceroy. They greeted each other at the door, and there was some conflict over who should enter the palace first. The Mestizo observed the scene, hoping the viceroy, as the higher-ranking man, would enter first.

"The marquis! The marquis!" the Mestizo heard some fearful voices exclaim, indicating that they wanted his younger brother to cross the palace threshold first. He saw his brother turn, smiling and greeting the entourage that had accompanied him. The Mestizo had no doubt that his younger brother had heard the voices. Without waiting, the marquis crossed the threshold first, with the viceroy following behind, smiling. The Mestizo noticed the viceroy's son watching the marquis's bold gesture with a displeased expression.

Several people who had stayed in the square approached Martín the Mestizo and his brother Luis, introducing themselves. Martín recognized their surnames from captains who had accompanied his father during the conquest. Although Luis and Martín were treated kindly, it was clear that the entourage was only interested in being with the marquis.

Soon, some scribes emerged from the viceroyal palace and read the list of guests invited to the banquet in honor of the marquis of the Valley. Luis and Martín entered the palace later, after spending some time in the main square exchanging words and greetings with other great lords of New Spain. The brothers, along with the rest of the guests, proceeded to the grand hall.

Settled in one wing of his brother's palace, Martín prepared the rooms to receive his children and wife in a few weeks. It had been two months since he had written to Bernardina, asking her to begin their journey to New Spain. The hurricane season was in the summer, so he told his wife to travel before June or after September.

"So you don't have to endure the extreme heat of a summer journey," he wrote, not wanting to frighten her with tales of storms.

His brother, the marquis, and Luis spent their days in celebrations, meetings, and banquets held in the marquis's honor. Martín the Mestizo, however, had always led a rather sober life and never cared much for celebrations. He preferred to visit his sister, María Jaramillo, who lived in the grand residence of Luis de Quesada, located behind the church. Martín spent most of his time with them, helping Luis de Quesada with various tasks and managing encomiendas or sugar plantations throughout the country.

"I'm worried about my sister Catalina," he confessed one May evening while dining with his sister and brother-in-law. "On my way back from Taxco, I detoured to Cuernavaca and visited Doña Juana, my father's widow. She informed me that Catalina had left for Spain around 1550. That was when I had lost contact with her. It's strange that she hasn't responded or sought me out all these years, knowing I lived there."

María Jaramillo glanced at her husband and made a subtle gesture that caught Martín's attention.

"Is something wrong, sister? It seems like you're hiding something from me."

"Dear, I beg you to tell my brother what you know," María said to her husband.

Luis sighed and took the last sip of his wine, finishing the little that remained. He wiped a drop that had fallen on his beard, placed the napkin on the table, and looked at Martín.

"What I'm about to tell you, I heard a few years ago. At first, I didn't believe it and didn't think it was important, but as time passed, I noticed that Catalina was no longer mentioned here in Mexico City. Which is strange, since Hernán Cortés's children are all well-known, and people like to keep track of them," explained Luis de Quesada. "If I hadn't told you before, it's because what I know comes from rumors and gossip."

"I understand, but please, tell me. I'm eager to know where my sister Catalina is, as well as her condition."

"Did you know Juan Altamirano well?"

"The last time I saw Juan, I was six years old. I lived with him for a time until my father took me to Spain. I wouldn't recognize him if that's what you're asking. Juan Altamirano was my father's cousin. He left me in his care when he went on the expedition to Honduras with our mother," Martín replied,

190

looking at his sister. "He lived near here, as far as I know, but I don't remember where."

"Altamirano died last year, and yes, he had a large house near the Zócalo where you spent a few years living with him," explained Luis de Quesada. "I know Doña Juana de Zúñiga was very displeased with the contents of the will. It seems that your father left a good dowry to all his daughters and the marquisate to his son, young Martín, but he didn't leave as much to her as she expected to receive."

Martín nodded, confirming the truth of his brother-in-law's account.

"Doña Juana didn't fare badly in the will, but she was annoyed that almost everything went to her eldest son, the marquis, and to her husband's natural daughter, Catalina Pizarro. As far as I know, she was the most generously rewarded daughter," Luis took the wine flask and poured a little more for his brother-in-law and himself. "From what I've been able to find out, two or three years after becoming a widow, Doña Juana began pressuring Catalina to cede the properties near Cuernavaca. The most valuable ones."

"But she didn't have to do that," Martín said.

"Of course not. Doña Juana claimed that Catalina had spent her entire life living under the roof of her palace and at their expense. She started harassing her and, as if that wasn't enough, she also received the help of Juan Altamirano, who knew the properties and assets your father had in New Spain well, as he had been a trusted man of his for some years."

"Catalina wanted to leave New Spain. She had asked me years ago to help arrange a marriage so she could live in Spain," Martín commented, puzzled.

"That's the thing. It seems they deceived her into believing that you, Martín, had arranged a marriage for her."

"That's not true."

"I thought the same when I heard it, but by then it was too late. Catalina left power of attorney with Doña Juana to act as executor in her absence. She boarded a ship in Veracruz and sailed to Seville," Luis de Quesada paused and took a sip from his glass. "Upon her arrival, the Duke of Medina Sidonia, in collusion with Juan Altamirano and your stepmother, had set a trap. They forced your sister into the Dominican Convent of Madre de Dios in Sanlúcar de Barrameda, against her will."

Martín collapsed at the news of what had happened to his sister. Overcome with sadness, he began to cry. María went to him and embraced him.

" If I'd known this before coming to New Spain, I would have gotten her out. Now that I think about it, I was just a few hundred steps away from the convent when I was in Seville," Martín murmured, holding his head in his hands as his elbows rested on the table. "Do my brothers know about this?" he asked, looking up at his brother-in-law.

"I don't think Luis knows, at least not before arriving here. The marquis almost certainly knows. He's been defending himself in the Audiencia of New Spain from numerous lawsuits filed by his mother. He has agents here keeping him informed, so he surely knows what happened to Catalina."

"And that dog never told me!" Martín exclaimed, clenching his fists.

Now that Martín knew where Catalina Pizarro was, he did not want to miss the opportunity to write to her. He imagined that any letters not from Doña Juana, Juan Altamirano, or the Duke of Medina Sidonia would be destroyed at the convent. He didn't know the mark those three used to seal their letters, but he remembered Juan Altamirano's study. It was there that he had received lessons from the tutor while under Altamirano's care. Martín discovered the house and learned that Juan Gutiérrez Altamirano, the licentiate's son, had inherited the property.

Through María Jaramillo's servants, he discovered the names of the old employees of the residence who still lived there until the heir returned from Spain to take possession of the large house in Mexico City.

Martín knocked on the door. An elderly lady opened it. Martín knew it was Mrs. Magdalena, the head servant. After asking about Licentiate Altamirano's son, the maid confirmed he had not yet returned from Spain.

"Are you by any chance Mrs. Magdalena?' Martín asked.

The woman looked closely at him but didn't recognize him—it had been forty years since she'd last seen Martín.

"I'm sure you don't remember me. My name is Martín Cortés, and the late Licentiate Altamirano had me in his care for a few years before I went to Spain."

The woman became emotional and embraced Martín, crying. She invited him into the house and offered him some honeyed sweets. Martín listened attentively as the old lady recounted many anecdotes from his childhood. He heard many stories from the time he lived there. Before leaving, he asked to see the room where he had studied as a child. Mrs. Magdalena told him he could enter Licentiate Altamirano's study, which was upstairs. It was where he had studied with the tutor as a boy.

Inside the study, Martín had a fleeting memory of himself studying at the round table, which had seemed so large to him as a child. On Juan Altamirano's elegant desk rested the iron seal next to the inkwell and quill. He dipped the seal in ink and pressed its mark onto a piece of paper.

The rest was simple. He had a seal made with the same mark and used it to seal the letter he sent to his sister Catalina at the convent in Sanlúcar de Barrameda. He doubted she would be allowed to send any reply, so he sent his best words of encouragement and love, along with a brief summary of his life over the past years. In his closing lines, he promised to visit her

when he returned to Spain and, if she wished, to take her out of
the convent.

New Life. February 1564.

Bernardina's reluctance to move to Mexico was eased by the warmth and friendship she received from her sister-in-law, María Jaramillo. The two women became close allies, though their happiness and friendship were short-lived. In the autumn of 1563, María Jaramillo passed away in her home, leaving her grief-stricken husband Luis and their two children.

On the last day of 1563, Martín the Mestizo was summoned before Viceroy Luis de Velasco and the royal auditor, Licentiate Jerónimo de Valderrama. Martín Cortés dressed in his finest clothes, which always bore the embroidered cross of the Order of Santiago. He had heard rumors that it was something important, so he was accompanied by his wife Bernardina and his brother-in-law Luis de Quesada.

He was received in the main hall of the palace, where the Audiencia and the viceroy met. Martín Cortés presented himself before Don Luis de Velasco and the auditors. A scribe who had been sitting in a corner of the president's table stood up and read a document aloud:

"I, Licentiate Jerónimo Valderrama of His Majesty's Council and his inspector here in New Spain, and since His Majesty has commanded me to take residence for the justice and councilmen and other officials of this city of Mexico, and during the time of said residence the wardens and bailiffs must not continue hold office and other persons must be appointed to hold said offices; trusting you, Don Martín Cortés, that you will perform the duties of chief bailiff as befits the service of God our Lord and the good execution of justice, in the name of His Majesty I appoint you chief bailiff of this city so that you may carry out all duties and cases annexed and concerning said office, as Juan de Sámano, the current chief bailiff, whose residence is under review, and other bailiffs have done... Done on the last day of December 1563."

Martín was pleased with his appointment as chief bailiff. He knew that Licentiate Valderrama had arrived weeks earlier to investigate the behavior of the wardens and bailiffs of Mexico, following complaints of certain irregularities. Reviewing the residence of those implicated would take at least a year, during which time Martín would have to cease attending to Luis de Quesada's business and dedicate himself to the duties of chief bailiff of Mexico.

He was well aware of the numerous reports about the extravagant parties and lavish galas held in honor of his brother, the marquis. Drunkenness was common at these celebrations, where Spanish wine and mezcal, the Mexican spirit made from the agave plant, flowed freely. It did not escape his notice that the marquis received great favors and exaggerated reverence. He even heard of many nobles and prominent men who mortgaged their estates to cover the expenses, as the parties were held in many houses and palaces by those who wanted to maintain good relations with his brother. Some of those who mortgaged their estates to host banquets, celebrations, and tributes failed to meet the deadlines and lost them, which were seized by creditors.

But what truly worried the Mestizo was the growing rumors that during those festivities and galas for his brother, meetings were held where there was talk of an uprising against King Felipe II, with the proposal to name Martín Cortés Zúñiga as king of New Spain. The Mestizo tried to ignore these comments, but he knew his brother's character well and knew that if there was any truth to these rumors, his brother would not hesitate to accept the title of sovereign of New Spain. The marquis and his wife's arrogance, pride, and vanity grew month by month. He hoped that his brother would have the sense to not be swayed by such ambitions of greatness.

196

As if it were not enough to hear rumors about his brother's involvement in a revolt against the king of Spain, there were also spreading rumors of an affair between the marquis and Marina Vázquez de Coronado. This Marina was the daughter of Francisco Vázquez de Coronado, the conqueror of New Mexico, and a married woman. The rumor spread so widely that one day, as Martín and Bernardina were leaving his brother's palace, where they lived, they found a graffiti was written with charcoal on the facade, making it clear that the marquis had a married woman as his lover:

"For Marina, I am a witness

that a good man won this land

And for a woman of the same name,

I swear it will be lost."

This message made it clear that his brother's lover was named Marina, just like Martín the Mestizo's mother. In the case of his mother, she was praised for having helped in the conquest of Mexico. Regarding his brother's lover, the warning was that through her imprudence, he could lose the throne of New Spain.

On July 31, 1564, Viceroy Don Luis de Velasco y Ruiz de Alarcón died in Mexico. More than a hundred thousand people attended his funeral, as he had gained a reputation in life as a just and fair viceroy. It bothered some attendees that Martín Cortés, the marquis, was accompanied by pages carrying spears with tips covered by sheaths adorned with silk tassels. The three auditors of the Royal Audiencia—Ceynos, Villalobos, and Orozco—constantly commented among themselves on the monarch-like gestures the marquis liked to display, and the entourage of nobles and principal men that always accompanied him.

The Conspiracy. July 1566.

Due to the recent birth of the marquise's twins, a masquerade was organized to celebrate their arrival. A corridor was constructed from the marquis's quarters to the main church, adorned with arches of flowers. In the plaza, a faux forest was set up with trees and shrubs, as well as birds, deer, hares, and other game animals.

Some guests dressed as Spanish conquistadors, with weapons and armor. Others played the role of Aztec warriors, waiting in the artificial forest set up in the plaza, as if preparing for an ambush. The pretend conquistadors carried the twins to the main church along the constructed corridor. Upon reaching the plaza, the faux Aztec warriors acted out an attempt to steal the twins. The performance concluded with the conquistadors triumphing over the Aztecs. The marquis and marquise, on the victorious side, proceeded to the church for the baptism of their twins.

Martín watched the florid battle between fake Aztec and conquistadors and felt ashamed. He could not stop thinking that his brother might be getting himself into trouble by being involved in the rumors of an uprising, especially now, with the suggestion that his brother's children could be the princes of New Spain. But Martín the Mestizo was not the only one offended by the spectacle. Luis de Velasco, son of the late viceroy, along with auditors Orozco and Villalobos, also observed the treatment given to the marquis and his wife. They left the plaza after the spectacle, avoiding the church and walking together to the viceroyal palace.

During the banquet later at the marquis's residence, Martín the Mestizo noticed Alonso de Ávila, son of the famous captain, placing crowns on his brother and his wife's heads. His brother's crown bore a prominent letter "R" in the center of his forehead.

"That 'R' on your brother's and his wife's crowns could be interpreted as 'king' and 'queen'," Bernardina whispered to Martín as the banquet began.

"He's a fool. His vanity, pride, and arrogance will cause him problems if he continues to indulge in this absurd game where he ends up as king of New Spain," replied the Mestizo, trying to contain his anger. "I just hope we don't get involved in whatever he's planning."

"Do you think we should leave?"

"Yes, Bernardina. It's better not to get caught up in this brewing trouble," replied Martín, rising from his seat, and helping his wife to do the same.

It wasn't long before a complaint reached the Royal Audiencia. Baltasar de Aguilar, a wealthy man in New Spain who had never approved of the treatment given to Martín Cortés, the marquis, brought the complaint. Baltasar de Aguilar appeared before the king's auditors and claimed to know of the uprising being plotted against King Felipe II, intending to crown Martín Cortés de Zúñiga, the Marquis of the Valley of Oaxaca, as king of New Spain.

To support his accusation, Baltasar de Aguilar was accompanied to the Royal Audiencia by Alonso de Villanueva and his brother Agustín, as well as Don Luis de Velasco, the viceroy's son.

"We have learned of the uprising being planned right under our noses," Luis de Velasco said before the auditors. "They intend to enter this palace on a Friday yet to be determined, taking advantage of the government agreement meeting. The insurgents will murder the members of this Audiencia, including your worships."

"And then?" asked Auditor Villalobos.

"With the members of the Audiencia dead, along with those opposed to the uprising, some of the insurgents will march to

200

Veracruz to prevent the news of the rebellion from leaving New Spain. The rest will take control of the main settlements,".

"And is the Marquis of the Valley involved in this uprising? Are you sure of the accusation you are making?"

"The marquis is the key figure. Once the insurgents take control, they will proclaim Martín Cortés Zúñiga, the Marquis of the Valley of Oaxaca, as king of New Spain. As king, he will appoint new nobles, both Creoles and some indigenous leaders, with whom he will distribute the lands."

With this information, the auditors had enough to take the complaint seriously and begin interrogating and gathering testimonies. The Royal Audiencia ordered investigations into the brewing rebellion. A few days later, Licentiate Espinosa and the brothers Pedro and Baltasar de Quesada increased the number of accusers against the Marquis of the Valley and the conspiracy to rebel against King Felipe II.

With the accusing testimonies, the Royal Audiencia acted. They were aware that the marquis was a beloved figure among many citizens of Mexico, and they did not want his arrest to cause alarm among the population. They took advantage of the fact that the last ship had arrived in Veracruz two weeks earlier to set a trap.

The marquis presented himself at the viceroyal palace on his black stallion. His presence had been requested before the Audiencia because a dispatch from His Majesty had been received, and as a leading figure in Mexico, he was often required to witness the reading of royal provisions.

He entered the audience chamber with his usual vanity. He was not surprised to find Juan de Sámano, reinstated as chief bailiff after his residency review, stood with several wardens.

"What good news has been received from His Majesty?" the marquis said as soon as he entered, addressing the table where the auditors sat.

Juan de Sámano, the chief bailiff, intercepted him halfway.

"Your Grace, give me that sword," he said, pointing to the Toledo sword the marquis wore at his belt.

The marquis was not surprised by the request, as it was customary to prohibit armed individuals from entering royal premises, although he did not recall it happening to him before. He unbuckled the sheath from his belt and handed the sword, in its scabbard, to the bailiff, who then gave it to a warden.

"You are under arrest by order of this Audiencia and His Majesty," the chief bailiff declared.

"For what reason?" the marquis asked, frightened.

"You will be informed in due time," Juan de Sámano replied, grabbing his arm and leading him out of the room, while the king's auditors watched the arrest from behind the table.

Once the marquis was locked in a room with a guard posted outside, the chief bailiff and his wardens continued the work entrusted to them by the Royal Audiencia.

"Martín, the chief bailiff Sámano is looking for you," said Bernardina.

"Please tell him to come up," replied Martín, who was reading in a room.

Juan de Sámano entered the stay. Martín did not know that the rest of the wardens were waiting downstairs in the house of his brother, the marquis, where the Mestizo and his family lived in one of its sections. The chief bailiff greeted Martín with seriousness.

"The king's auditors summon you," Juan de Sámano announced, surprising Martín with his formal tone.

"Of course, Juan, just let me put on a cloak," he replied, heading to his bedroom.

Martín put on his cloak and fastened his sword to his belt before leaving.

"You cannot take that," Sámano said, pointing to the sword, "because you are under arrest."

"I don't understand, Juan. What is the reason or accusation?"

"I do not know, sir. I was only ordered to arrest you and take you to the royal palace," Sámano responded, somewhat embarrassed.

"I was the chief bailiff when you were under review, Juan. It is mandatory that the bailiffs know the content of the complaints..."

"I can't tell you anything more," Juan de Sámano interrupted him. "Please, come with me," he said, motioning for Martín to leave the room.

Outside the palace, the Mestizo was surprised to find the marquis's horse prepared for him. He asked about his brother, but no one responded. He mounted the stallion and saw a warden take the reins and lead the horse, walking in front of it. On either side of the animal, beside the stirrups, were two other wardens, and behind the marquis's horse followed Juan de Sámano on another mount.

A large crowd had already gathered at the entrance of the viceroyal palace, guarded by riders and Audiencia servants. Upon seeing Martín the Mestizo enter, the people outside were astonished to see him being brought in as a prisoner. Word had spread that the Marquis of the Valley had been arrested earlier, though the Mestizo still did not know his brother's whereabouts.

Unlike the marquis, who was held in one of the rooms of the viceroyal palace, Martín the Mestizo was taken to the cells in the basement, without any notification or knowledge of the reason for his arrest. He was locked in a cell, and later that day, through the barred doors, he saw other men being brought into the dungeons. Among them was his brother Luis Cortés, as well as Alonso de Ávila and Gil González, the latter still in his field clothes, arrested just after returning from his estate. He saw Mayor Manuel de Villegas and Dean Alonso Chico de Molina on their way to their cells. Over the course of the day and into the next morning, eighteen more men were imprisoned. Martín did not know the content of the complaint or accusation, but he was smart enough to deduce, seeing who the other prisoners were, that it had to do with the much-rumored uprising.

The detainees were brought before the auditors one by one the next day. The first to be interrogated was Dean Alonso Chico de Molina. When he returned from questioning, Martín spoke with him through the bars. The dean confirmed that the accusation was related to the conspiracy of rebellion and the planned appointment of his brother, the marquis, as king of New Spain.

"They accuse me of participating in the rebellion and of presenting Martín Cortés's appointment as king to the pope," the dean said from his cell.

Martín did not ask about the truth or falsity of the accusation. The less he knew, the better. He knew that the dean had been inseparable from the marquis since his arrival in Mexico, participating in all the events and galas organized for him.

A scribe approached Martín's cell and asked him to accompany him before the royal auditors.

"You have been summoned before us due to accusations from several citizens that you participated in the conspiracy against His Majesty, King Felipe II. Do you swear to tell the truth before this Royal Audiencia?" asked Auditor Orozco.

"I swear to tell the whole truth before this Audiencia," Martín responded, placing his right hand over his heart, feeling the case with his mother's handkerchief under the fabric.

"What is your name?" asked the scribe.

"Martín Cortés Malintzin."

"How old are you?"

"Forty-four years old."

"Who are your parents?"

204

"I am the son of Don Hernán Cortés and Doña Marina, known as La Malinche. I am Hernán Cortés's firstborn son," Martín clarified for the scribe.

"How do you know Luis Cortés and Alonso de Ávila?" asked Auditor Villalobos, beginning the interrogation.

"Don Luis Cortés is my half-brother, and I have known him since his birth. I met Señor Alonso de Ávila upon my arrival in New Spain three years ago. I know he is one of the sons of Captain Alonso de Ávila, who served under my father during the conquest of Mexico," Martín replied, looking at the three auditors.

"What do you know about the rebellion that was being plotted, as well as the uprising and the plans to kill the members of this royal council?" Villalobos continued.

"I have not heard anything about it, but I am not oblivious to certain rumors and phrases overheard from various people at meetings. Snippets of conversations. It seemed frivolous to me, and I did not consider it to be true."

"Why had you accumulated weapons in recent days, and for what purpose?" Orozco asked.

"I have not gathered weapons, only some harnesses for a tournament in which I was to participate. I was going to share them with Don Alonso de Estrada and Don Luis de Ortega, among others. They requested arquebuses for a display, which only arrived yesterday."

"Had your brother, the marquis, suggested killing the members of the Audiencia and starting the uprising?"

"No, sir. My brother has never suggested such a thing to me. If anyone had, I would have reported it myself to your worships," Martín replied, offended.

"Have you ever seen people speaking secretly with your brother, the marquis?" Villalobos resumed the interrogation.

"I have never seen him speaking secretly with anyone, either by night or by day. Though, like anyone, he might have private conversations with a guest from time to time."

"Have you ever heard your brother talk about the matters we have mentioned?"

"I have never heard the marquis speak about it. I am sure my brother would have thought those rumors and gossip were nonsense, and if he thought they might escalate, he would certainly have avoided participating in such conversations. He knows King Felipe II well, having been close to him from a young age as a member of the prince's household. I am sure he would have thought the king would address any event that might arise."

The auditors concluded the interrogation and returned Martín to his cell. After him, the rest of the prisoners were called one by one to be questioned by the Audiencia.

Three days later, and having received no formal notification from the Audiencia, Martín requested paper and quill from the scribe and drafted a petition to the auditors.

"Powerful lords, I, Don Martín Cortés Malintzin, firstborn son of Hernán Cortés and a prisoner by your worships' order, having been held for three days without being informed of the reason, humbly beg your lordships to release me from this confinement."

Days passed without any response from the Audiencia. Six days later, he wrote again, pleading for his release, still uninformed of the charges against him. On July 30, fifteen days after his imprisonment, the scribe presented himself at his cell. Before Martín, in the prison hallway, the scribe read the document aloud.

"To Don Martín Cortés Malintzin, firstborn son of Hernán Cortés. This notice formally informs you that you have been accused of being aware for the past ten months of the uprising that Martín Cortés Zúñiga, along with Luis Cortés, was plotting in connivance with Alonso de Ávila and many others against His Majesty."

"I have been notified," the Mestizo responded tersely from behind the bars.

Martín realized that the accusation the scribe had read to him was severe. If found guilty, the punishment would be exemplary, possibly even leading to the death penalty.

At midnight, the auditors, along with the scribe and a priest, presented themselves before the dungeon occupied by the Ávila brothers. From his cell across the hallway, Martín could observe and listen to the proceedings. The scribe unrolled a sheet of paper and read the document in front of Alonso de Ávila and Gil González.

"This Royal Audiencia has rendered judgment regarding the accusation against Alonso de Ávila and his brother, Gil González. Having heard the testimonies of the accused, as well as examined the presented evidence and various testimonies of accusation, you have been found guilty. The sentence for this crime is death by beheading."

Silence filled the prison hallway. A faint groan escaped from Alonso de Ávila's lips.

"Following the execution, the heads of the condemned will be placed on pikes. Their residences will be demolished, salt will be scattered over their land, and a proclamation will be posted announcing the justice imparted by His Majesty's Audiencia against those who intended to rebel against the Crown." The scribe finished reading and withdrew behind the three auditors.

"Is this truly possible?" Alonso de Ávila asked, his voice trembling.

"Yes, sir," replied the priest who remained beside the cell. "What is advisable for your lordships at this moment is to reconcile with God and beg forgiveness for your sins."

"Is there no other remedy?" Alonso asked, gripping the cell bars, perhaps to avoid fainting.

"There is none, sir."

Alonso de Ávila began to cry silently. His brother, Gil González, remained seated with his back against the wall and his face buried in his knees. Both were young, around twenty years old. They were wealthy and handsome, owning estates, encomiendas, and vassals. Alonso had two daughters and lived in a large residence near where they were now imprisoned, and near where they would die.

"My dear wife! My children!" Alonso cried. Tears streamed down his face as he looked at the priest. "Is it possible that this could happen to someone who thought to give them rest and honor? Fortune has turned so that you will see my head on a pike, my children, exposed to the rain, as if I were the worst of criminals. I wish you were the children of a lowborn father who had never known honor."

"Sir, this is not the time for that. Look to your soul and beg God for forgiveness for your sins."

Martín watched from his cot as the events unfolded in front of his cell. He was deeply affected by the way the two brothers confirmed to the priest that the accusations against them were true. They admitted to plotting the uprising with the intention of making Martín Cortés Zúñiga the king of New Spain. From his cell, Martín heard their confession that his brother, the marquis, and Luis Cortés were aware of everything.

The indignation over what he heard and the sorrow of knowing the Ávila brothers would be executed the next day kept Martín from sleeping. They were the first to die for this cause, but Martín was certain they would not be the last. From his cot, he heard the curses that his brother Luis, imprisoned in the same jail, hurled at the Ávila brothers for accusing him of a crime that could cost him his life.

At midday, the scribe ordered the wardens to open the Ávila brothers' cell and escort them to the main square outside the palace. The brothers were still wearing the same clothes they had on when they were arrested. From his cell, Martín could hear the murmurs of the crowd that had gathered in the Zócalo to witness the execution of two distinguished citizens against whom there had been no previous reproach. Within hours, a wooden scaffold had been erected, with a large block on top, which would be used by the executioner to behead the brothers that very day.

Under the portico of the palace, the condemned were mounted on two donkeys, a final humiliation dictated by the auditors for the brothers who had never ridden such humble animals. The plaza was packed with tens of thousands of people. The bailiffs had to clear a path using their horses. Several of them guarded the condemned with weapons ready, fearing an uprising from the crowd attempting to free them.

They reached the scaffold, and Dominican friars who accompanied them helped the brothers down from the donkeys, as both had their hands shackled. They climbed the steps to the gallows, standing before the multitude that filled the entire main square, known as the Zócalo. The Ávila brothers looked at each other and embraced.

Gil González de Ávila was the first to approach the block. Standing before it, he made a final confession to a friar who came near. Due to the murmurs in the plaza, he had to raise his voice to confess, which allowed those nearby to hear his confirmation of participation in the conspiracy.

He knelt and placed his neck on the wood stump. The executioner raised the axe and brought it down, failing to sever the head with the first blow. Quickly, the executioner lifted the axe again, and with the second blow, he succeeded in decapitating Gil González. From the crowd, several voices protested the executioner's inability to prevent Gil González's suffering.

Alonso de Ávila instinctively turned and almost fainted upon seeing his brother's head rolling on the ground. Some attendants removed Gil González's body and placed his head in a basket. Alonso approached the block where his brother had just died and knelt.

"*Miserere mei, Deus, secundum magnam misericordiam tuam, et secundum multitudinem miserationum tuarum, dele iniquitatem meam,*" Alonso de Ávila prayed. "*Miserere mei, Deus, amplius lava me ab iniquitate mea et a peccato meo munda me...*"[18]

When he finished his prayer, he glanced toward where his house was, visible from a nearby street.

"My children. My beloved wife. To think that I will leave you in this manner..." he said, overwhelmed with tears.

"This is not the time to lament for them, your grace," said Friar Domingo de Salazar. "Look to your soul. Soon you will join Our Lord. I promise to say a mass for you tomorrow."

As his brother had done, Alonso requested the presence of the friar to confess. Like Gil González, Alonso reaffirmed his guilt, clarifying that no one else had supported the uprising. Friar Domingo de Salazar stood at the edge of the scaffold and addressed the crowd, raising his voice.

"Ladies and gentlemen, commend to Our Lord the souls of these two knights. According to their confessions, they die justly," and turning to Alonso, who remained kneeling, he asked, "Do you confirm this, your grace?"

"I confirm it," replied Alonso de Ávila, bowing his head, and resting his neck on the stump, in his brother's now-cold blood.

---

[18] The Miserere: O God, have mercy on me, according to your great mercy and according to your inexhaustible compassion, erase my iniquity. O God, have mercy on me! Wash me completely from my iniquity and cleanse me from my sin...

This time, the executioner did not need two strikes to sever the neck. It took three blows of the axe to separate the head from the torso, causing more protests and cries from the attendees due to the inhumane treatment.

On the rooftop of the viceroyal palace, the heads of the executed were displayed on pikes. They were impaled on a nail from the base of the severed neck, with the iron tips protruding through the crown of their heads.

Days later, the Ávila house was demolished, and after scattering salt over the land, a proclamation was posted on a pole:

"This is the justice ordered by His Majesty and the Royal Audiencia of Mexico, in his name, against these men for being traitors to the Royal Crown..."

Martín learned about everything that had happened to the Ávila brothers from the friar who came to give them daily confession. Alonso and Gil had not accused him at any point in their confessions before their execution. According to those testimonies, his brothers Luis and the marquis, Martín Cortés Zúñiga, were the main accused.

However, it seemed that the auditors were not satisfied with the confessions made by the Ávila brothers before their deaths, considered the most truthful from any man. They continued interrogating those imprisoned in the palace jail.

The first to resume questioning was Martín Cortés Zúñiga, the Marquis of the Valley.

"Did your grace return to New Spain to start a revolt against the Crown?" Villalobos began the interrogation.

"That is not true. I came to New Spain to manage the businesses my father bequeathed to me in his will. I brought my brothers to help me with this large task," replied Martín the marquis.

"Are you colluding with France and the Vatican? The dean has confessed that he would be responsible for communicating your appointment as king to His Holiness," Villalobos continued.

"I do not know what you are talking about."

"Why did you have a page carrying a banner in front of your grace?" Orozco added to the interrogation.

"I do not consider it inappropriate. I am the Marquis of the Valley of Oaxaca, the most important noble title in New Spain," the marquis responded proudly and arrogantly.

"What was your brother Luis Cortés's role in the attempted rebellion?"

"Nothing, I do not believe he is involved in any rebellion."

"And your brother Martín Cortés?"

"The Mestizo was just helping me prepare a tournament. I do not spend much time with him, even though he lives in my house."

"You were going to use that tournament to cover the uprising," Orozco accused the marquis.

"That is not true, your grace. I was not involved in it. If the Mestizo had planned it, I did not know. I thought he was doing it to celebrate my son's birth," the marquis replied, casting doubt on his older brother.

Luis de Quesada, brother-in-law of Martín the Mestizo, presented a declaration from twenty witnesses to the Royal Audiencia about Martín's always respectful conduct toward the Crown. He testified before the auditors that the accused had been a page knight in the House of Empress Isabel and later in the House of the Prince. He reminded them that Martín was a knight of the Order of Santiago and had participated alongside King Carlos in the Algiers expedition, the war in Piedmont, and the Battle of Mühlberg, where he had been personally rewarded by the monarch. He emphasized that Martín was a devout Christian and had never been accused by any of the detainees.

"On the contrary, the accusers of Martín Cortés Malintzin are known to have lived lives full of sins, vices, and accusations,"

Luis de Quesada declared in defense of his brother-in-law Martín.

The Audiencia had received the testimonies of the witnesses and heard the defense, but made no immediate decision regarding Martín the Mestizo.

A few days later, at midnight, the auditors arrived at the jail accompanied by a priest and the scribe. Everyone knew this had happened when they communicated the sentence to the Ávila brothers, so they understood what was likely to happen. As they walked past the Mestizo's cell, he noticed them glancing sideways at him. Though he could not see from his cell, he knew they had reached his brother's.

He could not hear the scribe's voice, but from Luis's shout and the curses he hurled, Martín knew they had informed his brother of his death sentence.

By divine providence, the next morning a message arrived from Veracruz, informing the auditors that the new viceroy of New Spain had arrived. It was the Marquis of Falces, Gastón de Peralta, whom Martín had met during the time he accompanied his father in Valladolid, where the Marquis of Falces had visited Hernán Cortés several times.

When the viceroy arrived in Veracruz and learned what was happening in Mexico City, he sent a message ahead, instructing the auditors of the Royal Audiencia to halt the process against Martín Cortés Zúñiga, the Marquis of the Valley, until he reached the capital of New Spain.

He was received with great celebrations and expressions of joy upon his entry into the city. Many of those who celebrated were friends and relatives of the many prisoners taken by the auditors during the investigations into the attempted uprising. They hoped the new viceroy would soon release them.

The same day he settled in the viceroyal palace, he summoned Martín the marquis, who had been occupying one of the chambers since his arrest. The two dined and spent several hours together. The next day, Viceroy Gastón de Peralta ordered his release and prevented the confiscation of the marquis's property.

"Your graces have too many ties with the accusers of the marquis and his associates," viceroy Peralta accused the auditors one day.

"They are enemies of Spain and a real danger to the Crown," Auditor Orozco defended.

"The only danger in this land has been caused by your graces by ordering the execution of Alonso de Ávila and his brother Gil González," the viceroy responded angrily.

The auditors felt slighted and humiliated by the viceroy's decision to release the marquis and annul some sentences. They drafted a letter to His Majesty, King Felipe II, expressing their anger over what they saw as collusion between the viceroy and the Marquis of the Valley, who allegedly sought to make himself king of New Spain through the uprising they had uncovered in their investigations.

Viceroy Gastón de Peralta reviewed the process and found many errors in the accusations. He summoned Baltasar de Aguilar, who had been the first to denounce Martín Cortés Zúñiga for attempting to establish himself as king of New Spain through an uprising. Baltasar de Aguilar recanted his confession, claiming unknown people had bribed him.

The death sentence for Luis Cortés was commuted by the viceroy to ten years of galley service in Oran. Others, including the son of Captain Andrés de Tapia, Pedro González and Oñate, were also sent to the galleys. As for Martín Cortés, the marquis, the viceroy ordered that he be sent to Spain to present his case before King Felipe II.

214

Martín the Mestizo was released, and weeks later, he was appointed governor of the province. His brother, the marquis, would be taken to Spain to face charges of attempted uprising and defend himself before His Majesty. The Mestizo did not wish to continue living in his brother's house. Luis de Quesada offered Martín and Bernardina to stay in his house while they prepared for their return to Spain, a decision they had already made.

It was a brief period of peace for the Mestizo's family. He had been exonerated by all the accused, and there was no testimony implicating him in the attempted rebellion against King Felipe II. His son Fernando was nineteen and a fine young man, so his wife Bernardina tried to arrange his marriage to the widow of Pedro de Paz, a cousin of Hernán Cortés, before they left for Spain.

"Martín, I have been informed that your brother, the marquis, sold the house your father built on the former palace of Moctezuma before departing for Spain," said his brother-in-law, Luis de Quesada.

"Why would he do that?" Martín asked, puzzled.

"It seems he sold it to pay for his sister's dowry."

"Wouldn't that violate my father's will?"

"That's correct," Luis said, pulling some pages from a folder. 'Here, I have a copy of the will. "I read: 'I want and command that said properties or any part of them cannot be alienated for any reason, not even for a dowry. Should this be violated, the offender shall be deprived of the entail for being unworthy.'"

"That's what I remembered," Martín commented.

"We could file a lawsuit. Perhaps the marquisate could pass to you," his brother-in-law suggested.

"I want no relation with him, Luis. It is best to put distance between us. The little marquis has caused me many problems, but now it's all over. In Spain, King Felipe II will administer justice," replied Martín the Mestizo.

The Torture. October 1567.

In Spain, the letter sent by the judges to Felipe II had been received, accusing Viceroy Gastón de Peralta of collusion with the Marquis of the Valley. The monarch dispatched new judges to investigate what was happening in New Spain. These new judges carried orders for the viceroy and the previous judges to return to Spain and present themselves at the Court. Investigations would be carried out into their conduct in New Spain.

The new royal judges arrived in Mexico. They were Doctor Luis Carrillo and Licentiate Alonso Muñoz. The third judge appointed by the king, named Jaraba, was supposed to arrive with them but had died during the voyage to New Spain.

Upon their arrival in Mexico City, and settled in the palace, they ordered the construction of a new prison, modeled after those used by the Holy Inquisition. It would have small, dark cells, each accommodating one or two men only. They also ordered the construction of a torture chamber. Nearly a thousand workers participated in the construction of the prison, completing it within two weeks.

The first prisoner locked in the new and grim dungeons was the man who had testified about the conspiracy: Baltasar de Aguilar. The judges accused him of giving two contradictory statements.

During the first week, prisoners who had been released by Viceroy Peralta and were still in New Spain were re-arrested and jailed. Among them was the Mestizo.

The new cells had solid doors, without bars, only a small peephole through which food and drink could be passed. The stone walls seeped water from the old lake of Texcoco, making the cell always damp and cold. A small oil lamp illuminated the confined space each prisoner occupied.

The Mestizo could not hear the voices of the interrogations, as they were muffled by the thick walls, but he could hear the screams and howls during torture. The newly arrived judges believed that torture would elicit better testimonies from the accused, which would serve to prosecute new individuals implicated in the uprising.

Baltasar de Aguilar could not endure the first interrogation. He confessed that the first of the two testimonies he had given was the true one, in which he claimed that the marquis was aware of the uprising and had participated in its planning.

Day and night, the Mestizo saw the accused being led past the peephole in his door for interrogations. He soon heard their screams, wails, and moans. After about an hour, they were returned to their cells, most often dragged by the jailers, as they could not stand after the interrogation and torment they had endured. On two occasions, the accused did not return to their cells. He learned from the notary Zavaleta, who was responsible for notifying the prisoners, that on both occasions, the men had died during the tortures.

The new judges, Carrillo and Muñoz, enjoyed announcing death sentences after midnight, perhaps to ensure the condemned suffered more by keeping them awake during their last hours of life. The next day, without delay, they were taken to the gallows in the plaza, which was no longer dismantled after executions, to keep it always ready.

November 15, the Mestizo was called for interrogation. Notary Zavaleta accompanied him to the torture chamber. Upon entering, Martín saw two men next to a wooden rack, beside which was a barrel of water and several piled ropes. Awls, braces, pincers, and bloodied knives rested on a small table next to the rack.

218

Judges Muñoz and Carrillo were seated behind a table. Notary Zavaleta sat at one end and prepared the papers, inkwell, and quill. He signaled the Mestizo to approach and sit in the chair at the table, facing the king's judges.

Alonso Muñoz, without uttering a word, handed Martín a sheet with a written declaration, with his name at the bottom, awaiting his signature. The Mestizo read it carefully. It was a confession drafted by the judges. In it, Martín admitted his participation in the uprising against His Majesty and acknowledged the intention to name his brother, the marquis, king of New Spain.

"Your graces, I cannot sign this declaration because it is not true," he calmly told the judges, handing back the confession.

Zavaleta took the testimony and escorted Martín back to his cell, without the judges having spoken a word to him. During his confinement, he could hear the laments in the adjoining cells of those who had already been tortured. Baltasar de Aguilar still could not get up from his bed due to the damage inflicted on him.

"I thought I would die from the pain," he repeated like a litany, "I thought I would die from the pain..."

Martín was unaware of the work his brother-in-law, Luis de Quesada, and lawyer Álvaro Ruiz were doing before the judges. They had repeatedly appealed the order for Martín Cortés to be tortured, succeeding only in postponing it to new dates without canceling it. They presented new witnesses, who testified under oath to Martín's innocence. They insisted again that he was a good Christian, loyal to the Crown, and a knight of the Order of Santiago, a person far removed from conspiracies and even from the celebrations and galas held for his brother, the marquis. But the appeals only served to give Martín a few weeks of respite.

On January 1, 1568, notary Zavaleta was sent to inform Martín Cortés that that night he would be taken for interrogation under the torment of water and ropes.

"I have heard. Let their will be done," Martín responded.

When he entered the torture chamber, everything was as it had been the previous time he visited it just over a month ago. There remained the wooden rack, the piles of ropes, and the barrel of water, as well as the torture instruments on a small table. Two executioners with uncovered faces awaited the judges' instructions from behind the long table. This time, they were accompanied by two witnesses, the Bishop of Puebla, Don Antonio Morales, and Don Luis de Velasco, son of the deceased viceroy.

Notary Zavaleta sat at the end of the table and again gestured for Martín to sit in front of the judges.

"We ask your grace to inform us of the names of the people involved in the uprising against His Majesty," said Doctor Carrillo.

"I do not know anyone involved in it, nor any conspiracy against the king," Martín replied firmly.

"We must inform the accused that, should he refuse to confess voluntarily, we will proceed with the interrogation under torture. We urge you to cooperate with this Court," Licentiate Muñoz remarked.

"I have already answered the question your graces asked me."

"If the accused dies or is gravely injured during the torment, it will be the responsibility of the accused, not ours," Doctor Carrillo informed him.

"I have told you the whole truth, your graces. I have nothing more to add."

They ordered him to undress. Martín stood up and stripped down to his undergarments. He felt the cold and dampness of the torture chamber, causing him to shiver. Executioners and judges observed the numerous marks and scars adorning the olive-toned body of the Mestizo, from neck to feet; signs of the many wars and battles in which he had fought, always in the name of the King of Spain.

The executioners approached Martín and motioned for him to go to the rack and lie down. Martín saw that a bull's horn, used as a funnel, rested on the water barrel. The ropes, two fingers thick, were piled under the table where he would soon be tortured. He felt the familiar twist in his stomach that always preceded entering battle, but this time, he had no weapon to defend himself, only the resilience of his own body and mind.

He lay on his back on the freezing rack. The executioners tied his ankles and wrists with the ropes, tightening them with a winch. He felt his arms stretch above his head and his legs in the opposite direction. The executioners nodded to the judges, indicating that the accused was ready to proceed with the interrogation under torture.

"Tell us the names of the conspirators before we begin the torment," Carrillo's voice came, though Martín could not see them due to his position.

"I have told you the whole truth, your graces. I have nothing more to add," he replied, starting to take deep breaths, preparing for the pain.

The judge nodded to the executioners, and they turned the roller, tightening the ropes bound to his legs and arms. His limbs were pulled from his body, each in a different direction. Martín felt as if he were being torn apart. He felt the burn in his joints, a chill of pain coursing through his body. In his head, he heard the noise of one of his shoulders dislocating. A lash of pain shot through his brain like lightning. He managed to stifle the scream.

"Tell us the names of the conspirators," ordered Doctor Carrillo's voice.

"I have told you the whole truth. I have nothing more to add."

The judges gestured again, and the executioners twisted the roller once more, tightening the ropes and bringing the pain back to Martín. A scream emerged from the depths of his being, escaping through his mouth.

"Tell us the names of the conspirators!"

"I have told you the whole truth. I have nothing more to add."

Once again, at a gesture to the executioners, the pain returned. Martín felt his dislocated shoulder being pulled further from his body, believing it would be torn off. He felt the ropes cutting into his skin, burning as they were pulled by the winch. He heard the crunch of an ankle dislocating and began to tremble from the pain.

"Tell us the names of the conspirators."

"I have told you the whole truth, and by the most sacred name of God, have mercy on me, for I will say no more until I die," Martín stammered between shivers.

There was a moment of silence. Martín could hear the murmuring voices of the judges and witnesses, though he could not understand what they were saying.

"It seems the accused is thirsty," Licentiate Muñoz said aloud. "Give him water."

One of the executioners stood by Martín's head and pinched his nose, preventing him from breathing through it. The other dipped a jug into the barrel and filled it with water, then grabbed the bull's horn funnel. His companion pried Martín's jaw open, forcing his mouth open while the other executioner inserted the funnel. At a signal from the judge, he began pouring water from the jug into the horn.

At first, Martín tried to swallow the water entering through the horn, but he could not swallow that much, that fast. Soon he began to cough, spitting out the water he could not swallow while trying to breathe through his pinched nose, causing water to enter his lungs as he attempted to breathe through his mouth.

The executioners removed the funnel and released the pinch on his nose. Martín breathed in the cold air of the room, but while doing so, he coughed and expelled the water he had inhaled.

"Tell us the names of the conspirators."

"I have told you the whole truth. I have nothing more to add," Martín responded, coughing and vomiting.

"Give him a bit more water."

Martín tried to resist, shaking his head. He tried not to open his mouth, but a hand pressing on his dislocated shoulder made him scream, a moment the executioners took advantage of to insert the funnel again. They pinched his nose, and the executioner began to pour water through the horn once more.

He had not yet recovered from the previous time when the funnel was already back in his mouth, pouring liquid into his body. It took less time for him to feel the cough coming from his lungs. As he coughed up the water, he tried to breathe, causing the water to enter again, making him cough once more. He felt his lungs burning under his chest, as if they were filled with pins.

"Tell us the names of the conspirators!" Licentiate Muñoz shouted when the executioners paused the torture.

"I have told you the whole truth… I have nothing more to add."

"Another jug of water."

As he resisted having the funnel inserted, they knocked out two of his teeth forcing it into his mouth. The water mixed with blood and teeth in his stomach, causing a great vomit he could not expel, as they held his mouth closed with a hand while water entered through the funnel. When the executioners released him, Martín felt blood mixed with water flowing from his ears, nose, and mouth as he desperately tried to breathe. He felt the warmth of urine spreading between his legs.

"Tell us the names of the conspirators," Doctor Carrillo insisted.

"I have said," Martín replied between violent coughs, "all…
all…" he vomited, "the truth. I have nothing more to add," he
said, the last words trailing off in a whisper.

"Give him more water!" Licentiate Muñoz ordered.

"He's going to drown. Let's give him a moment to recover."

"More water, dogs!" Carrillo shouted.

They inserted the horn into Martín's mouth again. This time
he did not resist. The executioners knew he was at his limit, but
they obeyed the judges. Martín tried to swallow the water as fast
as he could, but his body had less resistance, and it only took
moments before he began coughing and desperately trying to
breathe. Water splashed out through the fingers of the torturer
holding his mouth around the funnel, while Martín tried to expel
it. It trickled out of his ears. The executioners saw the Mestizo
lose consciousness and pass out. They knew this was the best
thing that could happen to him.

"Enough!" Judge Muñoz ordered.

At three in the morning, Martín's naked, unconscious body
was dragged back to his cell and thrown, limp, onto his cot. They
threw his clothes on the damp floor, wet from the water seeping
in from the lake.

Martín awoke from his faint. He did not know how much
time had passed. He shivered uncontrollably. He felt intense pain
and heat in his dislocated shoulder and ankle. He tasted blood in
his mouth. He sat up on his cot, and as he did, he began to vomit,
expelling a large amount of liquid into the corner where his waste
bucket was. The cell was dark; the lamp was out. He felt the pile
of clothes by his feet. He tried to dress as best he could, holding
his dislocated arm to prevent the unseated bone from rubbing
against the joint. He felt the case with his mother's handkerchief
and pressed it against his chest. He fell asleep clutching it in a
closed fist.

224

The cell door opened, and Martín could see a silhouette against the light in the doorway. He was terrified to recognize one of his executioners. It was the man who had held his head and pinched his nose during the torture. He pushed the fear aside and clenched his fists and jaw. This time he would not make it easy for them.

"Calm yourself, sir. I'm not here to take you, and even if I were, you couldn't stand," said the executioner, looking at Martín. "Though your resistance and courage are commendable."

"What do you want from me, then?"

"For one hundred pesos, I can set the bone dislocated last night," the executioner proposed. "I can also bandage the ankle I twisted."

"As you know, I have no money on me."

"Don't worry. You just need to send a message that someone close to you outside can identify, so they can be sure it's from you. They'll pay me."

Martín weighed the offer. Nothing assured him they wouldn't interrogate and torture him again. Or kill him.

"It won't be one hundred pesos; I'll give you two hundred. But it won't be until I leave this prison and can give them to you in person."

The executioner understood that Martín's proposal would, in a way, make him concerned for Martín's life during his stay in the prison. Two hundred pesos was no small amount, he thought.

"Agreed," the executioner replied, walking toward Martín.

Borrego, the executioner's last name, pressed on Martín's shoulder. He felt the inflammation and heat radiating from the area. He palpated to locate the head of the bone and determine the movement needed to return it to its place.

"First, I'll pull the arm to dislodge the bone from where it is now," Borrego explained. "Then I'll try to place it back in its socket. I'll have to do this as many times as necessary. If I don't set it correctly, the bone will start to fuse improperly, and you'll lose mobility in your arm for the rest of your life."

The Mestizo nodded. Borrego grabbed the arm and, with a strong yank, dislodged the bone from where it was stuck. He twisted the arm and pressed it against the shoulder, seating it in the joint on the first attempt. Martín could not hold back the scream in his lungs as he felt the pain when his arm separated again during the maneuver and was then replaced.

"You've been lucky. I managed it on the first try, and the bone is now in its place. Don't move it much for a few days because it will hurt," Borrego said, walking toward the cell door. "Two hundred pesos, Mestizo. When you get out of here," he reminded him.

"My foot still needs attention," Martín said.

"True, I almost forgot."

Borrego took out some cloth strips from his pocket and a small bottle.

"I'll rub some alcohol on it and then bandage the ankle so it won't hurt. It's important not to walk or put weight on it for as long as possible. A bad treatment will leave you limping."

Once he finished bandaging the foot, Borrego stood up, reminding the Mestizo of the payment he owed him.

"You have my word," Martín responded.

By the end of that week, four prisoners were notified of their death sentences. The judges did not wait for dawn. That same night, Gómez de Vitoria and Cristóbal de Oñate, son of the conquistador of the same name, were executed. The next day, January 9, two of the accusers, brothers Baltasar and Pedro de Quesada, were executed. Like the others, they confessed before dying.

One afternoon, Notary Zavaleta approached Martín Cortés' cell and spoke through the peephole.

"Your Grace will come out of these investigations unscathed. None of the accused, not even those executed in their last confessions, have implicated you as part of the uprising or as having knowledge of the conspiracy."

"If they had, it would have been a false confession. At least they died with the truth on their lips," Martín replied from inside the cell.

"Today, your brother-in-law and the lawyer appeared before the judges again. They requested your release based on the confessions and statements of the accused. I trust the judges will soon issue a verdict regarding you."

"Releasing me is the only thing they can do. My innocence has been proven, even under torture. As you said, not even the condemned confessed that I was involved."

Two days later, Notary Zavaleta, accompanied by the two judges, appeared at the Mestizo's cell. They opened the door, and Martín, struggling to steady himself, stood before them. He was about to be notified of something. The pain in his foot from putting weight on it made him dizzy; he could not even touch the ground.

The notary unfurled the rolled sheet he carried and began to read it aloud.

"In the case against Don Martín Cortés Malintzin, Knight of the Order of Santiago, who has been accused and judged of participating in the plot against His Majesty, this Royal Audience, after hearing the testimonies from both accusers and accused, condemns Don Martín Cortés to perpetual exile from the Indies. For this reason, it is ordered that he depart from New Spain on the first ship, accompanied by an armed guard, whose cost he will bear. We condemn him to pay a fine of one thousand gold ducats, half of which will go to His Majesty's treasurer and the other half to cover the expenses incurred by his imprisonment," Notary Zavaleta paused and then continued reading. "If the accused fails to comply with any of these terms, he will face the death penalty."

"I have heard the verdict," was Martín's only response.

At the end of January, Martín's lawyer, Álvaro Ruiz, presented Captains Juan de Nájera and Francisco de Granada before the judges. They testified and swore to Martín Cortés's innocence, as well as attested to his good conduct and nobility. The lawyer argued that Don Martín Cortés and Bernardina de Porras lived a humble life, residing in the house of his sister and her widower, Luis de Quesada.

Days passed and Martín remained imprisoned, placing his hopes on his lawyer's appeal. Meanwhile, new individuals had been sentenced to death by hanging, among them Bernardino Maldonado, Gonzalo Núñez, and Juan Victoria.

On February 16, the judges notified through Notary Zavaleta the resolution to the petition for clemency.

"Their graces confirm the perpetual exile from the Indies for Don Martín Cortés Malintzin and prohibit him from approaching within five leagues of the Spanish Court. Regarding the fine, it is reduced to five hundred gold ducats. From today, he will remain under house arrest at the residence of María Jaramillo and Luis de Quesada, until he must depart from New Spain."

Emaciated, feverish, and lame, Martín remained confined in his brother-in-law's house. Bernardina and her children tended to him constantly, as he lacked any strength during the first days. Luis de Quesada requested a postponement for Martín's journey, citing his weakness and poor health, but the judges denied it.

In early March 1568, Martín learned he was to go to Veracruz, as a ship was set to depart for Spain in the second half of that month. During that same period, the king's new judges, Don Vasco de Puga and Licentiate Villanueva, arrived. Upon their arrival in Mexico, they presented Licentiate Luis Carrillo and Doctor Alonso Muñoz with the king's writ, ordering them to return to Spain upon notification.

The king required the judges to appear before him in person.

228

"Bernardina, I have been thinking about the future of our family," said Martín, taking his wife's hands while they sat on the bed. "When I arrive in Spain, I will put our house and estate in Berlanga in order, where you and the children will stay. I cannot go near the Court, so I will have to enlist in another battle with the king's troops, hoping to meet him. I know there are uprisings in the south of Spain with the Moors and that there have been some skirmishes in Granada."

"But what if the king does not go to war, Martín?" Bernardina asked, her voice filled with worry.

"I must try. If I can approach him due to the circumstances of the war, I will not be violating the Audience's sentence. I will try to restore our honor and obtain a royal pardon."

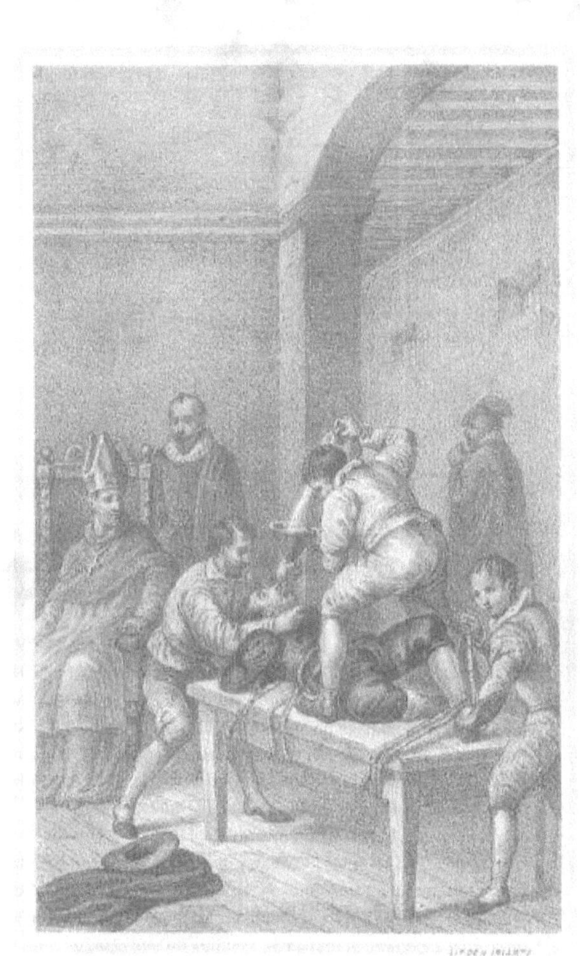

Water and Rope Torture

Rebellion of the Alpujarras. January 1569.

The journey back to Spain had been ironic, or at least it seemed so to Martín. On the same ship that took him to Seville, he had to share the voyage with Viceroy Gastón de Peralta and judges Luis Carrillo and Alonso Muñoz, the very men who had tortured and condemned him. All three had been ordered to present themselves before King Felipe II. Months later, Martín learned of their fates.

Gastón de Peralta, Marquis of Falces, and for a brief time, Viceroy of New Spain, was exonerated by King Felipe II after defending and justifying his decisions.

"Your Majesty, I did not go to New Spain to punish the sons of a man to whom the Crown owes the acquisition of such great and numerous kingdoms," the viceroy reportedly said to Felipe II.

His Majesty was less lenient with the judges, rebuking their conduct:

"I sent you to govern New Spain, not to destroy it!" Felipe II exclaimed to Carrillo and Muñoz. "You have condemned to death a great number of sons of conquistadors, nobles, and hidalgos. Your sentences caused great harm to the Crown and suffering to the citizens of New Spain."

Inexplicably, the following morning, Licentiate Alonso Muñoz was found dead in his chamber.

Martín also learned of the fate of his brother, Martín Cortés, Marquis of the Valley of Oaxaca. After his testimony was heard before His Majesty, and the accusations against him were read, King Felipe II sentenced him to permanent confinement in the castle of Torrejón de Velasco, where he was forbidden to receive any type of visit or communication from the outside.

The first thing Martín did upon arriving in Seville in July 1568 was to visit the Dominican convent of Madre de Dios in Sanlúcar de Barrameda. It had been eighteen years since his sister, Catalina Pizarro, had been forcibly confined there. Martín had managed to send her a letter using Juan Altamirano's seal four years ago, but he never received a reply. Perhaps she had already died.

He approached the grand stone entrance set in the white facade of the convent. A laywoman, who served the nuns living inside, attended to Martín. He requested to visit Catalina Pizarro, which had been his sister's name before she became a servant of God. The kind woman led him to a room with a floor of black and white tiles, like a chessboard. On one wall, above a stone bench adorned with gold and blue pieces, there was a small metal door, like a window.

"Please sit on the tile bench," the woman said. "If she is still alive or remains in the convent, you will be able to speak with her through the window."

"Can't I embrace her?" Martín asked.

"This is a cloistered convent. Fortunately for you, not many sisters here practice a vow of silence, so at least you will be able to speak with her," she said with a smile, retreating through a gated door locked with a key.

An hour later, he heard a bolt being drawn behind the small window. Martín pulled on the handle and opened the shutter. On the other side of a wooden grille, he could just make out the face of his sister Catalina. Because of her wimple, he could not see her hair, but he recognized her features. She seemed like an old woman to him.

"Is that you, Martín?" asked the woman on the other side of the grille.

"Catalina, it's me, sister, I've come to get you out of this confinement," said Martín, gripping the bars that separated them.

"Martín," said Catalina, beginning to cry silently. "I can't see you, I'm almost blind, but I recognize your voice. I know it's you, Martín, my dear brother."

Martín began to cry just like his sister. There were so many things he wanted to tell her, but at that moment no words came to his mind or lips. The siblings' hands joined between the bars that separated them.

"I received your letter a few years ago, Martín. By then, I could no longer read because my eyesight had begun to fail a long time ago. A sister from the convent has been reading your letter to me now and then. I've almost memorized it," Catalina Pizarro smiled through her tears.

The siblings spent several hours talking, separated by the bars that kept them from touching, embracing, and kissing. Martín knew when they said goodbye that it would be the last time he would see his sister. She had refused to leave the convent, despite having the opportunity to do so. In a way, Martín appreciated her decision, which would have been an obstacle to his plans.

Soon he learned about the uprising brewing in Granada. The Moors who had promised to convert to Christianity after the Reconquista by the Catholic Monarchs persisted in their customs. At the insistence of the Catholic Church, Felipe II had banned any distinctive elements of the Muslim religion, as well as their cultural markers such as language, ceremonies, baths, clothing, rituals, customs, festivities, and zambras with their dances and songs. The Moriscos[19] had tried to negotiate with the Crown's representatives several times, but they failed to overturn the ban. King Felipe II was determined to end that culture and

---

[19] Said of a person of the Muslim religion: One who converted to Christianity and remained in Spain after the Reconquista had ended.

social structure forever. If they refused to comply, war would be inevitable.

Thousands of Muslims rebelled against the ban, as the Crown had anticipated. They armed themselves and fortified their positions in the Sierra de las Alpujarras, near Granada.

Martín went to Toledo, where he joined the Royal Army as a captain, in the troops commanded by Don Juan de Austria, who would march to the Alpujarras of Granada in early 1569.

During the march to Granada, Captain Martín Cortés met Captain Gómez Suárez de Figueroa.

"I was told there was another mestizo in our army, and I didn't believe it. I came here to see if it was true," said Garcilaso de la Vega to Martín Cortés, who was warming his still-aching ankle by a fire, the cold winter causing it to hurt even more.

Martín turned to see who was speaking to him in such a manner and saw, despite the dim light of the evening, that the person addressing him was another captain who shared his skin color.

"In that case, you are looking for me," Martín Cortés responded, rising and approaching Garcilaso de la Vega, extending his hand in greeting.

The two men quickly developed a bond that went beyond the coincidence of their mixed heritage. During the breaks at the end of each day, they took the opportunity to talk with each other. Like Martín Cortés, Captain Garcilaso de la Vega was the son of a Spanish conquistador and an Indian woman from Peru. An avid literature enthusiast, Garcilaso loved discussing books of chivalry and the memoirs of great conquistadors with Martín. Garcilaso knew the story of Hernán Cortés and La Malinche and, like Martín Cortés, had read the *Conquest of Mexico* written by Friar Francisco López de Gómara before it was banned by Felipe II.

236

"Wouldn't you like to have your memoirs written down?" Garcilaso asked one night. "I think we could, together, do a work similar to what López de Gómara did in his book, speaking for hours and days with your father."

Martín liked the idea of putting his life in writing. He was realistic in thinking that he did not have many years left. He was forty-seven and had begun to feel worn out. The battles he had fought, the wounds he had received during them, and the tortures he had endured the previous year had taken a toll on his health and vitality. The limp he had since the torment in Mexico made the days on foot exhausting.

In the following days and weeks, Martín Cortés and Garcilaso de la Vega spent a few hours together after setting up the camp where the troops would rest. Martín narrated his memories to Garcilaso, who, by candlelight, wrote them down, using a large board from one of the carts to hold the paper and inkwell.

By March 1569, the troops under the command of Don Juan de Austria had reached the town of Órgiva, at the foot of the Sierra de las Alpujarras. Days before their arrival, they had encountered numerous churches and chapels looted, destroyed, and in some cases burned. Martín felt rage upon finding sacristans, friars, and priests dead, with clear signs of torture. Some had been flayed, others hanged with ropes. From some Christian villagers, they learned that the charred corpses they found were those of religious people. But what enraged Martín the most was finding the bodies of nuns who had been raped, tortured, and then murdered. He could not stop thinking about his sister Catalina, and what fate would befall her if the Moriscos succeeded in this uprising.

Since their arrival in the Alpujarras, not a day went by without encounters with the Moors, who came in two kinds: some were mere bandits seeking to harm Christians and receiving payment from the leaders of the revolt, but the most dangerous were the so-called mujahideen, infidel warriors fighting to impose their faith and establish an independent territory under Islamic rule.

Despite the daily skirmishes with those descending from the mountains and the atrocities inflicted upon Christians in the villages and against the clergy, Don Juan de Austria did not permit pillaging within his troops nor repression against the Morisco population that had not rebelled against the Crown. This fact pleased Martín Cortés. He had always respected the rules of war he had learned in the Royal Household and those of the Order of Santiago.

The marches became more arduous after leaving Órgiva due to the rugged terrain. Martín encouraged his men to climb the steep paths of the Alpujarras. They had information that the rebel Moriscos had fortified themselves in the town of Trevélez and intended to attack them.

As had always been the case when he commanded soldiers, worked with laborers in the field, or held the position of chief constable or even Governor in New Spain, the men under his command obeyed him willingly. The Mestizo was known for his firm and just character, his nobility, and his empathy when any of his men had a problem. He did not tolerate idlers or those who deceived their comrades, swindling or stealing from them. Against such men, Captain Mestizo's punishments were always severe and set an example.

They had rested in the town of Bubión, intending to continue through the mountains to reach Trevélez the next day. Bubión was a small village of whitewashed houses, so bright that the glare could be blinding when the sun shone directly on them. The village was nestled on a steep hillside, between the slopes of two mountains, forming a narrow valley.

238

"For now, Garcilaso, I have nothing more to tell you," said Martín, who had just recounted to Captain Garcilaso de la Vega his meeting with his sister in the convent of Sanlúcar de Barrameda. "I hope God grants me enough time to be able to tell you that after pacifying this Moorish revolt, I reunited with Bernardina and my children, resuming our life in Berlanga."

"Would that be a good ending, Martín?" asked Garcilaso de la Vega.

"The best, Garcilaso," he replied, smiling. "My memories and past haunt me. I look back and can say I have enjoyed and laughed, cried, and suffered. I have lived... and I have killed. I wish that the last pages of my memoirs could say that I reached old age, accompanied by my wife. That my children had good marriages and filled me with grandchildren. That would be a good ending. No more glory or wars. No more betrayals. Just peace."

They had spent many days together. Garcilaso de la Vega intended, once the Alpujarras revolt was over, to organize the memoirs Martín Cortés had narrated to him over the days. For a moment, he silently observed his companion and friend. The Mestizo was serving himself a second bowl of soup from the troop's provisions. He was not taking anyone else's share; everyone had already eaten, and the pot rested on a trivet over the embers.

Garcilaso de la Vega had never imagined that Martín Cortés would have had such an exciting life. He had not achieved the great feats of his father, Hernán Cortés, but... what other man had accomplished something similar?

In front of him, Martín Cortés drank the soup from his bowl, watching the flames of the fire. He did not need a spoon; there was little left to eat, and he could only drink the broth. This man, Garcilaso thought, was the son of Hernán Cortés and Doña

Marina, La Malinche, the Indian woman who helped that brave Spaniard conquer an empire for the king of Spain.

Garcilaso was surprised at how Martín recounted, without a hint of arrogance, that he had lived with Empress Isabel, her son King Felipe II, then a prince, and King Carlos himself. He learned from Martín's muted voice and evident shame about the failures in the Expedition of Algiers and in Piedmont. He listened in detail to Martín's successful maneuver in the Battle of Mühlberg, where he seized the pontoon, though Martín narrated it with humility, giving the glory to the men who accompanied him.

It became clear to Garcilaso de la Vega how much Martín loved his wife Bernardina, and how much he missed her and their children, Ana and Fernando. He saw Martín cry when remembering his father's death in Castilleja de la Cuesta, and become angry when recalling his brother the marquis's lack of mediation when he was involved in the uprising. He was outraged at the thought that there were people who believed the Mestizo would ever betray the king. Loyalty to both family and king were the main teachings his father had imparted.

"You'd better rest, Garcilaso," Martín said after finishing his soup. "Tomorrow will be another tough day. Some Christians living in the village have told us that the Moors plan to ambush us in the place they call Barranco Bermejo."

"Yes, we should lie down and get some sleep," Garcilaso replied, then tied the bundle of papers with a ribbon, as he had done each night for weeks.

Illustration #7

Massacre of Christians in Cádiar (Alpujarras). Engraving 1859

Inca Garcilaso de la Vega. March 1569.

My name is Gómez Suárez de Figueroa, but for some years now, I have come to be known as Inca Garcilaso de la Vega. I am a captain in the army of King Felipe II, commanded by Don Juan of Austria. Over the past few weeks, I have transcribed the words of Captain Don Martín Cortés Malintzin, firstborn son of Don Hernán Cortés and Doña Marina, La Malinche.

Yesterday, March 10, 1569, our troops ascended the Alpujarra mountains. I saw Don Martín Cortés, always at the forefront of his men, limping up the mountainside, encouraging them to fight against the Moors who awaited their arrival on that side of the mountain. His men were armed with arquebuses, lances, and swords. Don Martín never appreciated fighting with firearms, so he carried his unsheathed Toledo sword. At the Barranco Bermejo, where a stream flows through a narrow gorge, I lost sight of Don Martín and his men, as we were ambushed by another group of Moors hidden among the vegetation.

By midday, those who had attacked us had retreated, leaving the bodies of Christians and Moors on the ground, though more of the infidels lay dead. A young man accompanying Don Martín came to my men and asked for me, urgently requesting that I accompany him; they had lost Captain Mestizo. I ordered a camp to be set up at the base of the mountain, next to the stream that descended from the sierra, leaving space for Cortés's men who would join us at the end of the day.

I climbed the steep slope and reached the troops of Don Martín Cortés. His men did not know his whereabouts and feared that the Moors had taken him hostage, so I ordered a search before nightfall. I hoped to find him wounded, and God willing, not taken captive.

It was not long before I heard a call from the base of a waterfall formed by the gorge, where the stream fell through a cleft in the rocks. I ran toward the voices calling out to me, and as I approached, I came upon the body of Captain Martín Cortés lying on the ground among some rosemary bushes.

He had been shot twice in the back, where his half armor did not cover. Near him, two Moors lay dead with sword marks. Martín Cortés had killed them both with his Toledo sword, but another Moor had treacherously shot him in the back, ending his life.

The gold chain with the cross that his father had given him as a child was not around his neck. Undoubtedly, the Moor who had shot him, had stolen it after killing him. Martín had his hand clenched in a fist under his face. I knelt beside him while the men respectfully stepped back and murmured prayers. It seemed as if he had something in his closed hand. I gently lifted his arm from his body and pried open his fingers. Inside, I found a delicately embroidered cotton handkerchief. Some blood had stained one of its corners. I had no doubt that it was the handkerchief he had kept for so many years in a leather case. The same handkerchief that Doña Marina, La Malinche, had once tied around her hair or knotted across her forehead.

With his last strength, Don Martín Cortés Malintzin, the Mestizo, had managed to pull the case from inside his shirt. He had opened it and taken out his mother's handkerchief.

I ordered my men to bury Captain Martín Cortés next to a great oak tree near the pool formed by the waterfall. I brought a friar to the Tajo de Cortés, the name the men had begun to give the place. A mass was offered there for his soul, attended by all the soldiers under my command and those of Don Martín, who were truly mournful at his passing.

"Who knows?' I murmured beside my friend's body, just before they lowered him into the grave by the oak tree. 'Maybe, with your last breath, you caught the scent of avocado pit and

244

vanilla flower from her hair. The smell of milk, saltpeter, and smoke from her skin..."

Epilogue. January 2024.

When I finished reading the first draft of the story I had developed, based on the transcription of the manuscript that Inca Garcilaso de la Vega wrote from the firsthand account of Martín Cortés, I focused again on the last paragraphs.

"Could it still exist after five centuries?" I murmured, making my wife look at me as if I had lost my mind.

I opened the search engine on the computer and typed the reference mentioned by Garcilaso de la Vega After months spent confirming locations, names, and other details, this was the one I had yet to check.

The website displayed the listing for the reference I had typed. There it was: the Tajo de Cortés, in Sierra Nevada, in the Alpujarras. Nowadays, it was called Tajo Cortés, but I found no mention of the origin of its name, although I knew why. The Tajo Cortés, as seen in the images, was a beautiful waterfall of the Bermejo River, falling from about eight or ten meters high. At present, it was a popular destination for extreme sports enthusiasts. Near the waterfall, by the pool it formed, images showed a small forest, probably of pines and oaks.

No one knew that near the rocky hollow, where the waterfall broke, under the ground, rested the remains of Don Martín Cortés, the Mestizo.

"Mr. Palomares, I really liked the story about my ancestor. You treated it with respect and seriousness," Fernando Orozco said to me over the phone from Houston.

"I only added dialogues and some structure to the paragraphs. Everything else was told by your ancestor. The credit belongs to him, to Inca Garcilaso, and no one else," I replied, emotional, I admit. "I think it's time to return the manuscript to you, although…"

"What's wrong?"

"Where it belongs is in a national archive, either in Mexico, at the Chapultepec Archive, or in the Archivo General de Indias, in Seville. There it will be preserved for another five centuries, and everyone will be able to review it," I suggested.

"I've also thought about it over these months, but I will keep it with me for now. I've rented a safety deposit box at a bank here in Houston. I will store it there until I can pass it on to my children in the future, or until the executor I name in my will takes charge of those documents."

I asked my children to bring the parota wood box we had stored in the attic. The transparent sleeves with the manuscript pages were in order, and I thought it would be best to keep them as they were, without handling them again. In a few days, they would come to pick it up and send it to Fernando's home.

The children placed the box on the living room table and opened the lid. As I was about to place the pages inside, I saw that the cloth with which the bundle of papers had been tied was still at the bottom. I left the manuscript on the table and pulled out the cloth, holding it up to examine it.

I held it in my hand while I looked at it. It was a cotton handkerchief, worn by years, with a yellowish color. It had embroidered threads that had lost their original color, although the red, blue, and green tones could still be discerned.

My wife observed the cloth in my hands and looked at me, puzzled.

"Could it be?" she asked.

I spread the handkerchief, holding two of its corners, and held it up to the light, letting the sun illuminate it from the other side. In the lower corner, a dark stain appeared. Claudia approached and pointed it out.

"Martín's blood when he died?" she asked, closely examining the strange ochre-colored spot.

I folded Doña Marina's handkerchief and carefully placed it alongside her son Martín's memoirs. They had been together for five centuries, and so they should remain.

Mother and son, together at last, for eternity.

Acknowledgements.

Dear reader, this acknowledgment chapter is dedicated to you, who have made it to this part of the book.

Thank you very much for reading it!

Now, it would be perfect (taking advantage of the fact that the novel is still fresh in your memory) if you could go to the platform or online store where you purchased it and leave your opinion. This way, other people can read your comment and—if it's a good opinion—decide to buy the novel.

Manolo Palomares.
Twitter/X: @manpalomares

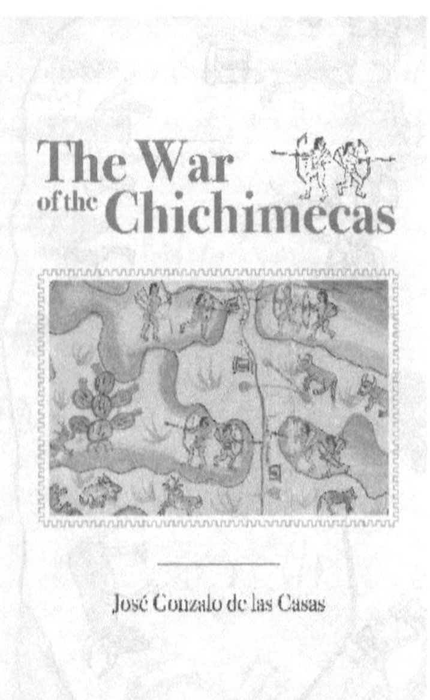

Transcription of the original 16th-century manuscript by the author, José Gonzalo de las Casas, narrating the war against the **Chichimecas** in New Spain. It describes the way of life of this **American indigenous nation**, as well as details the various tribes that composed it: **Jonaces, Pames, Guachichiles, Zacatecos, Caxcanes, Tecuexes, and Guamares.**